ELMORE LEONARD'S

Bandits

Quill
William Morrow
New York

Copyright © 1987 by Elmore Leonard

This book was originally published in 1987 by Arbor House/William Morrow and Company, Inc. It was previously published in paperback by Warner Books, Inc.

It is the policy of William Morrow and Company, Inc., and its imprints and affiliates, recognizing the importance of preserving what has been written, to print the books we publish on acid-free paper, and we exert our best efforts to that end.

The Library of Congress has cataloged a previous edition of this title.
Library of Congress Cataloging-in-Publication Data

Leonard, Elmore, 1925–
    Bandits.

    I. Title.
PS3562.E55B3   1987   813'.54   86–14104
ISBN 0-87795-841-6

Paperback ISBN 0-688-16639-3

Printed in the United States of America

First Quill Edition 1999

1 2 3 4 5 6 7 8 9 10

www.williammorrow.com

For Joan, Jane, Peter and Julie,
Christopher, Bill and Katy,
Joan, Beth and Bobi,
Shannon, Megan, Tim, Alex and Joan

ONE

Every time they got a call from the leper hospital to pick up a body Jack Delaney would feel himself coming down with the flu or something. Leo Mullen, his boss, was finally calling it to Jack's attention. "You notice that? They phone, usually it's one of the sisters, and a while later you get kind of a moan in your voice. 'Oh, man, I don't know what's the matter with me. I feel kind of punk.'"

Jack said, "Punk, I never used the word *punk* in my life. When was the last time? I mean they called. Wait a minute. How many times since I've been here have they called, twice?"

Leo Mullen looked up from the body on the prep table. "You want me to tell you exactly? This is the fourth time I've asked you in the past almost three years now." Leo

1

wore latex gloves and a plastic-coated disposable apron over his vest, shirt, and tie. He looked like a man all dressed up doing the dishes.

Jack Delaney stood in the open double doorway of the tiled room, about five feet from the head of the porcelain table—tilted slightly toward the sink—where Leo was preparing the body. It appeared to be a short balding man with a lot of body hair. The poor guy, his feet down at the other end pointing in at each other, a tag wired to his left big toe. Jack would never walk in here and look directly at a body. He'd take quick glances to guard against shockers, accident victims, sights that could remain vivid in your mind forever. This one seemed to be safe. Jack looked. Oh, shit. And looked away again. The guy must have been in a car wreck. He wasn't balding, he'd been scalped in front, given a sudden receding hairline through a car windshield. Jack ran a hand through his own hair. Then dropped his hand before Leo noticed and might tell him to get a haircut. He kept his eyes on Leo, who was squirting Dis-Spray, a disinfectant, into all of the guy's orifices, his nostrils, his mouth, his ears, all of his dark openings.

"All three times they phoned the times before," Leo said, "I seem to recall you came down with some kind of twenty-four-hour bug. That's all I'm saying. Am I right or wrong?"

Jack said, "I've been to Carville. When I worked for the Rivés we'd go up there once or twice a year, tune the organ. One of 'em, usually Uncle Brother, would be on the console hitting notes, I'm up in the loft by the pipes, way up on a shaky ladder making the adjustments on the sleeve. I was the one with the ear."

Leo looked like he was tuning the organ of the guy on the prep table, lifting his private parts to spray down in there good, Jack watching, thinking the guy might've been proud of that set at one time. A little guy, but hung.

Jack said, "Have I mentioned I'm sick or not feeling too good?"

Leo said, "Not yet you haven't. They just called." He picked up a plastic hose attached to the sink and turned on the water. "Hold this for me, will you?"

"I can't," Jack said, "I'm not licensed."

"I won't tell on you. Come on, just keep the table rinsed. Run it off from by the incision."

Jack edged in to take the hose without looking directly at the body. "There're things I'd rather do than handle a person that died of leprosy."

"Hansen's disease," Leo said. "You don't die from it, you die of something else."

Jack said, "If I remember correctly, the last time Carville had a body for us you had a removal service get it."

"On account of I had three bodies in the house already, two of 'em up here, and you telling me how punk you felt."

Jack said, "Hey, Leo? Bullshit. You don't want to touch a dead leper anymore'n I do."

Jack Delaney could talk this way to his boss because they were pretty good friends and because Leo was his brother-in-law, married to Jack's sister, Raejeanne, and because Jack's mother lived with Leo and Raejeanne part of the year, the four or five months they spent across the lake, at Bay St. Louis, Mississippi.

Leo was the last of Mullen & Sons, Funeral Directors, the fifty-year-old grandson of the founder; he had gone to work for his dad and an uncle and was now on his own, the end of the line. In ten years he'd sell and retire to the Bay, put out crab nets, and read historical novels. In the meantime he would appear dedicated, offer words of comfort, lead rosaries if he had to, and never duck upstairs for a drink until the bereaved had gone home. There were bartenders who thought Leo was Jack's uncle. Jack said to him one time at Mandina's, "You should never have been an undertaker." And Leo said, "Now you tell me."

Jack Delaney was all of a sudden forty but looked younger. His mother called him either her fine boy or her handsome son. She never mentioned Angola, the Louisiana State Penitentiary, where her boy had served thirty-five months working in cotton and soybean fields and clearing brush. Jack told his mom they had brush brought in from Mississippi when they ran out. His mom had seven framed photographs of him on her dresser, several of them she'd cut out of the paper when he appeared in fashion ads for Maison Blanche. She had one photo of Raejeanne, her daughter's Dominican High graduation picture. Girls loved Jack's mussed sandy hair, his slim build, his hint of a nice-guy smile. They said, "Oh, wow," when he told them he'd been a fashion model, sportswear mostly. They said, "Oh, my Lord," if he happened to mention he'd served time. The girls would wrinkle their noses, wondering what this cute guy could have done to be sent to prison. He'd tell them it was a long story but, well, he had been a jewel thief at one time. They'd want to hear it and he'd tell about some of the scarier situations, low key, having learned there were girls who were turned on by presentable ex-cons.

While he was living in medium-security at Angola it was Leo who did the most for him. Leo talked to some of the right people in Baton Rouge, told them his brother-in-law was a little wild, immature. You know, thought he was a hotshot, every girl's dream. Leo explained that Jack was intelligent but had lacked proper discipline as a boy; his dad had died in Honduras working for United Fruit when Jack was in the ninth grade at Jesuit High. Jack was the kind, he'd always been full of the devil. Like he'd go over to Manchac and hunt snakes and dump them into country-club swimming pools. But not poisonous ones. Leo told the people in Baton Rouge he'd give Jack Delaney a job in a profession that offered daily reminders of life's realities, its consequences, and get him straightened out. That is, once Jack spent some time in state rehabilitation, one month shy of three years out of the five to twenty-five of his sentence.

So going to work for Mullen & Sons, 3600 Canal Street, was part of Jack's parole deal. He didn't see working with dead people any more a career opportunity than picking cotton at Angola; but here he was living on the second floor of a funeral home, down the hall from the embalming room, driving a hearse, picking up bodies at hospitals and parish morgues, watching the door during visitation hours, sticking flags on cars in the procession. . . . Jack had said to his brother-in-law when he hired him, "You sure you know what you're doing?" And Leo said, "I know it isn't good for either of us to drink alone."

Leo said now, "If you haven't been to Carville since you worked for the Rivé brothers it must be six or seven years."

"Longer'n that," Jack said.

"They're not sure how you contract leprosy—I mean Hansen's disease—though I've read you can get it from an armadillo. So stay away from armadillos."

Jack didn't say anything.

"I know none of the sisters ever got it and they've been there since the place opened, almost a hundred years ago. The same ones that are at Charity Hospital. You recall if you met a Sister Teresa Victor?"

Jack didn't answer or say anything because he was staring at the face of the man on the prep table, recognizing familiar features beneath the lacerations, realizing he knew him, even without the dark hair that used to curl down on his forehead. Jack said, "That's Buddy Jeannette, isn't it?" Surprised, but quiet about it, a little stunned. "Jesus Christ, it is, it's Buddy Jeannette."

Leo turned to look at the death certificate, on the counter next to the Porti-Boy embalming machine. "Denis Alexander Jeannette," Leo said. "Born in the parish of Orleans, April twenty-third, 1937."

"It's Buddy. Jesus." Jack shook his head and said, "I don't believe it."

Leo had Buddy hooked up to the Porti-Boy now, the machine pumping a pink fluid called Permaglo through clear plastic tubing that snaked over Buddy's naked body and into his carotid artery, in the right side of his neck. Leo looked up, took time to study Jack.

"Why don't you believe it?"

"He was so careful."

Leo picked up the hose, began to play its gentle stream over Buddy Jeannette's shoulders and chest. "Where'd you know him, in prison?"

"Before," Jack said. There was a silence, Leo waiting, running the hose over Buddy, soaping him. "I'd see him downtown. Like a Saturday afternoon I might see him in the bar at the Roosevelt, we'd have a drink."

"Sounds like you were pretty good friends." Leo was massaging Buddy with the soap, kneading his flesh to help the Permaglo work through and give him a tint of natural color.

"We were friends when we saw each other," Jack said. "But if we didn't see each other it didn't matter."

"I don't recall you ever mentioned him."

"Well, it was a long time ago."

"What was?"

"When I'd run into him." He was getting used to looking at Buddy's wounds. The poor guy's head, skinned raw, looked sunburned. "He was in an accident, huh?"

"Went off the road into a canal. Early this morning," Leo said, "out on the Chef highway." He looked over at the death certificate again. "I see your friend was married. Lived in Kenner."

"Is that right?"

"Only he had somebody else in the car with him. A young lady," Leo said. "How'd you like to be his wife and you're told that?"

Jack said, "Well, that can happen, I guess."

"No matter how careful you are?"

"Maybe I was wrong," Jack said. "Maybe he wasn't careful. Or he was at one time but going through the windshield changed him. I don't know anything about him, what he's been doing."

"Sounds like we have a touchy subject here." Leo turned to check the pressure gauge on the Porti-Boy machine.

Jack knew he should leave, right now; but he continued to look at Buddy. "What happened to the person that was with him?"

"You mean the young lady that wasn't his wife? The same thing that happened to your friend," Leo said. "Cause of death, multiple injuries. Pick one. I'm surprised they didn't do a post on 'em at the morgue. All they did was take some blood. The young lady's out at Lakeview. You know where I mean? In Metairie, brand-new building. They must do two hundred funerals a year, easy. Mrs. Jeannette

7

requested your friend be brought here. But you act like you don't know her."

"I don't. I didn't even know he was married."

"How about the girl friend?"

"You mean the girl that was with him? What're you trying to find out, Leo?"

"You know lots of girls. I just thought you might've known the one he had in the car."

"Tell me what you're getting at."

"We're talking about girls, Jack. What's a good place to meet 'em these days?" Leo was reaching into the cabinet above the Porti-Boy now. "I hear the Bayou Bar at the Pontchartrain isn't bad."

"It's all right."

Leo turned to Buddy Jeannette with a sixteen-inch trocar, a hollow, chrome-plated brass rod with a handle at one end and a knife-sharp point at the other.

"You were there, weren't you, just a few days ago?"

"Leo, don't start with the trocar yet, okay? Let's get this cleared up. What day are we talking about?"

"You worked three nights this week, so it must've been Monday. I think around six o'clock."

Jack nodded, but not ready to come right out and admit anything, his conscience telling him he was innocent. "Uh-huh, and who was I with?"

Leo said, "You know who you were with." He picked up a length of plastic tubing coupled to a metal aspirating device that hung inside the sink and attached the tubing to the handle end of the trocar. "You gonna try and tell me you weren't with her? Kind of girl you can spot a mile away with that red hair?"

"Yeah, I was with Helene."

"You admit it."

"I want to know who told you."

"You admit it, what difference does it make?"

"Leo, you're not just saying I was with her, you're accusing me of it."

"If that's the way you take it."

"But what am I being accused *of*? I'm not a parolee anymore, Leo, I've been rehabilitated. I don't have to stand at attention and take any more shit, okay? I want to know what I did."

"I don't know. Did you take her up to a room?"

"I happen to run into her. I haven't seen Helene in, you know how long, it's been years."

"Since you went to prison."

"We had a drink, that's all."

"But did you have the urge?"

"To what?"

"Take her up to a room."

"Leo, you can't look at a girl like Helene and not get the urge, that's the way God made us." He watched Leo move toward Buddy with the trocar. "What it looks like to me, you're worried I could be getting into something," Jack said, "or I'm gonna screw up again because this guy used to be a friend of mine, years ago."

"About the same time as Helene."

"See, that's what I mean. They didn't even know each other. This poor guy, he's driving out Chef Menteur with a girl could be his sister-in-law, a friend of the family, you don't know. But you start imagining things. I'm guilty because he's guilty and you don't even know if he is. But the thing is, Leo, even if the young lady in the car *was* his girl friend, what's it got to do with me?"

"I worry about you," Leo said.

"Why?"

"I don't know, I guess it's your nature, your tendencies, make me a little nervous."

"We're two different people, Leo."

"We sure are."

"You like this work, I don't. You like to lie in the hammock at the Bay, read your book, smell the gumbo Raejeanne's fixing in the kitchen . . . "

"And what do you like to do, Jack?"

Jack didn't answer, looking at the spearlike trocar poised above Buddy Jeannette's belly, a few inches from his navel.

"See?" Leo said. "You don't think of normal things that'd be on the tip of your tongue everybody enjoys, you have to try and think of something crazy, huh?"

"I wasn't thinking anything at all. But if you don't mind my saying, Leo, I think this business ages you before your time. It's always serious. You know, there are very few light moments." He watched, with a sense of relief, Leo relaxing his grip on the trocar.

"You're right," Leo said, "I tend to jump to conclusions. I hear you're with that redheaded broad and right away I see you getting back in that hotel cocktail lounge routine."

"I bought her a drink."

"Yeah, well, even that. After what she did to you, you have to be out of your mind even to say hello to her."

"She didn't do anything to me, Leo. I did it to myself. The intellect presents it to the will, right? And the will says no way or let's do it. We learned that in high school. It means don't blame somebody else when you fuck up."

"As long as you realize," Leo said, "you start looking for that kind of excitement again there're only two ways you can end up. The one you know all about and the other way,

Jack, is on this table. Like your friend here has found out."

"I'll go to Carville tomorrow."

"I'd appreciate it," Leo said. He looked down and touched the sharp end of the trocar to Buddy Jeannette's belly, the point indenting soft flesh an inch or so above the navel.

Jack said, "Wait. What time should I go?" He saw Leo hunch over the instrument and said, "Leo, wait. Okay?" He said, "Oh, shit," turning away.

TWO

One of the bartenders at Mandina's, Mario, a young guy Jack Delaney knew pretty well, said, "You stick the thing right into the person, like you're stabbing him?"

"How else you gonna do it?"

"You poke the guy all over?"

"No, once you put the trocar in it stays in the same place. You change the angle. See, what you're doing is aspirating the viscera. You hit the liver and it doesn't give, you know the guy was a boozer, had cirrhosis."

"I could never do that. Jesus."

"You get used to it."

"You want another one?"

"Yeah, with three olives. Then I'll switch."

"Man, I could never do that."

"There free-lance embalmers that come around, trade men, they get about a hundred a job. What do you think? Make thirty to forty grand a year."

"Not me," Mario said, moving off.

Saturday afternoon the plain, high-ceilinged café was nearly empty, too far up Canal Street for tourists. Mullen & Sons was only a block away. After a funeral Jack and Leo would come in still wearing their dark suits and pearl-gray neckties, sit at a table, and gradually begin talking, polite to each other until, oh, man, the relief that would come with that first ice-cold vodka martini going down. Jack's with anchovy olives, Leo's a twist of lemon. Leo's eyes glistening as he'd look up at the black waiter with the beard who had been in that movie *Pretty Baby* and called them the funeral dudes. Leo would say, "Henry, why don't you do it again, the same way. Would that please you?" Leo settling in. "It would sure as hell please us, Henry." Then later on have the artichoke soup and the oyster loaf.

Mario came along the bar with the martini, placed it on the cocktail napkin in front of Jack.

"What I don't understand, how you can do that every day of your life. Fool with dead people."

Jack picked up the martini, about to say that for one thing the dead never complain or give you a hard time. But he stopped and thought a moment and said, "I don't know. I really don't." He sipped the martini, put an olive in his mouth, chewed it a few times and took another sip. Jesus, was that good.

"I heard you don't put any panties on the women, when they're in the casket."

"Where'd you hear that?"

"I don't know, I just heard it one time."

"We dress 'em right down to their socks. Shoes are optional, but everything else."

Mario picked up Jack's glass to place it on a fresh cocktail napkin. "You ever get like a real good-looking girl, I mean with a great body, you know, and you have to do all that stuff to her?"

"Now, it doesn't sound so bad, uh?"

"I still wouldn't do it."

"You know what the worst is? You look at a body that came in, all of a sudden you realize, Jesus Christ, the guy was a friend of yours."

"Brings it home, uh? Somebody you know."

"Even if you haven't seen the person in a while. Like this guy today. I see him lying there, I don't believe it. Not only is the guy dead, he's eight years older than the last time I saw him. You know what I'm saying? He's a different person. I look at him, guy named Buddy Jeannette, I know him but I don't know him. I don't know where he's been, what he's been doing."

"What'd he die of?"

"See, the thing is, this guy wasn't just an old friend. This's a guy when I met him, the first time I ever talked to him, it changed my whole fucking life from then on."

"Guy was what, like a priest?"

"He was a hotel burglar."

"No shit."

"You know I did time."

"You mentioned it once, yeah. Three years."

"Well, before that, when I met the guy . . . Wait, I have to tell you something else first. Right after I got out of school I worked at Maison Blanche, in the men's department, and they'd use me in ads. They said I was a perfect size forty and I had good teeth and they said they liked my

15

hair. But I quit 'cause it was a bunch a shit doing that, all that standing around in the lights. Now, this time I'm talking about . . . "

"When you met the guy?"

"Yeah, eight years ago. Now I'm thirty-two years old working for the Rivé brothers, barely making two hundred a week."

"They come in here. Emile and Brother."

"I know they do. They're my uncles. . . . Anyway, this particular night I come out of Felix's, there on Iberville, had my oysters, couple of beers, and this woman stops me on the street. She wants to know if I've ever done any modeling. I go, 'Yeah, you know Maison Blanche?' I can tell she's from out of town, the way she talks. She says they're here from New York doing catalog layouts for Hollandia sportswear—that's the one with the little tulip on the shirt —and she'll give me a thousand bucks for four days. Just like that. The thousand guaranteed plus overtime. But the way she's looking at me, touching my hair, I get the feeling she wants to do more than take my picture."

"Yeah, was she nice?"

"Attractive, very stylish, wore dark-tinted glasses all the time, and had the whitest skin I ever saw. She was maybe forty-two or three."

"That's not too bad."

"Her name was Betty Barr, she was the advertising manager. Only the other models and the photographer and his helpers all called her Bettybarr, like it was one name. I don't know why but I had trouble with that, so I didn't call her anything. We'd start in the morning and shoot all day, outside, at different locations. Jackson Square, naturally, Audubon Park, the lighthouse on the New Basin Canal, the docks down at Lafitte, Jesus, with the Cajun shrimpers standing there watching. Here we are posing, this group of us, like we're happier'n shit to have these outfits on, warm-ups, rugby shirts. . . . This other guy, Michael, who never said one fucking word to me, it didn't seem to bother him at all he looked like an asshole. You see the shrimpers making remarks. Or the girls, it didn't bother them, they were kids, sixteen, seventeen. . . . " Jack touched his glass. "Why don't you hit this again. Just vodka."

Mario stepped down the bar to get the bottle and Jack remembered the girls. The girls had no trouble becoming an instant part of it, slouching into poses with deadpan expressions or smiling or looking surprised. They fas-cinated him, their studied moves, girls being models, noth-ing else, able to lose themselves in their poses. He said to the girls, an aside, "You imagine a guy wearing this?" And the girls said, "Really." He liked them when they were posing and they liked him when he wasn't.

Mario returned and poured and Jack said, "We're out by Tulane, I have these real bright green fucking pants on with a pink shirt, the little tulip on it, and right there on Saint Charles Avenue these South Central Bell hardhats are digging up the street. Naturally they start making remarks, yelling different things. My regular job then, hauling around those goddamn organ pipes, I worked as hard as those guys any day. But I can't walk over and tell 'em that. See, that's bad enough, but then Bettybarr gets an idea, comes over and cocks this straw hat on the side of my head. I go, 'Excuse me, but you know anybody who wears a hat this way?' She goes, 'You do.' Sunday, the last day, we're shooting on the top deck of the Algiers ferry, riding it back and forth. Everybody on the boat was up there watching us. I see these two clowns drinking Dixie beer out of longneck bottles and I know right away I'm gonna have trouble. They come around to my side, I'm standing there grinning at the camera in this all-white outfit, and they start making these kissing-sucking noises, you know, and ask me if I'm dick trawling or what. Just then Bettybarr comes up to me with a yachting cap and I think, Oh, shit, here we go. She's about to cock the hat on my head and I say to her, 'Excuse me.' I turn to the two morons with the Dixie longnecks and tell 'em, 'I hear one more fucking word somebody's going over the side.' Bettybarr looks grim, like she's frozen, with no expression at all. She says, 'That's it for today. Pack it up,' and gets us all down below."

"What'd the guys do?"

"Nothing. The ferry docked and we left. But then we're in the bar that night at the Roosevelt, she asks me, 'Was that for my benefit?' Like was I showing off in front of her? I said, 'No, that was between those guys and me, something I had to do.' She goes, 'I see.' She finishes her drink, looks at me and says, 'Would you like to go upstairs?' "

"No shit."

"We go up to her suite."

"Yeah."

"She undresses me."

"No shit."

"She goes, 'You have a gorgeous body.' "

"Yeah?"

"I never had anybody tell me that before. I don't know what to say about hers. It's bigger, you know, looser, without any clothes on. And her skin was so white she looked more naked-looking than girls that have that real smooth skin and tan lines. Then when we did it it was weird to see this grown-up woman that smelled of bath powder moaning and carrying on."

18

"Yeah, but it was okay, uh?"

"It was fine. Then after, we're lying there, I bring it up again."

Mario grinned.

"I mean about the two morons, why I had to say something to them. She tells me to turn out the light. I go, 'You don't understand how I felt, do you?' She goes, 'Jack, I don't really care how you felt. If you don't want to be looked at, don't stand in front of a camera.' I try to tell her, look, when guys like that start mouthing off I'm gonna do something about it. And you know what she said?"

"What?"

"She said, 'Not on my time, you're not. Now please turn off the goddamn light.' "

"Man, touchy broad."

"You're right, this's a tough lady. And *she* was right. If I don't like standing around there feeling like an asshole, I shouldn't be a model. Even with the money they were paying. And I knew I could've got more work from her. I was living in half a shotgun double on Magazine with hardly any furniture, a job I hated, and I was thinking on and off of getting married. You remember Leo's Uncle Al? No, he was before you came here. It was Al's daughter I almost married. Maureen." Jack picked up his drink, took a slow, lingering sip. "I was gonna say I wouldn't be here if I had. But this's exactly where I'd be, in the fucking funeral business. I'd be over there right now with the rubber gloves on. Anyway . . . "

"You're in bed with the broad."

"Bettybarr. She's snoring by this time and I'm lying there wide awake trying to figure out what's more important, money or what you consider self-respect. See, I was leaving myself an opening. Maybe it wasn't a matter of self-respect. Maybe it was just a matter of being self-conscious I didn't like. I'm thinking maybe if I did ads for trucks or motor oil, you know, or chewing tobacco, something like that . . . when I hear a sound from over by the dresser. I raise my head up and, Christ, there's a guy in the room." Jack paused, touched his glass. "Why don't you hit it one more time."

Mario gave him a quick refill. "You want more ice?"

"No, this's fine." Jack took a sip. "I can't believe it, a guy standing right there by the dresser. Now I see him go past the window and out into the living room. I wait, I don't hear anything, so I get out of bed, put on my pants, and tiptoe over to the door. The guy has the desk lamp on and he's taking stuff out of the lady's briefcase and putting it in this flight bag he has with him. So, I start to sneak up behind him."

"No shit."

"He was about your size. What're you, five six?"

"Five seven and a quarter."

"He wasn't too big. Maybe a hundred and thirty pounds."

"I go one sixty-two," Mario said.

"So I don't see a problem unless he's got a gun."

"Yeah, did he?"

"Just then he turns around and we're looking right at each other. The guy says, very calmly, 'I bet I have the wrong room. This isn't 1515, is it?' I said, 'You aren't even close.' Then what does he do, he sits down in a chair, takes out a cigarette, and says, 'You mind if I smoke?' I said, 'Why, you nervous?' He says, 'This never happened to me before.' He lights up. I ask him if he's ever been busted. He says, 'Yeah, but no convictions. How about you?' I tell him, picked up once for scalping tickets at the Superdome and fined two hundred bucks. He says, 'I don't want to sound like a whiner, I hate whiners, but this was gonna be my last job. I'm supposed to go in the car-leasing business with my brother-in-law.' The way he said it you could tell he didn't want to. See, the thing was *my* brother-in-law, I'm talking about Leo, was trying to get me to be a mortician even back then. It was like we had something in common."

"You and the guy."

"Yeah, Buddy and I. See, that's who it was, Buddy Jeannette, the guy I just saw dead."

"But if he wasn't too big, why didn't you belt him?"

"For what?"

"And call the cops."

Jack paused, took a sip of his drink. "It was like—didn't you ever meet someone, right away you like the person, you feel a rapport, you feel you have something in common?"

"Yeah, but the guy broke in."

"And he starts talking like we're sitting in the lobby. This is something new; play it, see where it goes. At that point, why not?"

"Did he take any of your stuff?"

"I didn't have anything worth taking. He tells me he's been scouting Bettybarr 'cause she wore expensive clothes and had some gold that was nice. Then he tells me he was in this room once before, during the day. I ask him, 'What'd you come back for?' He goes, 'There's nothing in the room when the people are away. That's how you do it, man, get a reading of the layout. See, then I come back when she's here, she's sleeping, her wallet and jewelry are on the dresser, and I don't go around bumping into things.' He even knew I wasn't with the group, when they came from New York. I asked him, I said, 'What do you do, size people up?' He goes, 'I appraise them. Downstairs in the bar,

21

different places. You can generally tell who's got it. This one's borderline, but it would still be worth the trip. She's got over a grand in cash.' I asked him how he got in the room, he says with a key. Then he turns it around. He says, 'What happens if the lady comes out of the bedroom?' I said, 'I guess you'd be fucked.' He says, 'What happens if she doesn't come out?' I said, 'That's different. But tell me about this magic key you have.' "

"He got one at the desk," Mario said.

"No, what he does, he checks in, gets a room. Then late at night he pulls the lock out of the door, takes it all apart and figures out how to make a fire key."

"What's a fire key?"

"What it sounds like. It'll open any door in the hotel, in case of fire or some emergency they have to check every room. The guy use to be a locksmith. So I ask him, 'And how many fire keys do you have?' He says, 'You understand a fire key would be worth upwards of five grand or more to certain people.' I said, 'Yeah, or you might want to give it to somebody who's in a position to do you a favor.' He says, 'I thought you had something else in mind. You put the cash in your pocket, I leave with everything else, and she thinks that wad in your jeans is 'cause you love her.' "

Jack smiled, shaking his head. "Guy was something. High-class professional burglar, wore a suit and tie—it was like meeting a movie star and you find out the guy talks and acts just like a regular person."

"You took the guy's key," Mario said, "and let him go."

Jack held up his hand. "I said to him, 'First, you put everything back.' He says, 'You could still take the cash and I walk out with a few items.' I said, 'But then my name's in a burglary report, huh? Stuck in a police file they might happen to look at some time in the future. No, I don't think so.' Buddy goes, 'You might do okay, you're not dumb. But have you got the balls to walk in a room where you know the people are sleeping?' "

Mario shook his head. "Not me, man."

"Yeah, but what was funny, the guy's talking about balls while I have his right in my pocket. Still, I never threatened him. Give me the keys or I turn you in. Never, not a word. Later on, the next time I saw him, he said he was impressed I never tried to act tough. It showed class."

"Jesus," Mario said.

"And now he's dead."

"You want another hit?"

"No, I'm gonna switch."

Jack was at a table now, tired of standing. He looked up to see Leo coming away from the bar and noticed they'd turned the lights on. It was raining and looked greenish out on Canal Street, through the big plate-glass window, the sky pale green and everything else dark. Leo stopped and took a sip of the martini so he wouldn't spill any of it. His thin hair was pasted to his head, his raincoat soaking wet, his expression, Jack saw, concerned, very serious.

"You okay?"

Jack thought of saying, Compared to what? But kept it simple and said, "I'm fine," giving it just a hint of innocent surprise. He felt himself alert, his body floating comfortably while his mind buzzed with words and pictures, wide awake. He said, "How's Buddy doing?"

"Buddy's done," Leo said, "ready to receive visitors." He looked at Jack's glass. "What's that you're drinking?"

"It's a Sazerac."

"When'd you start drinking Sazeracs?"

"I think about an hour ago. I don't know—what time is it? It's getting dark out."

"Half past five," Leo said. He placed his martini on the table, pulled out a chair and sat down. "I'm driving over to the Bay. I told Raejeanne I'd be there for supper." With his serious expression. "You gonna be all right?"

"I know I'm safe here," Jack said. "I go outside I'm liable to get run over by a car."

"You're going to Carville tomorrow. You won't forget, will you?"

"I'm looking forward to it."

"I'll be back by seven. There'll be a rosary for your friend Buddy. Some priest from Kenner, Our Lady of Perpetual Help."

"Something he always wanted," Jack said, "a rosary."

Leo said, "Oh, I had a call from Sister Teresa Victor at Carville a while ago. There's somebody wants to go with you to pick up the body. You don't mind, do you? Have some company?"

Jack said, "Aw, shit, Leo. You know I can't talk to relatives, they're in that state. You're asking me to drive a hundred and fifty miles up and back, my head aching trying to think of words of consolation, Jesus, never smiling. Going to the cemetery's different, you don't have to say anything. Sometimes they even seem happy. . . . Shit, Leo."

Leo sipped his martini. He said, "You through?" and took another sip. "The one that's going with you isn't a relative, it's a sister, a nun, who knew the deceased when she was in Nicaragua and, I think, brought her up here for treatment. I was still prepping your friend while Sister Teresa Victor's telling me this on the phone. Then something came up, she had to cut it short."

"The one I'm picking up is a nun? The dead one?"

"Look," Leo said. "The deceased is a young Nicaraguan woman, twenty-three years old. I wrote her name down, it's on the counter in the prep room. Also the name of the person that's going with you, a Sister Lucy. You got it?"

"What'd she die of?"

"Whatever it was you can't catch it. Okay? You pick up Sister Lucy at the Holy Family Mission on Camp Street, tomorrow, one o'clock. It's near Julia."

"The soup kitchen."

"That's the place. She'll be waiting for you."

"We run out of conversation we'll say a rosary."

"There you are." Leo finished his martini. "You gonna be all right?"

"I'm fine."

"You won't forget. One o'clock."

"No problem."

"Wouldn't be a bad idea you stayed in tonight."

"You still worried about me?"

"You see your old pal on the table, the next thing I know you're eighty proof. Who drank the Sazeracs, Buddy or Helene?"

Jack smiled, feeling relaxed, wise, confident, in his favorite place to drink at the end of the day; rainy outside and growing dark, ideal conditions. He said, "You want me to tell you about Helene, don't you? What it was like seeing her again. You're dying to know, aren't you?"

"I told you," Leo said, "I was somewhat apprehensive when I heard."

"Then you'll be glad to know my heart didn't leap."

"How about any other area on your person?"

Jack shook his head. "The thrill is gone. She's got curly hair now and it makes her look different. Hey, but, Leo?"

Jack smiled. "Mmmmm, did she smell good. Had on a kind of perfume I know is expensive 'cause I picked up a bottle off a dresser one night in the Peabody Hotel, in Memphis, and gave it to Maureen."

"Guilty conscience," Leo said.

"Maybe. Maureen goes, 'Jack, this costs a hundred and fifty dollars an *ounce*. You bought this? Tell me the truth.' You know how Maureen looks you right in the eye? It was after I'd left Uncle Brother and Emile—"

"After they fired you."

"And everybody thought I was on the road selling coffee. There was a friend of mine did that, sold La Louisianne. I'd say good-bye to Maureen Sunday night and not see her again till Friday. I'm back in New Orleans or at the Bay while some conventioneer in Nashville is asking hotel security, 'But how could anybody get in the room when the chain's still on the door, when we woke up this morning?' "

"How did you?" Leo said.

Jack heard the clink of silverware—Henry the waiter setting a table—and in that pause realized he had never talked to Leo about details. Or told anyone before how he'd met Buddy Jeannette. Well, Buddy was dead. It was okay to tell about that night. But was he talking too much? He said to Leo, "The point I was making, I always felt Maureen suspected I was into some other line of work. I didn't know shit about coffee other than you drink it. But I know she never said a word to anybody."

Leo said, "Unlike another girl we could mention that we happen to be talking about, as a matter of fact."

"You get something in your head, Leo, that's it."

Leo said, "Jack, you've always been a little crazy, but you were never dumb. The Jesuits taught you how to think to some degree, put things in their proper order. What I'll never understand is how you could let that redheaded broad lead you around by your privates—"

"It wasn't like that."

"When you had a wonderful girl like Maureen dying to marry you. A girl that has everything, looks, intelligence, a good Catholic upbringing, she even cooks better than your mother or Raejeanne."

Jack said, "I saw you working for your dad and her dad, Leo. I saw if I married her I'd become a Mullen and Sons son-in-law, and I wouldn't need a Jesuit education to tell me I'd be stuck for good, committed. Like doing time."

Leo said, "Maureen wouldn't a cared what you did for a living. She was crazy about you."

"Maureen wants security and everything to be nice. That's why she married the doctor, that little asshole with his bow tie, his little mustache. But that's beside the point," Jack said. "You want to know why I didn't marry Maureen? It wasn't 'cause she was so sweet and nice. Hell, I could've changed that, got her to lay back and recognize the difference between bullshit and real life. You want to hear the real reason? Since I'm telling you my innermost secrets?"

"You mean since you're shitfaced," Leo said, "and won't remember it anyway."

Jack glanced around before leaning in close to the table. "I had the feeling Maureen, once she married and settled down, would have a tendency to get fat in her later years. I felt I could change her attitude about life, but not her metabolism."

Leo stared at him. "You serious?"

"I say that knowing my sister, Raejeanne, is no lightweight. She'd get me pissed off about something and I'd tell her, 'Raejeanne, you know what you look like? A waterbed wearing tennis shoes.'"

"That wasn't nice."

"No, and I don't mean to offend you, like it's something terrible. It's just I felt Maureen was gonna put on size."

Leo said, "I never heard of anything so dumb in my life."

Jack said, "Our preferences are different, Leo, what I've been trying to tell you. Our likes and dislikes, what we enjoy, what lights up our eyes. . . . You want me to tell you what attracted me to Helene? The first time I saw her? The very first thing I noticed about her?"

"I'm dying to know," Leo said.

"It was her nose."

Leo stared at him.

"That classic, what you'd call aristocratic, kind of nose. The most perfect fucking nose, Leo, I've ever seen in my life."

Leo said, "Do you hear yourself?" He said, loud enough for Henry and Mario to hear and look over from the bar, "You're gonna sit there and tell me you went to prison on account of this broad's *nose*?"

Jack said, "You don't know what I'm talking about, do you?"

Even half in the bag, talking too much, he didn't dare mention the fine spray of freckles or try to describe that pert tilt, that fragile beauty, her brown eyes . . .

Or the bare legs that went up into her skirt. Long slender legs, the high instep another delicate line with the high heel hanging from the toe, the young lady's legs crossed on the bar stool in the Sazerac Lounge of the Roosevelt Hotel. Or the Monteleone or the Pontchartrain, the Peabody in Memphis, the Biltmore in Atlanta. It was never just the nose. But why try to tell all that to a man who prepared dead bodies, read novels that took place in times gone by, and was not drawn to live girls in cocktail lounges?

Leo would still have said what he did. "You're never gonna grow up, are you?"

THREE

The bums in front of Holy Family, squinting in the sunlight, shading their eyes, said, Hey, it's the undertaker man. Who died? That ain't for me, is it? I ain't dead yet. Get outta here with that thing, Jesus. Come back after while. Hey, buddy, come back after we've et. They said, Here's one good as dead. Here, take this guy. Jack told them not to touch the hearse. Keep away from it, okay? He walked through them in his navy-blue suit, white shirt and striped tie, sunglasses, nodding with a faint smile, careful to breathe through his mouth. One of them said it must be good soup today, it wasn't all over the sidewalk. Most of them seemed to be hardcore alcoholics. They stood at the bottom of nowhere on a spring day, done for, but could make observations, even try to hustle him. Mister, gimme a dollar, I'll watch nobody pisses on your hearse. He got inside the storefront mission with only a couple of them brushing against him.

There were bums hunched over shoulder to shoulder along two rows of tables that reached to the serving counter, where a pair of round, gray-haired ladies wearing glasses and white aprons were dishing out the meal. Jack said to a little colored guy in bib overalls and an ageless tweed coat too big for him, "Which one's Sister Lucy?"

The man was coming out. He looked back over his shoulder, then turned all the way around and pointed to the line approaching the serving counter. "She right there. See?"

Jack said, "You sure?"

The man grinned, nearly toothless, at the way Jack was staring. " 'Nough to make you believe in Jesus, huh? She cook good, too. Come Monday for the red beans and rice."

Jack saw a slim young woman with dark hair brushed behind her ear in profile. He took off his sunglasses. Saw she was wearing a beige, double-breasted jacket, high-styled, made of linen or fine cotton, moving down a line of skid-row derelicts, *touching* them. He had posed with girls in designer jeans—but this was a nun wearing pressed Calvins, a straw bag hanging from her shoulder, long slim legs that seemed longer in plain tan heels. Across the room in a bare, whitewashed soup kitchen— look at that. Touching them, touching their arms beneath layers of clothes they lived in, taking their hands in hers, talking to them . . .

She came over with calm eyes to take his clean hand and he said, "Sister? Jack Delaney. I'm with Mullen's." And was surprised again to feel calluses that didn't go with the stylish look.

Though her face did. Her face startled him. The slender, delicate nose, dark hair brushed back though it lay on her forehead, deep blue eyes looking up at him. She was small up close and now that surprised him; only about five three, he decided, without the heels. She said, "Lucy Nichols, Jack. I'm ready if you are."

The derelicts outside told her not to go with him. Stay outta that thing, Sister. That's a one-way ride, Sister. Hey, Sister, you looking good. She smiled at them, put a hand on her hip, and let her shoulders go slack, like a fashion model. "Not bad, uh? You like it?" She stopped to look over the hearse, then at Jack, and said, "You know what? I've always wanted to drive one of these."

She blew the horn pulling away and the bums sunning themselves on Camp Street waved.

"You can handle it all right?"

"This is a pleasure. I used to drive a ton-and-a-half truck with broken springs. Last month, when we had to leave in a hurry, I managed to buy a Volkswagen in León and drove it all the way to Cozumel. That was a trip."

Jack had to think a minute. But it didn't do any good. "You drove from where?"

"From León, in Nicaragua, through Honduras to Guatemala. We wore what passed for habits and had papers saying we were going to the Maryknoll language school in Huehuetenango. Then we had to scrounge more papers to get us into Mexico. After that it was fairly easy, from Cozumel to New Orleans and then to Carville. We could have flown out of Managua to Mexico City, but it seemed risky at the time, waiting around the airport. That feeling you shouldn't be standing still. My one concern was to get

Amelita out of there, fast, and continue her therapy. You
know she's the one we're picking up."

Jack said, "Oh." The *one* they were picking up. Kind of
an offhand way to refer to the deceased. But that was the
name Leo had written down, Amelita Sosa. He wondered
if Sister Lucy thought he knew more about her than he did.
What she'd been doing down there. He wondered what she
did with the VW, if she sold it. It was like coming in in the
middle of a conversation. He didn't want to sound dumb.
He said, "You go around Lee Circle to get on the interstate.
Take it all the way to the Saint Gabriel exit. You get tired,
just let me know."

She said, "You don't know how much I appreciate
what you're doing."

He kept quiet. What was he doing? His job. Then
wondered if Leo had told them there'd be no charge. He
couldn't imagine it. Then looked out the window, trying to
think of nun-related things to talk about.

"I had sisters all the way through grade school."

She said, "You did?"

"At Incarnate Word. Then I went to Jesuit High."
Hearing himself it sounded like he was still going there. "I
went to Tulane one year, but I didn't know what to take,
I mean that would help me. So I left."

She said, "I did the same thing. Spent a year at New-
comb."

"Is that right?" He felt a little better.

"Before that I went to the Convent, Sacred Heart."

Jack said, "Yeah, I knew some girls that went there, but
they would've been before your time. Well, there was one.
Did you happen to know a Maureen Mullen?"

"I don't think so."

"She got out in, let's see, '70."

Sister Lucy didn't say when she got out.

He guessed she was somewhere in her late twenties, not more than thirty. Younger than Maureen.

"I almost married her. Maureen Mullen."

"You did?"

"But, I don't know. Everybody expected it, our families. I guess I felt pressured. Or didn't care for what I saw, looking into the future. So I made a run for it."

She looked at him and smiled. Then looked at the road again as she said, "It almost happened to me, too, the same kind of situation. I was at my own engagement party when I woke up."

"Is that right?"

"My family and his wanted to set the date."

"You felt pressured?"

"Did I. I thought, wait a minute. This isn't what I want, get married and join clubs. I guess I made a run for it, too. All the way . . . gone."

He laid his left arm along the backrest of the seat and took a good look at her profile. She had a wonderful nose. Jesus, and one of those lower lips you wanted to bite. Her nose wasn't quite as thin and delicate as Helene's, but it was a beauty. He liked her dark hair better. He liked red hair a lot, but not frizzy, the way Helene had it now.

"What happened to the guy you didn't marry?"

"He met someone else. He's quite a successful neurologist."

"Is that right? Maureen married a *ur*ologist."

This Sister Lucy didn't look anything like a nun; she looked rich. She had on a loose beige-and-white striped blouse, like a T-shirt, underneath the linen jacket. She was wearing, he decided, about three hundred dollars worth of clothes. He wanted to ask her why she became a nun.

Amazing, thinking that when she glanced at him and said, "How do you happen to be in the funeral business?"

"I'm not, really. I'm helping out my brother-in-law for a while. My sister's husband."

"What would you rather do?"

Jack edged up a little straighter. "That's a hard one. There isn't much I've done I cared for, or wouldn't bore you to tears." He paused, at first wondering if he should tell her, then wanting to for some reason, and said, "Except for a profession I got into when I made my run. There was sure nothing boring about it."

She kept her eyes on the road. "What was that?"

"I was a jewel thief."

Now she looked at him. Jack was ready, his expression resigned, weary, but with a nice grin.

"You broke into people's homes?"

"Hotel rooms. But I never broke in. I used a key."

There was a silence in the hearse as she passed a semi-trailer at 70 miles an hour.

"A jewel thief. You mean you only stole jewelry?"

Other girls, wide-eyed, had never asked that. They'd get squirmy and want to know if he was scared and if the people ever woke up and saw him. He said, "I'd take cash if I was tempted. If it was sitting there." Which it always was.

"You only robbed the rich?"

"There's no percentage robbing the poor. What was I gonna take, their food stamps?"

She said, without looking at him, "You've never been to Central America. There the poor are the ones who are robbed. And murdered."

That stopped him, until he thought to say, "How long were you there?"

"Almost nine years, not counting a few trips back to the States, to Carville for training seminars. There's no place like it. If your purpose in life is the care of lepers, and what's what the Sisters of Saint Francis do, then you have to go to Carville every few years, keep up with what's going on in the field."

"The Sisters of Saint Francis?"

"There're a bunch of orders named for Francis, the guy had so much charisma. He might've been a little weird, too, but that's okay. This one's the Sisters of Saint Francis of the Stigmata."

Jack had never heard of it. He thought of saying, I like your habit, but changed his mind. "And you were stationed in Nicaragua."

"The hospital, Sagrado Familia, was near Jinotega, if you know where that is. On a lake, very picturesque. But it isn't anymore, it's gone."

"You're a nurse?"

"Not exactly. What I did was practice medicine without a license. Toward the end we didn't have a staff physician. Our two Nicaraguan doctors were disappeared, one right after the other. It was only a matter of time. We weren't for either side, but we knew who we were against."

Were disappeared.

He'd save that one for later. "And now you're back home for a while?"

She took several moments to say, "I'm not sure." Then glanced at him. "How about you, Jack, are you still a jewel thief?"

He liked the easy way she said his name. "No, I gave it up for another line of work. I got into agriculture."

"Really? You were a farmer?"

"More of a field hand. At the Louisiana State Penitentiary. Angola."

She was looking at him again, now with a grin, showing dimples. It inspired him.

"Up the interstate to Baton Rouge, then Sixty-one till you get almost to the Mississippi line, turn off toward the river and you come to the main gate. Inside, you drive along a white rail fence. It's hard to see, through the wire mesh they have on the windows of the bus, but it looks like a horse farm. Till you notice the gun towers."

"Really? You were in prison?"

"A month shy of three years. Met some interesting people in there."

"What was it like?"

"Sister, you don't want to know."

She said, in a thoughtful tone, "Saint Francis was in prison. . . . " Then glanced at Jack and asked, "But how do you feel about it? I mean committing crimes and then being locked up."

"You do it and forget it." He hadn't heard about Saint Francis doing time. . . . But he was talking about himself now. "I have a healthy attitude about guilt. It's not good for you."

He saw her smile, not giving it much, but he smiled back at her, feeling a lot better, thinking maybe they should stop on the way, have a cup of coffee. She was nice, easy to talk to, and he was still a little hung over this Sunday afternoon. But when he mentioned coffee Sister Lucy frowned in a thoughtful kind of way and said they really didn't have time.

Jack said, "I've found one thing in this business, there's very little pressure. You go to pick up the deceased, and I don't mean to sound disrespectful, but they're gonna be there waiting."

She said, "Oh," in her quiet, unhurried way, her gaze lingering, "no one told you."

Jack said, "I had a feeling there was something you thought I knew. What didn't anyone tell me?"

She said, "I think you're going to like it."

He had to admit he liked the idea she was playing with him now, seeing a gleam in those calm eyes as she looked over again, about to let him in on a secret.

"The girl we're going to get—"

"Amelita Sosa."

"Yes. She isn't dead."

Seven years ago, when Amelita was fifteen or sixteen and living in Jinotega with her family, a National Guard colonel came along and put stars in her eyes. This guy, who was a personal friend of Somoza, told Amelita that with her looks and his connections she'd be sure to win the Miss Nicaragua pageant and after that the Miss Universe; appear on international satellite television and in no time at all become a famous film star. "You know, of course," Sister Lucy said, "what he had in mind." This was during the war. Before the Sandinistas took over the government.

Jack understood what the colonel was up to, but wasn't exactly sure about the war. He knew they were always having revolutions down there and did understand there was one going on right now. He remembered when he was little his dad, back from Honduras for a few days, telling them the people down there were crazy, hot-tempered; if they weren't fighting over a woman they were biting the hand that fed them. Jack would picture shifty-eyed guys with machetes, straw sombreros, bullet belts crossed over their shoulders, waiting to ambush a United Fruit train loaded with bananas. But then he would see Marlon Brando and a bunch of armed Mexican extras ride into the scene and government soldiers firing machine guns from the train. It was hard to keep the borders and the history down there straight. He didn't want to interrupt Sister Lucy's story and sound dumb asking questions. He listened and stored essential facts, picturing stock characters. The colonel, one of those oily fuckers with a gold cigarette case he opens to offer the poor son of a bitch he's having shot just what he wants in these last moments of his life, a smoke. Amelita, Jack saw a demure little thing with frightened Bambi eyes, then had to enlarge her breasts and put her in spiked heels and a bathing suit cut high to her hips for the Miss Universe contest.

But once he got her to Managua the colonel never mentioned beauty pageants again. The only feeling he had for Amelita was lust. Good word, *lust.* Jack couldn't recall if he'd ever used it, but had no trouble picturing the colonel, the son of a bitch, lusting. Jack put an extra fifty pounds on him for the bedroom scene: the colonel taking off his uniform full of medals, gut hanging out, leering at Amelita cowering behind the bed. Jack watched him rip open the front of her nightgown, show-class breasts springing free, as Sister Lucy said, "Are you listening?"

"To every word. And then what?"

And then, by the time the rebels had reached Managua, the colonel was in Miami and Amelita was back home, safe for the time being.

The next part brought the story close to the present but was harder to follow, Sister Lucy referring to the political situation down there like he knew what she was talking about. It was confusing because the ones that had been the government before, it sounded like, were now the rebels, the *contras*. The ones that had started the revolution back in the seventies were now running the country.

He got that much. But which were the good guys and which were the bad guys?

While he was still trying to figure it out Sister Lucy was telling how the colonel had now returned to Nicaragua as a guerrilla commandant in the north, came looking for Amelita in the dead of night and took her off with him into the mountains.

Say one thing for the colonel, he didn't quit. "Maybe the guy really liked her," Jack said, reserving judgment, still not sure which side the colonel was on, even taking off, briefly, the extra weight he'd put on the guy. And got a look from Sister Lucy; man, a hard stare. "Or he was driven by his consuming lust," Jack said. "That would be more like it, huh? A lust that knew no bounds."

She said, "Are you finished?" Sounding like Leo with that dry tone. He told her he was and she said, good. It was a new experience, the feeling he could say just about anything he wanted to a *nun,* of all people, and she'd get it because she was aware—he could see it in her eyes—and would not be shocked or offended. He had been to prison, but this lady had been to a war.

They came to the part where Amelita found out she had Hansen's disease. It was while she was still in the mountains with the colonel. Brown spots began to appear on her arms and face. She was scared to death. A doctor in camp—"Listen to this, Jack"—made the diagnosis and told the colonel Amelita would have to go to Sagrado Familia immediately, that day, to begin sulfone treatments. There

41

was no sensory loss, the disease would be arrested in an early stage, and the doctor was confident there would be no disfigurement.

Jack said, "It's hard to imagine a good-looking young girl like that—"

Sister Lucy said, "Listen to me, will you?" It surprised him and shut him up. "Where do you think the doctor was from he could take one look at her and make the diagnosis? Yes, absolutely, even before he did a biopsy and saw *M. leprae bacilli* and confirmed it, she had near-tuberculoid HD. Jack, he was *our* doctor, from Sagrado Familia. One of the disappeared ones."

There it was again.

"Well, he didn't just disappear then."

"Of course not. He was taken by force, guns pointed at his head. They kidnapped him."

"Then why do you call it disappeared?"

She said, "My God, where have you been? It isn't only in Nicaragua and Salvador, it's a Latin American custom. It happens in Guatemala, it's popular all the way south to Argentina. Don't you read? People are taken from their homes, abducted, and they're called *desaparecidos*, the disappeared. And when they're found murdered, you know who did it? *Los descomocidos*, unknown assailants."

Jack was shaking his head. "I'm not sure I ever heard about that."

"Listen to me." She snapped it at him. Then continued in her quiet tone. "The doctor, Rudolfo Meza, from our hospital, he told the colonel Amelita was in the early stages of leprosy. And you know what the colonel did? He drew a pistol and shot the doctor four times in the chest. Murdered him, standing close enough to touch him with the gun barrel. A witness told me, a *contra* woman who deserted a few days later and came to us. Amelita was there, of course. She saw it. . . . "

"I was gonna ask you."

"And she ran. The *contra* woman helped her get to Jinotega, then came to the hospital to warn us, the colonel had sworn to kill Amelita. . . . And you think maybe the guy really liked her. Is that right, Jack?"

He sat there in his navy-blue suit and striped tie and couldn't think of one goddamn thing to say back to her. This lady was not as nice as she appeared; she could show you a hard edge. They had left the interstate and were approaching the river, past chemical works in the near distance, the sight and smell of them along the flats.

"He murdered the doctor for telling him. Then came to the hospital looking for Amelita. He said she had defiled him." The sister's tone hushed in the quiet of the air-conditioned hearse. "He said she had allowed him to enter her body in order to give him the disease and he would kill her for that reason, trying to make him a leper."

FOUR

They passed through the main gate and she came to life, telling him that at one time it was called the Louisiana Leper Home. Her tone relaxed again, natural. And now it was the National Hansen's Disease Center. He knew that but kept quiet, still trying to imagine a man wanting to kill a girl he believed had tried to give him leprosy. Was that possible? She told him the administration building predated the Civil War, was once the mansion on a sugar plantation and all those mossy oak trees must be just as old.

He knew that, too.

Now that same girl, Amelita, was suppose to leave here in the hearse. They could have got a limo for the same price. So it must be somebody was watching. Or it was possible and they weren't taking any chances. Make them think Amelita was dead. . . . But would the staff be in on it? How would they work it?

Meanwhile his tour guide was telling him it amazed her that the world's most advanced training and research center for Hansen's disease was in the United States. And how many people knew about it?

Well, just about everybody in New Orleans did. He'd heard stories that in the old days lepers were brought here in a train with the windows covered, nailed shut; the whole place guarded so they couldn't get out and spread the disease. Somebody on his mother's side of the family, her aunt's father-in-law, had been brought here. . . .

She was saying now it reminded her of a small college campus. There, that view of the main buildings.

It looked to Jack Delaney like a federal correctional facility, minimum security, once you got past the older buildings that had that New Orleans look. The main buildings were all white three-story affairs laid out in rows and connected on all three floors by enclosed walkways that were like high walls with windows. The dormitories, the infirmary, the dining hall, the recreation building, all were connected by the walkways. Why was that? So nobody would see the lepers?

She told him the last time she was here there were about three hundred live-in patients.

The girl, he imagined, would be up on the top floor of the infirmary. If they were making this look real. That's where the morgue was.

New patients would come for sulfone therapy and have to stay only about a month. But there were some who'd been here for years and years, afraid to leave. Some were disfigured, some had lost limbs and got around in wheelchairs. That's why all the building levels were connected.

Oh.

Did he know there was a golf course? Yes, he did, and studied her calm expression, her smile as they passed a couple of sisters in white nurse uniforms. She waved . . .

While he sat here wired, trying to second-guess what was going on. Even a little annoyed. The sister giving him leper facts and the tour while a girl waited to be taken out in a hearse so a freaked-out Nicaraguan would think she was dead. That had to be it. Now she was waving to a guy in a lab coat . . .

And he thought, Yeah, but she got the girl out of Central America by herself under the gun and brought her all the way here, didn't she? So leave her alone. Don't rush her. She knows what she's doing. Look at her, Jesus, with that movie-star nose and the lower lip he wouldn't mind biting . . .

She looked at him just then and Jack said, "My mother's Aunt Elodie was married to a guy, I never knew him, but his dad was here back in the thirties. He was a building contractor and got the disease, according to my mother's aunt, from a colored fella that worked for him. She said he had a little cut on his hand, right here. I remember her telling me when I was little. She lived out Esplanade Avenue in a big frame house that was always dark inside. She kept the shades drawn during the day and it smelled old and musty. I picture her, I can smell that house. She believed that was the way you got leprosy, from a colored person. You had to be careful, she said, if you were around them and you had any cuts. I used to think about that old man, her father-in-law. . . . He died the same year I was born. I couldn't imagine a well-to-do man like that, in New Orleans, having leprosy. Lepers were always natives in Africa or Asia. . . . There was a movie we saw in high school about a leper colony in Burma that I'll never forget. When I think of lepers now I see those people. I mean they were in the worst shape you can imagine, really awful-looking. Some of 'em, I remember, didn't have noses." He paused a moment and said, "But what I remember most was this Italian missionary that ran the place. Guy with a full beard, real long, scraggly, wore a white cassock and a beret. But the thing about him, he was always touching the lepers, no matter how deformed they were. Like he was going out of his way to touch them. Taking hold of the stubs they had for hands, touching their faces . . . "

Jack paused again. They were on the tree-shaded drive that led to the infirmary building, Sister Lucy's gaze on the entrance, directly ahead of them.

He said, "You touch them, too, don't you? Not just the drunks at the soup kitchen, I mean lepers, at the hospital where you worked."

She came to a stop and turned off the ignition before looking at him with those quietly aware eyes.

"That's what you do, Jack, you touch people."

They sat in the hearse parked in the shade of old oak trees while she smoked a cigarette, Jack deciding it was no more weird for a nun than the way she was dressed. She had offered him one, a Kool Filter King. He told her he'd quit three years ago.

"In prison?"

"After I got out. When I was in there I smoked all the time."

Before lighting up she asked if he'd mind and he thought of Buddy Jeannette in the hotel suite that night his life changed. "You mind if I smoke?" Now wondering if the same thing could be happening with a nun, thinking that in the past week he had seen two old movies on TV where guys were with nuns in strange situations . . .

She said, "I left you up in the air. I come here and the place overwhelms me."

"It's a lot bigger than you think it's gonna be."

"What I should remember, it's also a public health service hospital."

"Why do you have to remember that?"

"It's operated by the federal government. Anyone with an *in* can find out things."

He said, "Yeah?" and waited.

"You don't see the connection, do you?"

He said, "We started out you thought I knew things I didn't. Well, if you're still under that impression then I'm sorry but I can't help you. I'm only the driver and I'm not even doing that." Letting her see some of his irritation. Why not? She was a sister, but she wasn't going to make him stay after and clean the erasers if he talked back. "You want the colonel to think she's dead, I can understand that. But why go to all this trouble if he's busy down in Nicaragua?"

"He isn't down in Nicaragua," Sister Lucy said, back to business, her voice quiet, in control. "He's in New Orleans."

"Guy's fighting a war, he drops everything to come after the girl, what'd you say, defiled him?"

"Jack, he was military attaché at the Nicaraguan embassy in Washington. He came here in '79, to Miami, when Somoza's government fell, and we know he was in New Orleans before he went back to Nicaragua. He has friends here. You must know they're getting all kinds of support from the U.S." She paused and said, "Don't you?" Frowning a little. She blew out a stream of smoke and said, "What we know is that the colonel traced us to Mexico and then here. Now *he's* here and has inquired about Amelita. He hasn't sent flowers, Jack, he wants to kill her."

Listen to the nun. He watched her mash the cigarette in the ashtray and close it.

"There's a doctor here, on the staff, who spent years in Nicaragua and was a friend of Rudolfo Meza . . . "

"The one the colonel shot."

"Murdered. At the time I arrived with Amelita I told him the whole story. So he knew the situation and got in touch with me as soon as he found out the colonel had called, asking about her. Right after that she had a visitor, not the colonel but a Nicaraguan. Sister Teresa Victor told him Amelita was seriously ill and couldn't see anyone."

"The whole hospital's in on it? What we're doing?"

"No, not administration; some of the staff. I think a few of the doctors and of course the sisters. There won't be a death certificate. But if anyone inquires the sisters will say they're not permitted to give out information about the deceased, well, other than she was taken to a funeral home."

"Wait a minute."

"Then all you have to do is put a notice in the paper that Amelita Sosa was cremated. She doesn't know a soul here, so anyone who inquires would have to be the colonel or a friend of his."

"I put a notice in the paper."

"Isn't that what you do? I'll pay for it."

"What're you getting me into?"

She said, "I don't think there's the least chance you'll be in any kind of physical danger."

"It's not the physical kind I'm thinking about."

"Sister Teresa Victor spoke to Mr. Mullen . . ." But

now she didn't seem too sure about it. "At least she said she did."

"She told Leo the whole story?"

"Maybe not all the details."

"Maybe not any of 'em. What you're talking about here, don't you think is illegal?"

She said, "A man has vowed to kill an innocent young girl and you want to argue the legality—if I understand you right—of placing a death notice in the paper?"

He liked that, the deadpan delivery. Jack said, "Well, I guess it's not something you could go to jail over."

"Who would know?"

He nodded at that. "You're right."

She said, "What else can I tell you?"

He thought a moment and said deadpan, giving it back to her, "If you saw the colonel right now, would you touch him?"

With just the barest trace of a smile she said, "You're having a good time, aren't you?"

"It's different," Jack said, with the same hint of a smile. "What's the guy's name, the colonel?"

"Dagoberto Godoy."   .

"Is he kinda fat and has a little thin mustache?"

"He has a mustache, but he's trim, you might say good-looking."

Jack said, "Oh."

He brought Amelita Sosa out in a plastic body bag on a wheeled mortuary cot, past empty cars parked along the back of the infirmary building, to the hearse standing in the sun, its rear door open. With the cot touching the step plate he squeezed the handles to collapse the front legs first, then the rear legs as he slipped the cot into the hearse, pushed down the lock button on the door, and closed it firmly.

Jack glanced over at Sister Lucy in her Calvins and heels talking to the doctor who had been in Nicaragua and two Daughters of Charity, the little bowlegged one Sister Teresa Victor, who had been here about fifty years. Jack stood for several moments looking off, hands clasped behind his dark suit in a patient funeral director's pose, thinking that was quite an attractive girl he'd helped into the body bag, not like any leper he had ever seen in pictures. He had touched her zipping up the bag, making sure the zipper didn't get snagged in her flowery shirt. He hadn't noticed any brown spots on her face or arms. He gave Sister Lucy another look before strolling up to the driver's side of the hearse and getting in. By the time he'd started the engine and revved it a couple of times the passenger side door opened and Sister Lucy got in.

"I don't mean to rush you, but Amelita's back there in a plastic bag."

"Oh, my God." She turned in the seat.

"Not yet. Wait'll we're out."

"Can she breathe?"

"Enough, I imagine."

A car came from the drive in front of the infirmary and fell in behind them. There were three cars in line by the time they passed through the gate. Jack watched them in his outside mirror.

"Okay. Now."

Sister Lucy turned to slide open the glass partition, then got all the way around, up on her knees.

"Can you reach it?"

"Barely."

"Pull the cot toward you."

She said, "There." Then began speaking in Spanish to Amelita, hunched over the seat back, her linen jacket pulled up and the curve of her hip in the tight jeans right there next to him. This was different, all right. He glanced at her hip, the neat round shape, without really looking. She was the toucher—what would she do if he touched her? There was touching and there was touching. He could touch the girls he knew bent over the seat and not one of them would think anything of it. They might say, "Hey," but they wouldn't be surprised. It wouldn't mean anything. An affectionate pat. Maybe a little squeeze.

He kept his eyes on the road and began to think about the two movies he had seen on TV in just the past week. In one of them Richard Burton and two other guys are on a life raft with Joan Collins after the ship they were on is torpedoed by a Japanese submarine. She seems to go for Richard, but holds him off when he makes the moves and Richard can't figure out why this girl in the strange-looking playsuit would turn him down. It's not till the end of the picture you find out that Joan Collins is a nun and the strange-looking white outfit she has on is probably nun underwear. Joan Collins was pretty young then. The other movie was the one where Deborah Kerr, in a pure white nun's habit framing her face, her nice nose, is with Robert Mitchum, a U.S. marine, on an island in the South Pacific during the war. Most of the time they're hiding from the Japs in a cave, Deborah and Robert Mitchum alone, looking at each other. You know sooner or later he's going to make the moves on her, but you don't know what she's going to do. Both movies about guys and nuns in intimate situations facing danger together. Something else occurred to Jack while he was thinking about it. He remembered from the TV listings that both movies first came out in 1957. He wasn't sure why he remembered it, though he did notice that kind of thing. And in 1957, when he was twelve years old, he was in love with his seventh-grade teacher, Sister Mary Lucille. Lucille? Lucy? Take it another step. Ten years or so later he fell sort of in love with Sally Field, with her cute little nose, who happened to be in that television series "The Flying Nun" and wore that gull-winged wimple, the head covering, that was not unlike the one the Daughters of Charity used to wear, the same Daughters of Charity that were at Carville.

For whatever that was worth.

There were girls he knew who loved to speculate about signs. Helene would say, "Hey, spooky," if he told her about it. Especially if they were smoking a little dope.

The leggy Calvins came around on the seat.

"Amelita has to go to the bathroom."

"We just left the place."

"Does that mean you won't stop?"

They weren't even to St. Gabriel. It was there ahead of them, a block of storefronts and a few cars, the town half dead on a Sunday afternoon. He crept through the main intersection and kept going until he saw the Exxon station on the right, no cars at the pumps, and rolled toward the shade of the canopy. Restrooms would be on the other side of the station. He'd pull around and back in, like he was getting air for the rear tires and sneak Amelita into the Women's.

There was a café across the road, four young guys between a car and a pickup truck, hanging out, looking this way now. He could give St. Gabriel something to talk about all week. This girl, honest to God, gets out of the back end of a *hearse* . . .

"I don't think it's open."

He braked to a sudden stop near the row of gas pumps and Sister Lucy reached out to the dashboard.

"You see anyone around?"

No, he didn't and the service doors were down. He should've noticed that, no business, nobody home. They'd left a light on inside the station. He could see it through the BIG SPRING TIRE SPECIAL painted on the window. There were credit card emblems on the glass door and another decal he knew something about: VAS, black letters on a gold field, VIDETTE ALARM SYSTEMS guarding the place against breaking and entering. The place looked old, run-down, not the kind you'd bother with.

Now what? There was the café across the road, the farm boys still looking this way. He glanced at the outside mirror and his gaze held on a car parked directly behind them even with the gas pumps.

A black Chrysler sedan. One of the cars that had followed them out of the center. A guy in a tan suit came out from behind the wheel. Now another guy joined him at the front of the car. Dark-haired guys, Latinos. Now they were out of sight, behind the hearse.

"Tell Amelita to play dead and lock your door. Right now. Quick."

Sister Lucy did, just like that, without looking at him or asking questions. She straightened around again as one of the Latinos appeared at her window looking in. A little guy. He touched the window and said something in Spanish. She said in English, "I can hear you. What is it?" The guy began speaking in Spanish again, Sister Lucy looking up at him about a foot away from her, listening.

Jack turned as the other one came up on his side, past him and around to the front of the hearse. Both were little guys, 130-pounders. Jack liked that. What he didn't like were their suit coats and open sport shirts. Not migrant bean pickers, were they? The one on Sister Lucy's side wore sunglasses, his print shirt was silk and his hair was carefully combed. The other one was Creole-looking, a light-skinned black guy with pointy cheekbones and nappy hair. He stared at the windshield of the hearse while the face close behind Sister Lucy continued to speak to her in Spanish.

"He wants you to open the back. He says they're friends of the deceased and would like to see her a last time before she's buried. It has to be now because they have business, they're unable to come to the funeral."

Jack said, "How does he know who's in there? Ask him." He waited while Sister Lucy spoke to the face with sunglasses. The guy said something, one word, and hunched over trying to see into the back of the hearse, squinting, shading his eyes against his reflection in the glass.

Sister Lucy looked at Jack quickly, about to speak. But the face with the sunglasses straightened and began talking again, his expression solemn.

"He says they want to say a prayer for the departed. He says they're determined to do this, or they wouldn't be able to live with themselves."

Jack waited because she kept looking at him, her eyes alive, as though she wanted to say more but couldn't, the face so close behind her. Jack nodded, taking his time, making a decision. "Tell him I wish I could help him, but it's against the law to show a body on the street." She started to turn and he said, "Wait. But tell him he's gonna see one if his partner doesn't move out of the way, now, 'cause we're leaving." He saw her eyes, for a moment, open wider and saw the guy's face staring at him. Jack said, "He understands, but tell him anyway. Put it in your own words."

She said, "Jack," her voice low, "look at me. He has a gun." The fingers of her right hand slipped inside her jacket at the waist. "Right here."

The man was talking again and she listened, still looking at Jack. "He wants to know why we're being difficult." Translating as the face with the sunglasses spoke through the window. "He says it will only take a minute. He wants you to turn off the motor and get out. With the key." She listened again and then said, "If you try to drive off someone will be dead in this coach. If there isn't someone already."

He saw her eyes and then she was turning away, saying something back to him now in rapid Spanish, fluent, an edge to her tone. The window framed the face with the sunglasses and the BIG SPRING TIRE SPECIAL behind him, lettered on the window of the empty station with the light on inside and the decals on the door.

Jack said, "Don't get him mad, okay?" He took the key from the ignition and she turned back to him as he opened the door. "But keep talking." He got out, pushed the lock button down and closed the door.

The farm boys across the street were uncapping beers in the sunlight, still watching, a boy turning his head to remark, speculate, force a laugh, fool with the bill of his tractor cap. Trying to liven up a Sunday afternoon in St. Gabriel. Jack had known some farm boys at Angola, one who'd killed a man with a beer bottle, drunk.

He'd known guys like the face with the sunglasses and the Creole-looking guy standing in front of the hearse, the guy turning to face him as he came around. They'd stand like that in the Big Yard looking for some new guy to turn out, give him that sleepy mean look and not move out of the way. The dead-eyed stare saying, Walk around me, man. But knowing if you did you might as well hand over your balls, they weren't yours anymore. He would walk around this one; there was nothing to prove. But you didn't have to walk around any of them in the yard if, one, you walked over them or, two, you used your head. If you knew before they tried to turn you out you were smarter than they were, smarter than at least 95 percent of the entire prison population . . .

Smarter than these two assholes giving him that old familiar look. Jesus, he hoped so, if he had learned anything of value in those thirty-five months. A good rule was, whenever you were with people whose intentions were in doubt, the first thing you did was look for a way out or something to hit them with.

He nodded and smiled at the Creole-looking guy with the nappy hair as he walked past him. "How you doing, partner?" And said to the face with the sunglasses, the guy stepping away from the hearse, "This never happened to me before. Long as I've been in the funeral business." Jack kept moving toward the station.

The guy said, "Hey, where you going?" Coming after him now, the Creole-looking guy closing in, too.

Jack stopped at the door and half turned. "I have to get something."

The face with the sunglasses, close to him, said, "No, you can't go in there. Look." He reached past Jack and tried to turn the knob on the glass, wood-framed door. "See? Is locked. You can't go in there."

Jack said, "Yeah, I guess you're right." He looked around, frowning, and said, "Shit. Now what am I gonna do? I have to go the toilet and the key's inside there. See, it's on the desk. Has a hunk a board wired to it so nobody'll steal it. Toilet keys being as valuable as they are."

The face with the sunglasses said, "Go someplace else. Tha's no problem for you."

They stood close to each other. Jack said in a quiet voice, "I think we both have a problem. You want my car key and I want the key to the toilet. We're a couple of desperate characters, aren't we? Desperadoes. You know what I'm saying to you?" The face with the sunglasses staring at him, not answering. "Only I'm more desperate than you are, partner. You don't believe it I'll show you."

Jack turned to face the door, took a short place-kick sort of step, his eyes on the VIDETTE ALARM SYSTEMS decal, and punched the sole of a black loafer through the plate glass.

The blast of sound from the burglar alarm was so immediate and loud he barely heard the glass shatter. Even louder than he'd expected. He looked around at the guy in the sunglasses edging away. The Creole-looking guy didn't move and the other one had to gesture to him. Jack watched them move off in a hurry, turned, and there was Sister Lucy's face in the side window, staring. And beyond the hearse the farm boys across the road, their heads raised to the clanging racket, heads turning now to follow the black Chrysler peeling its tires out of there, from shade into sunlight and gone, down the blacktop toward the inter-state. Jack watched too, thinking, Well, there were other roads home, with bathrooms along the way. He had not felt this good in . . . he couldn't remember.

The sister had a different look for him as he slipped in behind the wheel. Not exactly wide-eyed, but sort of stunned, lips parted, eyes staring in what he would like to think was respectful amazement. She didn't say a word. He didn't either until they were pulling away from that urgent sound and he gave her his nice-guy smile.

"That's why I only went into hotel rooms."

FIVE

As soon as Jack turned onto Camp Street he saw the white Cadillac stretch limo in front of the soup kitchen.

Right away he tried to think of a clever line, a quick, offhand comment. He would have said to Helene the first thing that came to mind: "Boy, you must really cook good." For Lucy he'd try a little harder.

But then, when he saw the way she was looking at the car, not the least bit surprised, curiosity messed up his concentration. So he didn't say anything. He angled across the one-way street to bring the hearse in close behind the limo. Then, just as Sister Lucy was saying, "That's my dad," a black guy in a tan chauffeur suit was getting out.

Giving Jack a crack at another line. There was another obvious one. But now he was thinking that if her dad rode around in a stretch limo this was a nun from a very wealthy family. Which he'd never heard of before. But could explain how she'd bought the VW in Nicaragua—something he'd been wondering about. Except she would have taken a vow of poverty along with chastity and obedience. . . . And by this time it was too late to think of anything clever. She was out of the hearse as her dad made his appearance.

He came ducking out of the car quick and agile, that wiry kind who reaches his fifties with still a lot of boy in him. Jack saw his energy, then his confidence in the relaxed way he stood: arms open to his daughter but with the elbows tucked in, cocking his head now, holding that pose as he called to her. "There's my girl. Sis, I mean to tell you, you look just great." He seemed easy to type, coming out of a limo in his soft calfskin jacket and tailored jeans down on his hips, his cowboy boots. But Jack wasn't sure if he looked like a retired rodeo star or a movie producer. He had seen movie producers on location in New Orleans, had watched them shoot in the Quarter realizing, shit, *that's* what he should be, a movie actor. It was strange to see Sister Lucy going into a man's arms, giving him a kiss on the cheek. He held onto her, patting her back with big hands for a man his size, a ring gleaming there, which Jack squinted to appraise. Now they were talking face to face—she didn't have his nose—her dad keeping a hand on her arm.

Jack turned to slide open the glass partition. He could see the crown of Amelita's head, her body encased in the plastic bag. "You okay?" She murmured something and he saw her move. "Hang on. It won't be long." Amelita seemed like a very patient girl. She didn't have Bambi eyes, but they were nice ones, a liquid brown.

The plan was to drop Lucy off so she could get her car. She'd said "my car," which had sounded strange, vow-of-poverty-wise, another one to add to the list of questions he might ask her sometime. He'd take Amelita to the funeral home and Sister Lucy would call later with the next move. Some plan. Leo would be there by seven. It was now a quarter to—

Sister Lucy was motioning to him, her dad looking this way. Jack got out and walked over. She said, "Jack Delaney, my dad," letting it go at that.

Her dad put his hand out and said, "Dick Nichols, Jack. It's a pleasure." Rough hand and a rough face up close; he had curly hair going gray but a dark mustache. Rodeo star, not a movie producer. "I don't envy you your job, caring for the dead, but I guess somebody has to do it. My broker and'n accountant I had one time were buried from Mullen's. I 'magine you've heard of the Saint Clair funeral people in Lafayette . . . "

Jack said, "I don't think so." Her dad's driver, standing by the car, was watching him. Young black guy with shoulders in that tan double-breasted suit.

"Way the oil business is causing heart attacks those people stay busy, I mean to tell you."

Sister Lucy said, "My dad lays pipe," with her dry tone, "and builds those offshore platforms."

"Uh-unh, I got shuck of that, Sis, before I had to eat it." He grinned, shaking his head, and looked at Jack. "There was a time—see, I started out I was selling oil leases, then I got into drilling and lost two, what you might consider, fortunes before I was thirty years old. Blowouts, both times, wiped me clean. But back starting out, man, I scraped, borrowed, signed notes on everything we owned to put two hundred fifty thousand in a lease block. Sis's mom says, 'But, honey,' "—changing his tone to sound vague—" 'if the deal goes bust how do we eat?' I said, 'We eat *it,* sweetheart. That's the business.' "

When Sister Lucy said, "How is mother?" Jack looked at her. She didn't sound too interested.

But then when her dad glanced at his driver and said, "Clovis put her on the plane to New York this morning, she's just fine," Sister Lucy seemed to perk up. Jack caught it.

She said, "To buy clothes, I imagine."

Dick Nichols said, "She isn't going all that way to buy toothpaste. You see the light on in my office late at night, that's me turning out hundred-dollar bills. Hey, but it's fun. I'm in the helicopter end of the business now." He said to Jack, "Tell you what, I'll lease you a 214 Super-Transport Bell for ninety-five grand a month. How's that sound? Mullen could be the first funeral home in New Orleans to offer burial at sea. Take 'em out over the Gulf a few miles, the priest reads the prayer, sprinkles on some holy water, and out they go. Listen, I'd rather have that'n get taken to Saint Louis Number One and stuck in a vault. All those people crowded in there with their statues and monuments, uh-unh. I like the country, Sis, I always have."

She said to Jack, "My dad lives in Lafayette and my mother lives here in New Orleans."

"I have visiting privileges. If I call first and talk sweet."

She said to Jack, "My dad can get you into Galatoire's without waiting in line."

Giving him that quiet look, something between them he could feel, as her dad checked his watch and said, Hey, he'd told them seven, and told Jack he and Sis were going over to Paul's have them some crabs and shrimp and good conversation; stay away from politics they might just find something they could agree on—her dad grinning—now that she had her head on straight again. What did that mean? Jack wanted to look at her, frown, make a face, but her dad had him locked in, shaking his hand, saying it was awful nice talking to him and hoped they could do it again real soon. There. When that was done and Jack was finally able to turn to her, she was still looking at him with that quiet look. She said, "My dad can even get into K-Paul's without waiting in line," touched Jack's hand and said, "What do you think of that?"

Buddy Jeannette's rosary was going on in the small parlor, the mechanical drone of fifty Hail Marys recited by family and those who hadn't got out in time. Jack, watching from the front hall, counted thirty-seven sitting and kneeling, the priest leading the rosary from the prie-dieu at the casket—a Batesville made of hand-rubbed walnut with the Cameo Crepe interior. Buddy had apparently left his widow in good shape. She was older than Jack had imagined her, a petite little thing, sitting on the edge of a wing-back chair saying her beads, somewhat apart from the others. What was she thinking about with that faraway look, lips barely moving? He wanted to hold her hand and say something to her. He had seen more than a thousand people in these visitation rooms and was never sure who was mourning and who wasn't. He wanted to tell her what a nice guy Buddy was, that everybody liked him, a lot . . .

Leo said, "You want to tell me what's going on?"

Jack turned from the doorway. "What's wrong?"

Leo said, "I go up to the bathroom, there's a girl in there brushing her hair's supposed to be dead. I've never had that happen before."

"If I remember correctly," Jack said, "you're the one sent me to get her. You said you'd talked to Sister Teresa Victor."

"I did, yesterday. I was prepping your friend in there."

"Well, you better talk to her again." He took a step to walk off.

"Jack, I'm busy, I've got people here."

"Then call her later. If I tell you why I picked up somebody who isn't dead you'll say it was my idea. Talk to the sister and I'll see you after while." Jack walked across the hall and up the stairway.

He found Amelita in the casket selection room, browsing, running her fingers over the parquet finish of a Batesville done in solid oak. Jack said, "That's the Homestead model, with your Tawny Beige interior. We can give you fiberboard, plastic, metal, or hardwood, from sixty to sixteen thousand dollars, depending on your budget and how sorry you are to see the loved one go. I'm glad we're not putting you in one, you look too healthy." She did, the overhead light shining in her dark hair, long, down to the middle of her back in the flowery shirt, reflecting in her dark eyes as she looked at him.

"They so nice inside"—touching the tawny crepe now —"so soft."

"Like you could sleep forever in there, huh? Do you know where you're gonna be staying?"

"I'm going to L.A. sometime, but I don't know when. I hope soon, I always want to go there."

"To Los Angeles?"

"Yes, I have two of my aunts and a grandmother live in L.A. I hear is pretty nice there. When you put people in this, do they have all their clothes on?"

"Yeah, they're completely dressed. Did Sister Lucy say where you'll be staying in New Orleans?"

"She said she find a place. I like this pink color inside, very nice."

"Well, Sister Lucy seems to know what she's doing. You've known her a few years . . ."

"Yes, a long time."

"She told me what happened to you. That was awful, the guy taking you away from your home. Twice, in fact, huh? The first time you must've been just a kid."

"You mean Bertie?"

"What's his name, the colonel."

"Yes, Bertie. Colonel Dagoberto Godoy Diaz. He was very important in the government. I mean before, the real government. He could buy one of these, even the one you said, sixty thousand."

"Sixteen, not sixty. He *killed* a guy. The doctor."

"I know. He had so much anger, it was terrible."

"And you saw him do it."

"Tha's what I mean, to see him like that." She hugged her arms and seemed to shudder. "Not the same man I knew in Managua." She reached into the casket to feel the pillow, once again relaxed. "He was going to enter me in the Señorita Universo, but the war became worse and he had to leave, so I went home." She seemed fascinated by the pleated material covering the pillow.

Jack took his time. "But now, the way I understand it, Amelita, he wants to kill you."

"She tole you that, uh? Yes, he was so angry he thought he would get leprosy, but he won't. You don't give it to a person that way, you know, like that disease now is popular, or the old one they call the clop. Someone has to

tell Bertie he won't get it. Though I heard the Comman-
dante Edén Pastora, also with the *contras,* has mountain
leprosy, but I don't know what kind that is. Perhaps only
from insect bites."

Jack said, "Wait. Okay? This guy kidnapped you. I
mean before. He disappeared you, came at night and
grabbed you and took you up in the mountains. Is that
right?"

"Yes, of course," turning to him with a look of surprise. "He want me to be with him." Her gaze softened
then as she said, "When you like a girl very much, don't you
want her to be with you? You have girl friends, I bet all
kinds of them." She smiled, moving closer. "Good-looking
guy with expensive clothes," taking his seven-dollar striped
tie between her fingers, feeling it. "I saw your nice rooms
you have, with a big refrigerator has beer and a bottle of
vodka in it. Sure, I bet you bring girls here for the evening.
Maybe stay all night. . . . Oh, you look surprise. I know
American guys in Managua when I was there would do that,
open their eyes. Who, me? Like a little boy. I think only
American guys do that, but I'm not certain. Want you to
believe they always so good. But you bring girls here, don't
you? Tell me the truth."

"Once or twice I have."

"Tell me something else, okay? You ever get in one of
these with the girl?"

Jack said, "Are you serious?"

"I jus' wonder. It so nice and soft," touching the
Tawny Beige crepe again.

He said, "Amelita, that's a casket."

"Yes, I know what it is. But I never look inside one or
feel it. Like a little bed, uh?"

He said, "Why don't we go sit down, take it easy."

She gave him a sly look over her shoulder. "In your room? Yes, I think that would be nice."

He thought a moment and said, "If I was the one pulled you out of the situation you were in . . . "

"Yes?"

"I'd seriously consider throwing you back."

She frowned. "You mad at me? Why?"

No, he wasn't, really; but all he said was, "Come on," and turned out the lights in the casket selection room. They walked down the hall past his apartment and the prep room to Leo's office.

"Sister Lucy'll get in touch as soon as she's free. If she doesn't, you'll have to sleep on that." He nodded toward a cracked and creased leather sofa that was old as Mullen & Sons.

Amelita sat down in it, saying, "Why do you call her that?"

Jack said, "What?" looking at the mess on Leo's desk, letters and invoices, blank *First Call Records* lying by the phone. No new business.

"I say why do you call her Sister Lucy? She's not a sister no more. She jus' Lucy. Or Lucy Nichols, if you want to say all her name."

Jack looked up, stared at the girl sitting in the middle of Leo's worn-out sofa. He took a moment.

"What're you talking about, she's not a sister? That's what I called her . . . " He took another moment to think about it. "I'm sure I did, and she didn't say she wasn't."

"Maybe she so use to it."

"All the guys at the mission when I picked her up, they called her sister. I can hear 'em. And Leo, the guy I work for . . . " Jack paused, not sure if he could count Leo. Leo might've assumed she was a nun, because she'd been at a mission in Nicaragua.

Amelita said, "I don't know who you talking about, but I know she isn't a sister. She quit being one. You think if she was a sister you see her dress like that, with those Calvin Kleins? I'm going to buy a pair when I go to L.A."

"I wondered about that."

"Sure, soon as I go there."

"How do you know? Did she tell you?"

"When we lef' Nicaragua in the car. She say to me, I'm not going to be a sister no more. I can't do it."

"She said that?"

"I jus' tole you she say it."

"I mean, are you sure?"

Amelita shrugged. "Ask her, you don't believe me." Her gaze roamed over the office, to Leo's mortuary science license framed on the wall, before returning to Jack, standing by the desk. "She was nice when she was a sister. She was the nicest one at Sagrado Familia."

"Don't you think she's nice now?"

"Yes, but she's different. I think something is happening to her."

When she called she said, "Jack? It's Lucy." He waited and she said, "Jack?"

"How was dinner?"

"I'd like to tell you about it."

"Boiled shrimp and beer?"

"I may never see my dad again. How's Amelita?"

"She's okay. What happened?"

"I really would like to talk to you." It was her voice, but it was different, strained; she was keeping it in control. "If you could bring Amelita here. . . . I'm at home, my mother's house, 101 Audubon, on the uptown side of the park."

"I know where it is. Are you alone?"

"The housekeeper's here, Dolores. . . . If you could come as soon as you can. . . . But not in the hearse. Just in case . . . "

He said, "No, I have a car." He waited a moment and said, for the first time, "Lucy?"

"What?"

"We'll be right over."

SIX

She brought him through a hall of dim portraits and framed pictures of Carnival balls, past sitting and dining rooms that were dark, formal, to a sun parlor that was startling, the atmosphere suddenly tropical as he looked at walls papered in a blaze of green-and-gold banana trees. Lamplight reflected on giant green fronds, on green-cushioned wicker, a ceiling fan, baskets of fern, a bar with bottles displayed against tinted glass. On the wicker coffee table was a glass of sherry. She was quiet, polite, wearing a white shirt now with tan slacks and sandals. She asked him if he'd help himself to a drink, then asked if he was sure he wasn't hungry—as he poured vodka over ice—Dolores was fixing something for Amelita and it would be no trouble. He shook his head. She said Dolores had been to church. She said Dolores had been attending the African Baptist Church on Esplanade as long as she could remember. She said Dolores used to teach her hymns and it disturbed her mother to hear Protestant songs in the house. Jack took a sip of the drink and looked at her and said, "You're not a sister anymore."

She said, "No, I'm not."

"I called you Sister."

"Once or twice."

"You sound different."

She seemed to smile.

"I mean since this afternoon."

She was looking at his drink and said, "Let me try that." He handed her the glass. She took a sip of the vodka and looked at him with that round lower lip pouting as she swallowed, then shook her head. "I still don't like it."

"You're trying different things again?"

She said, "The day I got back to New Orleans I called my mother for the name of a hairdresser. I'd made up my mind, after thinking about it for at least a year, I was going to get a perm. Curl my hair and change my image. I felt I needed to pick myself up. So I made the appointment. . . . It wasn't until I was in the chair, looking at myself in the mirror, I realized that a perm wasn't going to do it."

"Do what?"

"I mean it wasn't necessary. I'd already changed. You said I sound different. I am, I'm not the same person I was a year ago or this afternoon, or the same person right now that I'm going to be."

She was close enough to touch; not as tall as earlier today, in the heels. He said, "I think you made the right decision. That's the way your hair should be, natural." He thought a moment and said, "The day I got home from Angola, the first thing I was gonna do was get dressed up and head for the bar at the Roosevelt, like I'd never been away. But I didn't. My parole came up the same time as a friend of mine, guy named Roy Hicks." Jack felt himself start to smile. "Roy had a way of looking at you, with this cold stare, not putting much into it at all, but it was like he was asking if you wanted to die. He wasn't that big, either."

Lucy had started to smile because he did, but now the smile left her eyes. "I thought you said you were friends."

"We were. Roy taught me how to jail. No, he didn't give *me* the look, it was for guys who came onto him or got out of line. . . . You know what I'm talking about?"

"I think so."

He started to smile again, knowing what he was going to tell, and saw Lucy ready to smile, he was pretty sure. It encouraged him, made it all right to show off a little, slip into a role with her that was comfortable, natural; the feeling he could tell her anything he wanted.

"We get to New Orleans, Roy says he has some business to tend to and wants me to come along. We take a cab over to the projects, you know, off Rampart? We go up to a door, Roy bangs on it with his fist. . . . I forgot to mention, Roy Hicks was a New Orleans cop at one time, but that's another story."

"What was he doing in prison?"

"That's what I mean it's another story; but a good one. We're in the projects, this black guy opens the door I think I recognize. He doesn't invite us in, but he knows us and we go in, and I see three more black guys sitting there. The place, I find out later, is a dope house. I'm thinking, what am I doing here, as Roy says to the black guy that runs it, 'Shake hands, dude.' But the guy doesn't want to. By then I realize I know the guy; he was at Angola and got his release about six months before us. He ran a still while he was inside, made home brew out of fruit cocktail, rice, raisins, whatever he could find. It was terrible stuff. He'd sell it and give Roy a cut, something like half, 'cause Roy had given him permission to make it." He saw Lucy frown and said, "Roy ran the dormitory we were in, Big Stripe, medium security." He didn't know what else to tell her. "It's the way it is, part of the convict social structure. . . . Anyway, Roy goes, 'Shake hands, dude.' Says it a couple more times and finally the guy sticks his hand out. Roy grabs it, gets an armlock on him, pulls a gun out of the guy's pants, a P.38, with the three guys sitting there watching. Roy tells the guy he's got in the armlock he left owing Roy money, and with accumulated interest the amount was now two thousand dollars. The guy told Roy he was crazy, couldn't he see they were outside now? That kind a deal was over with. Roy goes, 'It ain't over till I say it is. Pay up, dude,' never raising his voice or threatening the guy, and the guy finally gave him the money."

Lucy was staring at him. "Amazing."

"You understand, the guy might've owed him a few bucks, but this was a shakedown. Or with the gun you could even say it was a thinly disguised stickup. We get in the cab I ask Roy if he's flipped out. He goes, 'It's like you fall off a bike you have to get right back on it again.' I said to him, 'Yeah, we took a fall, but I don't see ripping off a dope house the same as getting back into what we were doing.' Meaning neither of us, strictly speaking, had ever been into armed robbery. Roy goes, 'What difference is it what statute you break, B and E or going in with a gun? You think you're ever gonna live like a civilian?' I told him I had every intention of trying. He goes, 'Well, here's a start.' Counts out half the money, a thousand bucks, and hands it to me."

She said it again. "Amazing."

"I was thinking, that kind of scene is enough to curl your hair, if you don't want to pay to get a perm."

Lucy's eyes raised. "It looks fairly straight now."

"Yeah, well, that's from working in a funeral home, seeing unexpected sights that get it to stand on end."

"What's your friend Roy doing?"

"He's a bartender. Works in the Quarter."

She took his glass and poured another vodka before looking up at him again. "Let's sit down. I want to tell you something."

"When my dad put up his new office building in Lafayette, he told me this at dinner, it was going to cost just over three million dollars. But they'd have to remove a live oak that was about a hundred and fifty years old. So my dad had the plans changed. He built his office at right angles, sort of around the tree, and it cost him another half million. . . . What do you think that says about him?"

It was quiet in the room. Jack could feel the vodka, a good feeling in soft lamplight. He liked the fit of the deep-cushioned wicker chair; he could fall asleep here. Lucy waited, not far away, on the end of the sofa close to his chair, legs crossed. She leaned forward now to reach her sherry. He thought of ways to answer, moved only his arm, slowly, to raise the glass, and gazed at banana trees before taking a sip.

"He loves nature."

"Is that why he's contaminating the Gulf?"

"I thought he leased helicopters."

"He's in the oil business. He's been in the oil business all his life. My mother calls him Texas Crude. Men in her family wore white linen suits and owned sugar plantations in Plaquemines."

"I'm not good at environment," Jack said. He could fall asleep by closing his eyes. "Or, what's that other word, ecology. I'm weak in those areas."

"You see my dad as a nice guy."

"I think he works at it some. Wants to give you that impression, one of the boys."

She said, "Then you know he's not just good old Dick Nichols, he's Dick Nichols Enterprises. He sings Cajun songs, eats squirrel and alligator tail, but he's also been to the White House for dinner, twice. He loves nature as long as he and his pals can suck oil out of it and he doesn't give a damn about that tree. He's using it. He's the guy at the Petroleum Club with the live oak that cost him a half million dollars. Not a yacht or a plane, they all have those, including my dad. No, this is a tree."

Jack said, "Well, it's nice to be rich."

"Buy anything you want," Lucy said. "My dad came to visit me in Nicaragua, seven years ago. An embassy limousine arrives, a long black Cadillac, and my dad steps out, the last person I ever expected to see. Except that he loves to surprise you and act very nonchalant about it. 'Hi, Sis, how are you? Nice day, isn't it?' He knows he's obvious, so it's funny. I showed him around and he seemed interested enough, he was cordial. But he'd pretend not to see the lepers, the ones who were crippled or disfigured."

"Wouldn't shake hands with 'em."

"Not even with the staff. He kept his hands behind his back. He said, 'Sis, this place is awful. What do you need?' I said, 'How about giving the patients a ride in your car?' I told him it would be an experience they'd never forget. He gave me a check for a hundred thousand dollars instead."

Jack took a sip of his drink, wondering if her dad had

kissed her when he arrived. He could understand her dad not being a toucher. How many people were? He said, "I know what you're getting at."

She said, "No, you don't."

"It's easier to give to 'em than go near 'em."

She said, "Jack," not reacting, but with her quiet manner, knowing what she was going to say, "last week he wrote another check, this one for sixty-five thousand."

"For the hospital?"

"For the man who destroyed the hospital, the man who burned it to the ground and hacked ten of the patients to death. I was there, Jack. I saw them drive up in a truck. . . . The men got out and began firing, all of them with automatic weapons. They shot our dogs, they shot out the windows of the hospital. . . . I came out of the sisters' house and heard him yelling at them and thought he was trying to stop the firing. He was, he was yelling at them in Spanish, 'With machetes! Do it with machetes!' Some of the patients ran or were able to hide. I brought a few of them into our house. But the ones in the ward, who couldn't run, were hacked to death in their beds, screaming. . . . You know who I'm talking about, Dagoberto Godoy and his *contras*. When he came to kill Amelita and didn't find her." She paused and said, "I had never laid eyes on him before that day, and now I'll never forget him." She paused again and said, "Excuse me," getting up now. "I'll say good night to Amelita and fix you something to eat, if you're hungry."

She came back with a pack of Kools, tapping one out. Jack picked up the silver table lighter and held it to her cigarette. He watched her sit back blowing a slow stream of smoke, relaxing in the green cushions of the sofa, and he said, "You mind?" Picking up the pack of cigarettes and getting one for himself. He'd have *one*, and inhaled for the first time in nearly three years, telling her he still wasn't hungry, not the least bit. He was keyed up and told her he was a little confused, trying to get all of it straight in his mind. He said it seemed like whenever she told him something else he'd have more questions and not know where to start.

She said, "What would you like to know?"

"This guy tries to kill Amelita and she says, well, he was angry, but he really wants her to be with him. She even calls him Bertie."

Lucy's head remained against the cushion. She said, "I know. Amelita's a little screwed up. *Bertie,* I love it. He changed her life and she doesn't want to believe he murders people. But she wasn't at the hospital when he came. She was with her parents. That's why I was able to get her out of there."

"It doesn't make sense."

"Of course not."

"He killed them because they were lepers?"

"With machetes—he doesn't need a reason. He shot Dr. Meza to death. He assassinated a priest while he was saying mass and formally executed six catechists in Estelí. They killed an agrarian reform worker with bayonets, shot his wife in the spine and left her for dead. . . . She watched them strangle their year-old baby. Ask Bertie why he let his men do that. They slashed the throats of nine farmers near Paiwas, raped several of their daughters, raped and decapitated a fourteen-year-old girl in El Guayaba. Murdered five women, six men, and nine children in El Jorgito. . . . Do you want a complete list? I'll give you one. Do you want to see photos? I'll show you those, too. Have you ever seen a little girl's head on a stake?"

There was a silence in the room that seemed to Jack, for a moment, like a stage set: the backdrop of wallpapered banana trees as she told him about death in a tropical place.

"He did all that?"

"I haven't counted the disappeared," Lucy said, "or the ones who were only tortured. Or the ones who were killed with more sophisticated means. A priest in Jinotega opened the trunk of his car and was blown to bits. Bertie killed him. He found out it was the priest who drove us to León to buy the car, when we escaped. I have a letter from one of the sisters; I'd like to read it to you sometime."

Jack felt awkward, not sure what to say.

"But what can you do? It's a war."

"Is that what you call it? Killing children, innocent people?"

"I mean you can't have him arrested."

"No, not even if he were still in Nicaragua. But now he's here, raising money to buy more guns and pay his men. Three days ago in Lafayette my dad had Bertie to lunch, listened to the guy's pitch, and gave him a check for sixty-five thousand dollars."

"Your dad's helping him? Why?"

"There are people, Jack, who believe that if you aren't for Bertie you're for communism. It's much the same as saying, if you don't like Dixie beer then you must like vodka." She said it with that dry tone, the quiet look, her head resting against the cushion. "My dad and his friends are passing Bertie around, inviting him to their homes—he's a celebrity. He has a letter from the President and that's good for a check every time he shows it."

"The president of what? You mean *the* president?"

"Of the United States of America. He calls the *contras* our brothers. 'Freedom fighters.' Quote. 'The moral equivalent of our Founding Fathers.' And if you believe that you can join my dad's club. But here's the part you're not going to believe."

He watched Lucy lean out of the chair to stub her cigarette in the ashtray, the light touching her dark hair. He was glad she didn't get the perm.

"At dinner my dad began telling me about the Nicaraguan former embassy attaché war hero he invited to lunch, a personal friend of several important people in the White House." As she sat back, Lucy said, "And anyone affiliated with *that* club is more than welcome at my dad's, no questions asked. My dad hadn't told me the hero's name, but I knew it was Bertie. First, my dad tells me how this guy is a guerrilla commander, leading a dedicated fight against the Communists. And then he puts on his nonchalant act and says, 'Oh, by the way. The colonel mentioned that you two have met, or you know each other from somewhere.' I haven't said a word yet. But now I'm pretty sure that when I do I'm going to let him have it. I could feel it tightening up in me. My dad says, 'Yeah, he's looking for some girl up here, a friend of his or used to be his sweetheart, and wonders if you might be able to help him find her.' " Lucy paused. "You like it so far?"

Jack didn't say a word, waiting.

"I said, 'Did the colonel tell you where we met?' My dad shook his head. 'No, he didn't.' I asked if the colonel had told him why he wants to find the girl. My dad said, 'No, I don't believe he did.' I said, 'Do you want me to tell you why?' He said sure. I said, 'Because he wants to fucking kill her, that's why.' "

There was a silence. Jack didn't move. She kept looking at him and he said to her, "So you let him have it."

"I gave him every murder and atrocity I could remember. My dad said, 'You don't believe that stuff, do you?' I said, 'Dad, I was *there*. I saw it happen.' He didn't like that. He said, 'Yeah, but it's a war, Sis. Awful things happen in a war.' I said, 'How would you know? You don't fight wars, you finance them.'" She raised her sherry and took a sip. "So much for dinner with dad. . . . I had softshell crabs."

Jack said, "Lucy Nichols, you've come a long way from the nunnery."

She said, "But not from Nicaragua. He's brought it here."

Jack said, "Bertie knew it was your dad, huh?"

"He's given a list, rich guys in the oil business. He looks at the names, he knows Amelita and I flew to New Orleans, he finds out I live here. I don't think it's a coincidence, I think the idea of using my dad has enormous appeal. He could be in Houston raising funds, but he's not, he's here. New Orleans is a *contra* shipping point; they have arms and supplies stored here waiting to go out."

Jack felt an urge to get up, move. He reached for a cigarette instead. One more. If he ever started smoking again it wouldn't be Kools. He sat back looking at her legs stretched out on the coffee table now, ankles crossed. One sandal was loose and he could see the curve of her instep. He wondered what she was like, when she was a girl, before she became a nun.

She said, "Sometime, within the next few days, I have to get Amelita on a flight to Los Angeles."

"That doesn't sound too hard."

He wondered if she'd ever suddenly with somebody gone swimming in her underwear at night, in the Gulf of Mexico off Pass Christian.

She said, "I suppose not. If I'm careful."

He watched her draw on her cigarette, turn her head slightly to exhale a slow stream.

"And somehow, before Bertie gets ready to leave with his funds, I have to think of a way to stop him."

Jack waited a moment. He said, "And"—feeling himself alive but not wanting to move now, not wanting to ruin the mood—"you're wondering if a person with my experience, not to mention the kind of people I know, might not be able to help you."

Lucy's eyes moved, her quiet gaze coming back to him. She said, "It crossed my mind."

He wondered if she had ever made love on a beach. Or in bed. Or anywhere.

"What you're saying," Jack said, "you don't care if Bertie leaves . . ."

"As long as the money stays here."

Jack drew on his cigarette, taking his time. Shit, he could play this. This was his game.

"What does he do with the checks?"

"They're made payable to, I think it's the Committee to Free Nicaragua. Something like that."

"He puts them in the bank?"

"I guess so."

"Then what? Where would he buy the guns?"

"I suppose either here or in Honduras—that's where their arms depots and training centers are. But I'm sure he'd take American dollars and exchange them for cordobas to pay his men."

"How? By private plane?"

"Or in a boat."

"From where?"

"I have no idea."

"Ask your dad."

"We're not speaking."

"Both of you aren't, or just you?"

"I'll see what I can find out."

"Ask him where Bertie's staying."

"He's at a hotel in New Orleans."

"You're kidding."

"But I don't know which one."

"You're gonna have to kiss and make up with your dad before we can start to move."

Now Lucy was hesitant. "You're saying you're going to help me?"

"I'll tell you the truth, I've never heard of one like this before. You're breaking the law, a big one. But you can also look at it another way, that you'd be doing something for mankind." Jack paused, realizing he had never used the word *mankind* before in his life. "I mean if you want to rationalize. You know, tell yourself it's okay."

"I don't think we need to look for moral permission," Lucy said. "I can justify this in my mind without giving it a second thought. But if the idea of saving lives doesn't move you enough, think of what you might do with your share. I'd like to use half the money to rebuild the hospital. To me, that would seem all the justification we need. But the other half would be yours, if that's agreeable."

Jack took his time, wanting to be sure of this. "You're telling me we're gonna keep it?"

"We can't very well give it back."

"How much are we talking about?"

"He told my dad he'd like to raise five million."

"Jesus Christ," Jack said.

Lucy's eyes smiled. "Our savior."

SEVEN

Jack pulled up to the front entrance of the Carrollton Health Care Center. He was out of the hearse when the young light-skinned black guy dressed in white came running through the automatic doors waving his arms, telling him, "Get that thing out of there. Man, those old people look out the window, they have a fit and die if they don't fall down and break their hip."

Jack looked at the name tag on the guy's white shirt. "Cedric, I'm picking up . . . " He had to get the note out of his suit coat pocket then and look at it. "I'm picking up a Mr. Louis Morrisseau."

"He's ready, but you have to do it 'round back."

"How about the death certificate?"

"Yeah, Miz Hollenbeck has it."

87

"Where's Miz Hollenbeck?"

"She in the front office there."

"Why don't I go in and get the death certificate and then drive around back? How would that be?"

"But was Miz Hollenbeck say for me to tell you," Cedric said, holding his shoulders hunched, the building behind him, then moving his head, giving it a slight nod to the side. "You see anybody in the window look like an alligator? That's Miz Hollenbeck."

Jack looked over at a row of front windows.

"You want people to die?" Cedric said. "You want that woman to climb on my ass?"

Jack said, "Hey, Cedric, turn around."

"She watching?"

"Look, will you—the second window, there's a guy in a maroon bathrobe. You know his name?"

"Where?" Cedric said, coming around casually. "In the bathrobe, yeah, that's Mr. Cullen."

Jack said, "I knew it," grinning, and yelled out, "Hey, Cully, you old son of a bitch!"

"Oh, man," Cedric said to him, "would you leave. Please?"

Jack took care of Mr. Louis Morrisseau, got him on a mortuary cot tucked away inside the hearse, now parked at the service entrance. He locked the door, hurried back inside, and there was Cullen waiting for him.

The bank robber. Angola celebrity.

"You're out," Jack said. "I don't believe it."

They hugged each other.

"My boy wanted me to stay with them, I mean live there," Cullen said. "It was Mary Jo was the problem. She'd been thinking about having a nervous breakdown ever since Joellen run off to Muscle Shoals to become a recording artist. . . . See, Mary Jo, all she knows how to do is keep house. She don't watch TV, she either waxes furniture or makes cookies or sews on buttons. I never saw a woman spend so much time sewing on buttons. I said to Tommy Junior, 'What's she do, tear 'em off so she can sew 'em back on?' I got a picture in my mind of that woman biting thread. First day I'm there, I look around, I don't see any ashtrays. There's one, but it's got buttons in it. I go to use it, Mary Jo says, 'That is not an ashtray. We don't have ashtrays in this house.' I ask her, well, how about a coffee can lid I could use? She says if I'm gonna smoke I have to do it in the backyard. Not in the front. She was afraid the neighbors might see me and then she'd have to introduce me. 'Oh, this is Tommy's dad. He's been in the can the last twenty-seven years.' See, it's bad enough Joellen takes off with this guy says he's gonna make her a record star. Mary Jo sees *me* sleeping in her little girl's bedroom with the stuffed animals and Barbie and Ken and she can't handle it, even sewing on buttons all day. She keeps sticking her finger with the fucking needle and it's my fault. So I have to leave. Tommy Junior says, 'Dad, Mary Jo loves you, but.' Everything he says ends in 'but.' 'You know we want you to be happy, *but* Mary Jo feels you'd be much better off in a place of your own, with people your own age.' How do you like it? This's the place of my own."

Cullen and Jack Delaney were walking along a wide hallway, past open doors and the sound of television voices, that would take them to the nursing home's lounge: Cullen wearing a velour bathrobe over his shirt and pants, running his hand along the rail fixed to the wall; Jack feeling awkward, holding back to stay with Cullen's slow pace. The hall smelled to Jack like a Men's room.

They came to an old woman tied in a wheelchair. Jack saw her reach for him, her hand a claw with veins and liver spots. He slipped past her with a hip move and saw another old woman in a wheelchair, waiting.

"What do you mean, people your age?"

"I'm sixty-five. Mary Jo thinks that's old enough."

Jack touched the sleeve of Cullen's burgundy velour robe. "What're you wearing this for?"

"I can't take a chance. I wear the robe and move slow, so I'll look sick. You were paroled. I got a medical release. They call it *de*carceration prior to sentence termination, make it sound official. But I don't know if I look okay they can put me back in or not."

"Cully, if they gave you a signed release, you're out. Christ, you had a heart attack. . . ."

"Yeah, and they took me to Charity in leg irons and handcuffs, with a lock box over the cuffs in case I tried to pick 'em lying there with a oxygen mask on my face trying to fucking breathe. All the time I was in the hospital they had me shackled and chained to the bed, up until I had the bypass. That's the way they do it. Doesn't matter how sick you are."

They came to the lounge that was like a church social hall with its tile floor, an array of worn furniture, hand-drawn announcement posters on the cement-block walls; a bunch of gray heads, some of them dozing, some watching television. " 'General Hospital,' " Cullen said. "That's the favorite. Me, I like 'The Young and the Restless,' they get into some deals." Jack steered Cullen to a sofa. A bare maple coffee table stood close, a small glass ashtray on it filled with butts. When Jack brought out his cigarettes Cullen said, "Lemme have one." He said, "Kools, uh? I'm not particular; shit. I'm suppose to quit, but we all have to die of something. When I got sick up there I wrote to Tommy, I said, 'Promise me if I die in this place you'll bring me home to New Orleans, I won't have to be buried at Point Lookout, Jesus, and never have any visitors.' Next thing I know I'm in Charity."

"Tommy come to see you?"

"Yeah, he comes. I've only been here, be a month tomorrow. Mary Jo never comes. I think she's saying a rosary novena I don't fuck up here and they have to take me back. With my cigarettes."

"Can't you leave if you want?"

Cullen thought about it, looking off. "I'm not sure. I guess I could. But where would I go?"

Jack hesitated before he said, "Maybe I've got something might interest you . . . the old pro, huh? You don't look sick to me."

"No, I'm feeling pretty good." Cullen leaned toward Jack, lowering his voice as he said, "I'll tell you something. Place like this, you wouldn't believe it. There's more pussy around here'n you can shake a stick at."

Jack looked over the lounge, saw nothing but little bent-over ladies with gray hair, some of them tied into their wheelchairs.

"I think I'm about to get me some," Cullen said. "See the one right across from us? The one reading the magazine? That's Anna Marie; she's in a private room. See how she sits with her legs apart and you can see London? That's body language, Jack. I read a book on it. You can look at people and tell what's on their mind. Like the body is speaking to you."

Jack looked at little Anna Marie, who had to be at least seventy-five years old. "What's her body telling you, Cully?"

"You kidding? Look. It's saying, 'Put it to me, kid, it's been a long time.' You know how long it's been for me, since I got laid? . . . The last time was December the twenty-second, 1958. I went in my last bank January the third, 1959. Art Dolan, the fuck, breaks his leg going over the teller's counter—I should've known he was too old—and I spend the next five months in Central Lockup, no bond. They knew I'd have left facing fifty to life, no chance of parole, and they were right. Oh, well, that's what I get helping out a pal." Cullen exhaled, sounding tired, his stomach filling his shirt in the robe hanging open.

Jack said, "I might have something to talk to you about. Depending if you're up to it."

Cullen, still watching Anna Marie, began to smile and leaned toward Jack again. "There was a woman, a new one that came in the other day. The story gets around how a young guy broke in her house, stole seventeen bucks she had in her purse, and raped her three times in three different places. I mean different rooms, on the floor, on the bed and somewhere else. The woman's seventy-nine years old. I'm listening to these ladies talking about it. Anna Marie says, 'Well, for seventeen bucks she sure got her money's worth.' You see what I mean? She's got it on her mind."

Jack said, "That's interesting, Cully. I don't doubt for a minute you're gonna get Anna Marie to ring your bell. You have a nice way about you."

"Well, I try not to give anybody any shit. You know. What's the percentage?" Cullen's gaze moved off and stopped. "You know who that is? Jack, look. The guy in the wool shirt hanging out? That's Maurice Dumas. You've heard of him, Mo Dumas, one of the great trombonists of all time. He played with Papa Celestin, he played with Alphonse Picou, with Armand Hug. . . . You'd see all those guys at the Caledonia Bar on Saint Philip. Go in there after a funeral you'd see every one of 'em there. You know what he does now? He goes in people's rooms and steals clothes, puts 'em on. Go on over and look at him, he'll have about three shirts on and a couple pairs of pants. He doesn't think anybody notices."

Jack said, "I'm looking for a guy that's a little more professional, Cully. How many banks was it you've done in your life, about fifty? You know, it's amazing, if I hadn't stopped there in front and saw you in the window . . ."

"I think it's sixty something. You get around these people you start to forget things. Old guy's son comes in to see him, the old man looks at him, says, 'Who the fuck are you?' This simp says, 'It's me, dad, Roger. Don't you know me?' I think this particular old man is faking. That's one way. Or you make excuses for your kids. Tommy Junior's sold out, he's scared to death of Mary Jo, a broad that goes through life sewing on buttons for something to do. But I don't say nothing. What's the percentage? She thinks I'm dying to live there, blow smoke all over her fucking house."

"You know how to read people, Cully."

"I knew when to get my ass out of a bank if it didn't feel right. And I always looked like a customer, too. None of this going in with a shotgun and a ski mask. That's the wild-ass amateurs. They go in and start screaming and everybody in the place turns around, they take a good look at the guys and then make 'em in a show-up."

"There you are, what I'm getting at," Jack said, "you're a pro."

"Yeah, but I'm not doing any more banks. They got

tricks now, they hand you a stack of taped bills that's hollow inside, with a dye in there that's set off by some kind of a timer. I don't know how it works, this fish was telling me about it. Not here, Christ, Angola. The teller picks the stack up off a battery plate in the drawer and the guy says 'it starts to think.' You put the take in your clothes or in a bag and as soon as you get outside, like in twenty or thirty seconds, the thing pops and you got red dye all over you. And tear gas, all this shit going off. It's like you come out of there with a sign, I just robbed the fucking bank."

Jack said, "Cully, I'm not talking about a bank. This is much bigger than a bank."

"I thought you were an undertaker."

"I'm taking a leave of absence or I'm quitting. I don't know yet."

"I'm not doing any armored cars, either. Christ, I'm sixty-five years old."

Jack said, "Cully, I'm looking at a score where if you plan it out carefully, as you know how to do, not miss anything that could blow up in your face, we walk off with five million. Cash."

"Jack, what's money? I got enough to last me the rest of my life, if I die Tuesday." Cullen paused. "I can't do another twenty-seven. I come out I'd be . . . Christ, ninety-two. Broads'd be saying, 'Look out for Cullen, he hasn't been laid in fifty-four years.' "

"I'm gonna get some more information and then . . . I could make you a proposition. If it looks right. But I think you have the head for this kind of a deal."

"Speaking of which," Cullen said, and gave Jack a nudge.

"What?"

"Head. I'll see if Anna Marie wants to give me some.

I hear it's becoming the thing even outside, girls getting to like it. I mean nice girls."

"You're feeling pretty frisky, aren't you?"

Cullen turned to look at him. He said, "Jack get me out of here, will you?"

At Mullen & Sons, backing the hearse toward the rear door, it opened and there was Leo waiting for him. Jack saw him in the outside rearview mirror, Leo motioning to him now to come on, hurry. By the time Jack had the hearse positioned, Leo's face was right next to him in the side window, Leo tense, all eyes.

"Will you get out of there?"

"I would, Leo, if I could open the door without breaking your nose." Leo stepped back and Jack slipped out from behind the wheel. "What's the matter?"

"There two guys just came in. They want to see Amelita Sosa."

"She isn't here."

"*I* know she isn't here, for Christ sake."

"Leo, calm down. What'd you tell them?"

"I said she wasn't here."

"Then what's the problem?"

"They don't believe me. They want to look around."

"Couple of Latin dudes?"

"*I* don't know what they are."

"Little black-haired fellas . . ."

"Jesus Christ, will you go in and talk to them?"

"Wait. First, what'd you say? She's not here and never was? I hope that's what you said."

"I told them I don't know anything about it, I wasn't here yesterday. I was across the lake. I drove over there Saturday evening and didn't get back till last night."

"Did you sweat when you were telling 'em all that?"

"You think it's funny. We could get in a lot of trouble doing this."

"Doing what? We've never even heard of Amelita. Amelita what? No, sorry, nobody here by that name."

"You don't care—that's the trouble, how we get involved in something crazy like this. You don't care or have any feeling about this business."

"Leo, I've been trying to tell you that for three years."

He found Colonel Dagoberto Godoy in Buddy Jeannette's visitation parlor, saw him from behind and then in profile and knew it was the man without ever having seen him before. It was in the way he moved, with a lazy, confident stride, like he was inspecting the premises and should have a swagger stick under his arm. There was even a military look to his tan, mod-cut suit, his black tie and aviator glasses.

Standing still the guy didn't look very mean or nasty. If anything he looked like Harby Soulé, the husband of his old girl friend, Maureen; and Harby had always seemed to Jack to look more like a headwaiter than a urologist—whatever urologists looked like—with his thin slicked hair and little pencil mustache. The colonel was maybe five seven and would go about a hundred and a half. One thing that could be said in favor of this deal, all the bad guys so far were little fuckers.

Now the colonel was inspecting Buddy Jeannette, looking closely into the open casket. Concentrating as he was, he jumped as Jack said, "Pretty nice work, uh? You should've seen him when he came in." Jack, gazing down at Buddy's waxen face, stood next to the colonel. "I think we took ten years off him, not to mention how we had to, you know, fix him up."

Close by, the colonel's voice said, "Are you the one I should talk to?"

"His funeral's tomorrow morning. Going out to Metarie Cemetery for his final resting place."

"I ask you a question."

Jack turned, looked at a glistening cap of hair before lowering his gaze to the man's rosy-tinted glasses.

"I heard you. I'm the one you should talk to if that's what you have in mind. What do you want to talk about? A deceased member of your family?"

"A deceased friend," the colonel said. "You brought her here yesterday from Carville, the leprosy hospital."

"I did? Or somebody else?"

"You or somebody—what difference does it make? I want to see her. Amelita Sosa."

"We don't have anybody here by that name. We have this gentleman here and that's it. No, I take that back; we also have Mr. Louis Morrisseau. But no Amelita Sosa. I'm sorry."

The colonel stared, giving him a haughty look, and said, "If you aren' sorry, you going to be." He walked off across the parlor. As he reached the open doorway he called out a name that sounded like Frank something. Frank Lynn? Jack, following him, wasn't sure.

As he reached the opening he saw the Creole-looking guy from the Exxon station coming out of another visitation room. Shit, it was the guy, all right. The one with the nappy hair who stood directly in front of the hearse and didn't say one word.

The colonel said the guy's name again. It was "Franklin." And then began speaking in rapid Spanish, ending it with a question. The guy frowned without changing his expression much and said, *"Como?"* The colonel began again in Spanish, then broke off and said in English, "Is this the one who brought Amelita from Carville or not? . . . *Amelita,* the girl yesterday."

Jack watched the guy's eyes come over to look right at him and hold without much of an expression—the same expression as yesterday, when he got out of the hearse and walked past the guy, that deadpan look that told nothing.

The guy, Franklin, said, "Yes, it's the same one that drove the coach. But I don't know if the girl was in it."

There was something strange here. The guy had a distinct accent. There was no doubt in Jack's mind the guy was some kind of Nicaraguan. But why would he have trouble understanding the colonel's Spanish, if they were both from down there?

"He wouldn't let us look in the coach to see if she was inside."

"That's enough." The colonel snapped it at him and turned to Jack. "You drove to Carville. You pick up a body. All right, where is it?"

"Who said I went to Carville?"

"He did, Franklin. You heard him."

"I think Franklin's mistaken. Where's he from?"

"Where is he from—he's from Nicaragua. Where you think he's from?"

"I don't know," Jack said, "that's why I asked. How long's he been here?"

Franklin was looking from one to the other.

"What are you talking about? What difference does it make?"

"Maybe, you know, we all look alike to him. Maybe the guy he saw resembled me."

Jack believed the colonel would like to hit him with something.

"You going to say there was another guy look just like you, but in another coach went to Carville yesterday?"

"Well, you know the coaches, as you call them, all look alike. Am I right? Why couldn't it have been another guy that looked just like me?"

"Because it wasn'."

"You're not positive though."

"This is Mullen and Son."

"That's right."

"Then it was you, no one else."

"I'll tell you, chief, I'd remember going to Carville. You say it was yesterday? No, I'm afraid I was right here the whole day."

"You lying to me."

Jack gave him the Big Yard stare, cold and hard, set his tone low, and asked, "What did you say?"

The colonel hung in, didn't budge, stared back at him through tinted glass and Jack began to think he might've made the wrong move with that Big Yard bullshit; it worked right away or it didn't. When the colonel said, "Franklin, show him your gun," Jack was sure he had made the wrong move. He looked over to see the bluesteel pistol in Franklin's extended hand.

Jack said, "Well, I think I'd better call the police." Something he had never said before in his life.

The colonel said, "How you going to do that?" Jack didn't have an answer, but it didn't matter; the colonel was anxious to tell him what he had said earlier. "In case you didn' hear me, I said you a fucking liar. What do you think of that?"

This was not Big Yard stuff; this was different. There

was no manhood to prove here. What he had to do was
. . . handle it, that's all.

"I think," Jack said, "that is, I have to assume, you're
distraught over the death of this person you mentioned.
I've seen many people in your state, mourning a tragic loss,
and I can understand. After all, it's my business." Jack
paused. "I wonder if you'd mind telling me your name."

The guy's suspicious mind, behind those rosy glasses,
wouldn't let him come right out with it.

"If you would, please. I know this is Franklin. Franklin,
how you doing?" The guy didn't seem to know how to
answer. Jack turned back to the colonel saying, "And you're
. . ."

"Colonel Dagoberto Godoy."

Man, and proud of it. The guy straightened and there
was a very faint but sharp sound as though he might have
clicked his heels. Jack wondered. He couldn't remember
any heel clicking since grade school. It made him think
these guys were from some world he knew nothing about.
The only thing to do was get them out of here.

"Colonel," Jack said, "if your buddy will put his gun
away I'll show you around, let you look in every room in
this place, and if you see the person you mentioned . . .
What was the name?"

The colonel didn't want to say it, but he did. "Amelita
Sosa." Snapping the name.

"If you see her, then it will be the first time in mortuary
history," Jack said, "the deceased ever walked in on his or
her own. If you'll follow me, please . . ."

Leo had brought Mr. Louis Morrisseau upstairs and
was working over him in the embalming room, head down,
concentrating to find that carotid artery in the old man's

neck, Leo's rubber fingers probing into the incision he'd made. It caught Colonel Godoy's eye. He approached the doorway from the hall, where Jack and the Creole-looking guy, Franklin, waited. Leo still didn't look up. Not even when the colonel asked him what he was doing and Leo told him.

"Drain the blood, uh?" the colonel said. "I always wonder how you do that. I don't understand why you don' make more holes, do it quicker."

Leo mumbled something. The colonel said, "What?" as he moved in closer. "This is a very old man I see. But yesterday you had a young girl, uh? Very nice-looking one."

Leo said, "I wasn't here yesterday. I told you that." Still not looking up, his shoulders hunched, his rubber fingers working away.

"But you do get young girls who die."

"Once in a while."

The colonel glanced over his shoulder at Franklin and gestured for him to go down the hall. "See if she's in a room somewhere, hiding."

Jack turned to follow Franklin. He heard the colonel saying to Leo, "When you place a young girl in the coffin, you don' dress her completely, do you?"

Jack said to Franklin's back, "Will you please put your gun away."

He was glad Leo hadn't noticed it. Leo might have come apart and told them anything they wanted to know. He watched Franklin take a look in Leo's office, then come back along the hall to the two-room apartment. The door was closed. Franklin stepped aside for Jack to open it. That surprised him. He waited in the doorway as Franklin looked at the old sofa and refrigerator. When he went into the bedroom Jack stepped over to the refrigerator, opened it and looked in, then waited for Franklin to peek in the bathroom and appear once again.

"You want a cold one?"

The guy stared at him.

"That means a beer. You want one? You like beer?"

The guy shook his head and Jack closed the refrigerator. The guy had really weird hair. Not so nappy up close, rounded in a semifro, but all of it was above his ears in sort of a bowl hairdo, no sideburns. He looked as if he'd just stepped off the banana boat and somebody bought him a suit of clothes, guessing the size: a black suit with pointy shoulders, meant to be snug and mod, but at least a size too big, the sleeves almost touching his knuckles. The guy had the hands of a stonemason, the nails cracked and ridged. It was hard to guess his age, other than he was full grown but not too big. Now, with time to look at him, he appeared different than he did yesterday, when Jack was picturing him in the Big Yard. The guy looked like he was out of the fucking Stone Age, wearing a white regular shirt buttoned at the neck but no tie. Jack thought of asking the guy who dressed him, but then came up with a better question.

"What do you carry a gun for?"

"They gave it to me to use."

There was the accent that made no sense. If the guy had trouble with Spanish, what was he? Maybe Jamaican. Except it wasn't quite that kind of accent and the colonel had said he was from Nicaragua.

"To use how?"

"To use, to shoot it."

"Well, I guess that's what I'm asking. Who you gonna shoot in New Orleans?"

"I don't know. They don't tell me if I am."

Jesus Christ. "You mean if the colonel, Godoy, he told you to shoot somebody you'd do it?"

"That's why they give me the gun. If I have to use it."

"Yeah, but it's against the law. You can't just shoot anybody you want."

It seemed as if the guy had to think that one over. Finally he said, "If I'm told to shoot . . . You understand it isn't the same as I want to shoot. Uh? It would be I have to do it."

"If you *have* to . . . You realize this is hard for me to understand. What you're talking about."

"Why is it?"

A simple question. The guy waiting for an answer.

"Well, I guess it's different here than in Nicaragua."

"Much different, yes. But I think I like it here."

"Well, that's nice." The guy seemed so easy to talk to, but he wasn't, he didn't make sense. The guy was studying him now, beginning to nod.

He said, "That was you, yesterday."

"You think so?"

"Yes, in the coach. I know it was you."

Like stating a simple fact, nothing more to it than that, nothing in his expression. . . . The Creole-looking guy stared at him and then walked out.

Jack waited. He looked at the phone, on the end table next to the sofa. He walked over and put his hand on the phone, then took it off. He couldn't think of anyone to call who'd do him any good. He thought of Leo's trocars, in the cabinet in the prep room. He had been good yesterday, wide awake. But a failure today. He was slow today. He wasn't thinking. He thought, Well, you better start now, quick. And began to think, Take 'em. Just fucking take 'em, that's all. You see 'em, hit. Take the guy with the gun first.

Unless they both have a gun. Shit. Then had to get ready again, work himself up. . . . It was so quiet before the sound from the hall reached him, the hurried steps coming this way . . .

Leo said, "Hey!" Stopping dead and bringing his hands up as he came in the room. "What's wrong with you?"

"Where are they?"

"What were you gonna do, hit me?"

"Leo, where are they?"

"They had a cab waiting, they left. What's his name, that colonel? He seemed like a nice guy."

EIGHT

"**I** think they're watching the house," Lucy's voice said. "We've been sitting at a window most of the day. Dolores and I take turns. She's there now, writing down what goes by. There aren't that many—the street doesn't go anywhere. The trouble is, all the cars look alike, the new ones."

"The one yesterday," Jack said, "was a Chrysler Fifth Avenue, I'm pretty sure. But you're right, they all look alike. It was black."

"Are you working?"

"I was. I'm at Mandina's now. I wanted to call you before, but Leo kept coming in. You know Mandina's, on Canal?"

"I've passed by it. Hang on a minute."

He heard Lucy's voice, away from the phone, call

Dolores and then heard steps on a hardwood floor. Dolores had opened the door last night when he brought Amelita: Dolores a slim black woman in a flowery print dress and high heels, not looking anything like a housekeeper. When Lucy introduced them she said, "Jack Delaney, Dolores Wilson," and Dolores gave him a nod, closing her eyes, then gave Lucy a strange look—What's going on here?—no doubt the first time she'd ever been introduced to company. He heard steps again on the wood floor and then Lucy's voice.

"Jack? The black Chrysler. It drove by twice and then parked down the street, toward the river."

"How many people in it?"

"Dolores thinks just one."

"You could tell the police."

"I don't think it's a good idea. If I cause a scene I'm not sure what might happen. I don't want the guy in the car to think I'm, you know, sitting in the window. How about you? Anyone come to the funeral home?"

"Only the colonel himself. He's a little guy, isn't he?"

"Jack, really? What did you tell him?"

"He was there when I got back from picking up a body. Listen, I think I might have us another guy, too."

"Jack . . ."

"I told him we didn't have an Amelita Sosa. He goes, what're you talking about? You picked up her body yesterday, at Carville. I said no, it wasn't us. Must've been some other funeral home."

"But did you put the notice in the paper?"

"No, see, then you're admitting you have her, or you did. Then they want to know what you did with the body. You say you had it cremated or you sent it somewhere, they can check. There all kinds of records would be involved.

I've found it's best, something like this, to open your eyes real wide and play dumb. You don't know anything. Amelita Sosa? No, I'm sorry, you have the wrong place."

"But if they check with Carville . . ."

"So, one of the sisters wrote down the wrong funeral home. They're human, aren't they, can make mistakes? I never met a sister who did, but it must be possible."

"What'd he say, the colonel?"

"He had a guy with him. You remember the other one yesterday who didn't say anything?"

"He stood in front of the hearse."

"Yeah, did you get a look at him?"

"I saw him, that's about all."

"He's a weird guy. You didn't notice his hair? Like he might be part colored?"

There was a pause on Lucy's end. "Yeah, I did notice him. He looked different."

"His name's Franklin. You ever hear of a Nicaraguan named Franklin?"

"Sure, it's possible." She paused again. "Or he's Indian. They live along the east coast, near Honduras."

"He looked more black."

"Well, there're Caribbean Creoles mixed in with the Indians. Yeah, and some have unusual names, you're right, they got from Moravian missionaries. There was a Miskito Indian at the hospital, his name was Armstrong Diego." She said then, "But when you told the colonel she wasn't there, what'd he do?"

"Well, he didn't believe me. Especially when the guy, Franklin, says I was there, he saw me. But he didn't do anything about it."

"What do you mean?"

"I said, okay, take a look around. We go upstairs, the

colonel sees Leo preparing a body and forgets all about Amelita."

"It didn't make him ill . . ."

"No, he loved it. But after a few minutes that was it, he left. Told Leo he had an appointment. See, when I first got there I thought Leo was gonna have a heart attack. He talked to Sister Teresa Victor on the phone this morning and then he and I talked and he did *not* know how to handle it. The colonel comes, Leo's scared to death. Afraid to even look at him. The colonel leaves and Leo says, 'He seems like a nice guy.' "

"He didn't . . ."

"You have to understand, anybody that'd want to watch an embalming becomes Leo's friend for life."

"That was all? They left?"

"I guess he had to be somewhere. But the guy, Franklin . . . he was weird."

"I have to learn how to lie," Lucy said.

"You tell a big one. The bigger the lie, the better chance you have they'll believe you."

"But if they believe she's alive and she's not at your place, then she must be here. Bertie and his guys. He seems less of a threat if I think of him as Bertie. I found out he's staying at the Saint Louis. You know where it is?"

"It's in the Quarter. Very nice hotel, small."

"Did you ever . . . pick up jewelry there?"

He said, "I don't think it was a hotel back then," picturing the open hallways on each floor that looked down into a center courtyard. Why didn't the guy stay at the Roosevelt? "You talked to your dad, huh?"

"I called him this morning and apologized. Probably the most deceitful thing I've ever done in my life."

"Yeah, but were you convincing?"

108

"He said, 'Don't give it another thought, Sis.' I said, 'If I decide to borrow one of your guns and shoot the son of a bitch, where would I find him?' He thought that was funny, his daughter the nun turned reactionary. Or whatever I am, I don't know. I put him down, criticize his business, his politics, but I used money he gave me to buy the car in León."

"You shouldn't have trouble with that. You don't have to like him just 'cause he's your dad."

"But I do, he's a nice guy. . . . Except his values are all screwed up."

"Wait'll you meet Roy Hicks."

There was a silence on Lucy's end.

"If you're having second thoughts, I can understand."

"No, I want to meet him."

"I might have another guy, too. The only problem is, he doesn't have a place to live. But we can talk about that later. If the guy in the Chrysler comes to the door, don't open it."

"I won't. But I'd like to get Amelita out of here tonight, if possible. There's a late flight to L.A. with a change in Dallas. But we'd have to leave here by nine-thirty."

"We'll work it out. I'll call you by eight."

Jack had a couple of beers and an oyster loaf at the bar, talked to Mario on and off about nothing, and in between thought about the guy, Franklin, and his bluesteel automatic. That was one weird fucking guy. Jack finished eating and drove downtown.

Roy Hicks was putting together an array of pastel-colored drinks in stem glasses along the inside edge of the bar, topping them off with cherries, orange slices, and tiny parasols.

Jack watched him from the front end of the bar, near the entrance to the International Lounge, "Featuring Exotic Dancers from Around the World."

The way Roy was concentrating, that hard jaw line of his clenched, Jack wouldn't be surprised to see Roy finish making the drinks and then sweep them off the bar with one of his hairy forearms. Roy always wore short-sleeve shirts, even with the formal black bow tie and the red satin vest. The owner of the club, Jimmy Linahan, had told Roy he'd have to wear long sleeves with French cuffs, but Roy wouldn't do it; he kept showing up for work in his short-sleeve shirts. Jimmy Linahan said to him, "I don't want to have to tell you again." Roy said, "Then don't," and went on making drinks.

Jack remembered that day, sitting on this same stool when it happened and Jimmy Linahan coming over to him. They had known each other since they were fifteen years old and used to swim off the levee in Audubon Park and get in fights with black kids or Italians, whoever happened to be there. Jimmy Linahan said, "What's with this guy?" Roy had given Jack's name as a reference.

Jack said to him that time, "Jimmy, if I were you I'd let the guy wear a jockstrap with sequins on it if that's what he happens to show up in. A joint like this, you need Roy more than he needs you. And I don't mean 'cause he was a cop and knows how to use a stick. Roy has a knack of getting people to agree with him."

Jimmy Linahan came to appreciate Roy: the fact he never drew complaints or had to give refunds. Roy could put together a drink he'd never heard of without referring to the *Bartender's Guide.* And if the patron said, "This isn't a Green Hornet," Roy would look at the patron and say, "That's the way I make 'em, pal. Drink up." And the patron would see Roy's eyes, the dead dark stones in there, and say, 'Mmmmm, it's different, but good.'' Or if the patron bought one of the Exotic Dancers from Around the World a split of champagne and made a fuss when he got a tab for sixty-five dollars, Roy would look at the patron and say, "I bet you can have the money out, plus tip, before I come over the bar. Huh?''

Jack could hear conventioneers behind him having fun, several tables of middle-aged men and women wearing big ID badges. There were a few thousand more of them out on Bourbon Street and it wasn't yet eight o'clock. Roy was working days this week and would be off at eight.

One of the International girls took the stool next to Jack saying, "Hi, how you doing?" With an accent that would make her an exotic dancer from around the East Texas part of the world. She said, "My name's Darla. You want to pet my monkey?"

Roy was at the cash register punching keys. He looked over his shoulder and said, "Hey, Darla? Get your hand off his dick. That's a friend of mine." He punched some more keys, took the check out of the register, and walked up the bar to the service station.

"He's an old sweetie, isn't he?" Jack gave her a nice smile as he said it. He had watched her perform, up on the stage back of the bar, the Exotic Darla naked except for a silver G-string and pink pasties centered on tired, impersonal breasts that looked too old for her. Poor girl trying to make a living. "I tell people," Jack said to her, "if you're ever behind Roy at a stoplight and it changes and he doesn't start up right away, don't honk your horn."

The Exotic Darla said, "Yeah?" Waiting for him to continue.

So Jack said, "We were on a 747 one time going to

Vegas, one of those junkets where everything's included, the flight, the hotel. . . . We've been drinking for about two hours, Roy decides he has to go to the bathroom. I'm on the aisle, so when I get up I decide, well, I may as well go too. We get to the back of the plane and see these little signs on all the lavatories, occupied. Roy goes over to the other side of the plane where there three more, but they're occupied too, so he comes back. I'm standing there, he knows these three are occupied, he can see the little signs, but he tries the doors anyway, jiggles the handles. He stands there for about a half a minute and all of a sudden he kicks the door of the one I'm standing right in front of. He kicks it and says, 'Come on, hurry up!' The door opens like only about ten seconds later. This guy comes out, big guy, and gives me the dirtiest look you ever saw in your life. Not Roy, *me*, 'cause I'm the one standing there. The guy walks off, up the aisle, and Roy goes, 'What's the matter with him?' "

The Exotic Darla said, "Yeah?"

"That's the end of the story."

"You're not gonna buy me a drink, are you?"

"No, I'm not," Jack said. "You want to hear another Roy story?"

She thought a moment. Maybe that's what she was doing, Jack wasn't sure. She said, "No, thank you," swiveled around on the stool, looking over the room, raised both arms to adjust the halter holding her tired breasts, and left him.

Roy came down the bar holding a bottle of vodka by the neck. He poured a shot into Jack's glass, then twisted off another one, Jack saying, "Darla's got bruises on her arm. You notice?"

"Bumping into the wrong guys. That girl's a sack of roaches."

"I read in the paper that in the U.S., I think it was just this country, a woman is beaten or physically abused something like every eighteen seconds."

Roy said, "You don't tell me."

"Somebody made a study."

Roy said, "You wouldn't think that many women get out of line, would you?" He walked off.

Jack watched Roy making a drink down the bar. He wondered why he remembered a short piece in the paper about women being abused but hardly anything at all about Nicaragua.

When he came back Roy said, "Delaney, you know what broads do when they get sick? I've never seen it to fail, they throw up in the washbasin. They don't throw up in the toilet, like you're suppose to."

"That's interesting," Jack said. "You think that's why they get beat up?"

"Who knows why. They're all different and they're all the same."

"Still hate women, huh?"

"I love women. I just don't trust 'em."

"I met one you can."

"Yeah? Good for you."

"And heard an amazing story you aren't gonna believe."

"But you're gonna tell me it anyway."

"You'd be hurt if I didn't. You'd pout and probably never speak to me again. It's an opportunity story, as in chance of a lifetime."

"Is it about money?"

"Five million, give or take a few bucks."

"That's money. Where is it?"

"You're jumping to the best part. It belongs to a type of individual, Roy, that if you can take it from him you'd not only never have to work again as long as you live, you'd be performing a service to humanity. The kind a thing that makes you feel good all over."

Roy said, "You understand I serve humanity every day for eight hours and it doesn't make me feel worth a shit. They come in, a guy wants a Sazerac. He has no idea in the world what a Sazerac is, but he's in New Orleans. I serve him something with a lot of bitters in it. Another guy comes in, looks around, he whispers to me, 'You got any absinthe?' He says, 'They don't have none at the Old Absinthe House. They tell me it's against the law to serve it.' I say how do I know, to this little pussy fella, you're not a cop? He shows me he's from Fort Wayne, Indiana. I glance around the bar, get out a clear bottle I make up that's got Pernod in it and a piece a deadwood with a caterpillar stuck on it. Asshole drinks five of 'em at five bills a shot. Serve humanity, I serve 'em any fucking thing they want."

Jack said, "That's why I'm talking to you, Roy, you're a sensitive, understanding person. This guy gets finished collecting his five million he's most likely gonna hop in a private plane and leave the country with it. We get a half share we split three ways."

"Who's we?"

"You and I, maybe Cullen."

"Cullen, they let him out?"

"Medical release, so he can get laid."

"What was he in, twenty-five years?"

"Twenty-seven."

"Jesus, they'd a had to shoot me off the fence."

"Well, he's out and feeling pretty good."

"What're we talking about, a bank, for Christ sake?"

"Not anything like it."

"Then what do you need Cullen for?"

"I think he'd enjoy it. Why not?"

"You're feeling pretty good yourself, aren't you?"

"I've been born again. Since yesterday I have an entirely new outlook on life."

"This guy's gonna collect five mil you say, give or take. . . . Are we talking about cash, with bank straps on it?"

"You've never heard of one like this, Roy. It's never been done before."

"It has to do with the funeral business."

"Not unless somebody gets shot."

"This doesn't sound like you atall, Delaney."

"I told you, I'm a different person. You want to know what it is, or you rather guess?"

"I know every kind of scam or heist there is grown men have tried to pull and fell on their ass doing."

"All except this one."

"Have you seen the guy? You know who he is?"

"I met him today."

"Yeah? . . . Well, what is he?"

"He's a Nicaraguan colonel."

Roy stared at Jack. He turned then, walked down the bar, made a drink, rang it up, and came back.

"You met a woman you say you can trust and she told you an amazing story I'm not gonna believe. How to pick up five mil."

"Give or take."

"How come she gets half? The guy her husband?"

Jack shook his head. "She needs it to build a hospital, for lepers."

Roy paused, then nodded. "A leper hospital, yeah,

that's a good idea. You know why lepers never finish a card game?"

"They have to quit," Jack said, "when they throw in their hands." He looked at Roy with the same deadpan expression, because he knew he had him and knew they were going to play this one and might even have a pretty good time working it out.

He said, "What I need at the moment is a police officer. Or someone who knows how to speak in that same ugly, obscene way they have of addressing offenders."

NINE

Roy's killer look didn't work on lavatory doors or in creeping traffic, so he'd have to kick something or pound the dashboard of Jack's VW Scirocco with the edge of his fist. It was a tan '78 Scirocco, faded but still mean-looking, Jack Delaney had bought used and now had 153,000 miles on the odometer. He wasn't worried Roy could hurt the car hitting it, but he'd jump when Roy yelled, "Move it, goddamn it," the man's impatience coming out unexpectedly, in spurts; then Roy would be quiet for a while. Jack got them out of the narrow streets of the Quarter, across Canal, and through the new downtown that looked like every other big city. They were heading uptown on St. Charles Avenue, once again in New Orleans, before he told Roy about the deal, why the guy was collecting five-million dollars.

Roy would say, "Now hold on a minute," and ask a question. Jack would answer it or he'd say, "Don't you know what's going on in the world, Roy? Christ, don't you read the paper? You never heard of the Sandinistas, for Christ sake?" Lucy had given Jack a book of color photographs called *Nicaragua* that showed all these young guys in sport shirts and baseball caps wearing masks, hoods with holes, or scarves tied around their faces, and armed with all kinds of dinky weapons, Saturday Night Specials, .22 rifles . . . A pickup army fighting well-armed uniformed troops wearing helmets, and it was a kick looking at pictures of these guys in print sport shirts and bandit masks. Jack could see himself one of them if he were Nicaraguan and had been there in '79. There were pictures of bodies, too, death and destruction, fires, refugees running and crowds of people waving red and black flags. There was a picture of the guy they hated and finally overthrew, ran out of the country, Somoza, wearing a white suit with a sash. Jack could tell by looking at Somoza he was that type of person who was set in his ways and didn't know shit.

Roy said he had a snitch one time who was a Nicaraguan. When he was working undercover with the felony action squad. He said there were plenty of Nicaraguans in New Orleans.

Jack said, "Yeah, and I think you're gonna meet a couple of them pretty soon."

With the windows open they would quit talking as Jack passed a St. Charles Avenue streetcar clanging along the median. It was his favorite street, overgrown with oak and all kinds of shrubbery, palm trees in the yards of old shuttered homes. He rode the streetcar for fun when he was little. The tracks ran all the way to the levee and then up

Carrollton Avenue to a point where the motorman would flip the seatbacks, walk to the other end of the car, and drive it downtown to Canal.

Roy said, "I hope some guys I know don't find out what this Nicaraguan's up to. They'd be standing in line to take a swipe at him. Is the guy really as bad as you say?"

"Ask Lucy. She'll tell you."

"I mean this guy is *bad.*"

"That's what's good about taking his money."

"But if he's *bad* . . ."

"Yeah?"

"How come he doesn't keep the money for himself? What is he, just bad in certain areas?"

"I wondered about that, too," Jack said. "Maybe he's got all the money he needs."

"Or why would he want to go back and take a chance getting killed"

"Why were you a cop?"

"It wasn't for the money, I'll tell you that."

Jack said, "Well then."

He took the Scirocco rumbling in second gear down Audubon, the street full of trees and the dark shapes of big homes, warm lights in windows here and there, a few porch lights showing through hedges and shrubs. He said, "There, on the left. That's Lucy's house, her mother's."

Roy said, "Get Lucy to buy you a muffler. I think she can afford it."

"There's the car. What should I do?"

"Keep going."

"It's the same one, the Chrysler. . . . Jesus, the guy behind the wheel, that's the one named Franklin. The colored guy, or whatever he is. Creole, I don't know."

"Go down the end and turn around."

"The other guy, I don't think it's the colonel." Jack felt a need to talk. "But Franklin, Christ, he's the one that was with him and put the gun on me."

"I love that kind," Roy said. "Come on, turn around."

"I have to get down there first, don't I?"

Near the river end of the street the dark mass of trees opened to show bare telephone poles and vacant lots that extended to the levee, a grassy barrier against the night sky. Jack circled one of the poles and his headlights again probed the aisle of trees.

Roy said, "Ease up behind them."

"I get out, too?"

"You come up on the curb side. Stand close to the car but a few steps back, so they can feel you but can't see you. It might confuse 'em otherwise. What is this guy, an undertaker or a cop? Before you get out, write down the license number."

"I don't have a pen."

Roy said, "Jesus Christ," took one out of the inside pocket of his corduroy jacket, pulled out a bunch of folded papers then, looked through them, and handed Jack the pen and an envelope that said *The International Lounge Featuring Exotic Dancers from Around the World* across the flap. "From now on you carry a pen and a notebook. And you wear a suit or sport coat any time we have to pull this kind of shit."

Jack said, "What do you think I have on, pajamas?" He was wearing a tan cotton blazer with jeans.

"You look like an undercover fed trying to pass as a fucking yuppie. I get their IDs, I give 'em to you. You come back to the car like you're gonna call it in, see if they're felons or they're wanted for anything, and you write the names down. Then tomorrow I'll have 'em checked out."

"Still have friends on South Broad."

"I still have snitches, too, if I need 'em."

"You gonna show these guys a badge or what?"

"Why don't you wait and see what I do? Then you'll know. Go on, pull up right behind 'em."

"Should I give 'em a bump?"

"Yeah, whiplash 'em. They'll be more cooperative."

Jack could see the two guys inside looking back this way, into his headlights. He said, "Louisiana plate," stopped close behind the Chrysler's shiny black rear deck, and wrote down the number as Roy said, "It's a rental," and got out. By the time Jack was approaching the curb side of the car Roy was asking the driver to see his operator's license, the Creole-looking guy. The other one was leaning forward, saying to Roy, "He don't have to show you no license. We have the permission. Who the fuck are you, you don't know that?" He was the one who had done all the talking at the Exxon station. The dude in the sunglasses, though not wearing them now.

Jack heard Roy say, "Sir, he may not want to remove it from his person and show it to me him*self.* But I'm gonna see it, one way or the other. Are we clear on that?"

The Creole-looking guy took out his wallet, saying something to the other guy Jack couldn't hear. And then Roy said to the other guy, "You too, sir, if you don't mind. I'm curious to know who you assholes are you think you can sit here any time you want." The guy on the passenger side began talking about "the permission" again, mad. Jack didn't catch all the words. Now the two guys were talking to each other in Spanish, Roy waiting. Finally the guy in the passenger seat took a billfold out of his coat and Jack looked up the street toward Lucy's house.

121

The idea was, she'd drive off with Amelita while they kept the two guys busy. He had phoned her with the plan after talking to Roy. Lucy said, as long as they left by nine-thirty. It was now about twenty after.

Roy handed him both guys' driver's licenses and the rental car envelope across the roof of the Chrysler, the one who'd been talking saying something now about calling the district commander of police and they would see.

Jack walked back to his car and got in, leaving the door open so he'd have light to see what he was doing. He wrote down Crispin Antonio Reyna. This was the dude, not the driver. He was thirty-two and lived in Key Biscayne, Florida.

Something to think about, huh? Why did the colonel bring these guys all the way from Florida?

The National Car Rental agreement was also in his name. It appeared Crispin Antonio was the boss. It made sense, he was the mouth. The Creole-looking guy was Franklin de Dios—the hell kind a name was that?—forty-two. His home address was in South Miami.

Jack got out to approach the Chrysler. He saw Roy look back, then step away from the side of the car and come to meet him at the rear deck.

"They're from Florida, both guys."

It didn't seem to surprise Roy. He said, "They're try-ing to tell me it's an immigration matter and they have police permission to sit there all they want."

"You believe it?"

"That's neither here nor there. We'll go on the as-sumption they're full of shit. Don't say a word if they ask you anything, if you talked to the captain. Okay?"

Roy walked back to the driver's side as Jack moved

between the cars to the curb. He looked toward Lucy's house, the third one up past dense shrubbery. Not a light showing. He heard Roy telling the driver, "You're giving me a bunch of shit, aren't you? I think you better step out of the car."

Jack heard Roy's voice, with that easy cop drawl he put on, and was looking at a car all of a sudden popping its lights and coming out of the shrubs where Lucy's driveway would be, a dark-colored Mercedes. Jack watched it turn into the street going away from them, toward St. Charles, its red taillights becoming tiny dots up there in the dark, almost to the point of disappearing, gone, when Crispin Antonio Reyna began yelling in Spanish. Jack turned to see Franklin de Dios of South Miami hunched over the steering wheel, reaching for the ignition.

There was no doubt they were leaving, with nothing in front of the car to keep it there. Until Jack saw Roy reach in, grab a handful of nappy hair, and pull Franklin de Dios's head out to lay it on the windowsill, Roy saying, "You trying to run on me?" Roy was reaching in again, now with his left hand, and came out holding a pistol, Roy saying, "Uh-oh, what have we here?"

Jack was moving toward the other one now, Crispin Reyna, having seen how it was done. He heard Roy telling Franklin de Dios he could step out of the car or get pulled clear through the window, heard that and saw Crispin Reyna's hand on the glove box, punching the button to open it. Jack reached in and grabbed a handful of Crispin Reyna's hair and yanked him back against the seat, hard. He changed hands then, learning how to do this as he went along, pressed the palm of his left hand against the guy's face, to hold him there, while he felt inside the glove box with his other hand. Jack stepped back from the car with a bluesteel automatic, holding it lightly, looking at its dull sheen in the streetlight. He liked the feel of it. He stepped back in when he saw Crispin Reyna turn to look at him. Jack motioned for him to face straight ahead and touched the barrel to the guy's right ear.

Roy had Franklin de Dios out of the car now, telling him to lean against it and spread his legs apart, "Come on, spread 'em," the guy doing what he was told without expression, his Creole-looking face with its pointy cheekbones carved from some kind of smooth, hard wood.

"Should we take these fuckers to Central Lockup and then have to do all that paperwork, or what?"

Jack said, "I hate paperwork."

Roy said, "It perturbs me off, too. What do you think? The river's right there."

Jack saw Franklin de Dios's calm eyes staring at him and he put his hand to his face, elbow on the roof of the car. "The mighty Mississippi, that's a thought. The current'd take 'em clear down to Pilot Town. If they can swim."

"You wouldn't want to weight 'em down none?"

"I thought we might give 'em a chance."

Now Crispin Reyna was speaking, saying they were fucking dumb cops and they had better call their superior right now. "I tell you we have the permission to be here."

"On second thought," Jack said, "how about drop 'em in the Outlet Canal? They'll be in the Gulf before morning." He saw Roy, taller than Franklin de Dios, nodding.

"Less you want to take 'em to the graveyard of strangers."

"Where's that?"

"John the Baptist Parish, in the swamp. They say if all the bodies dumped there ever stood up, man, you'd have a crowd could fill the Superdome."

"It's hard," Jack said, "isn't it?"

What they couldn't do was let them go just yet. Lucy would need an hour or so free of worry and looking over her shoulder. So they put Franklin de Dios and Crispin Reyna in the trunk of the Chrysler, Crispin bilingual in his protests, but finally got them spooned against each other like a couple of Angola sweethearts in the Big Stripe dorm, Roy telling them to mind and he'd let them out after while.

They discussed the guns for a minute, both 9-millimeter Berettas. Beauties, Roy said, better than those six-shooter Smiths cops had to pack when he was on the force. They stuck the guns under the front seat of Jack's car, then had a discussion on the best place to leave the Chrysler, with the key in the ignition. Jack mentioned City Park, West End. Roy mentioned out toward Chalmette in St. Bernard Parish there were a lot of good places. Jack said, Yeah, and nobody would ever find them either. Roy said, Well, where we going after? Jack said he thought they may as well get the show on the road; stop by the St. Louis Hotel, find out what room the fundraiser was in and what the setup looked like. Roy said, Well, shit, we'll drop these dudes off on the way.

That's what they did. Roy drove the Chrysler with Jack following behind and left it on Tchoupitoulas near Calliope, where they used to park cars for the World's Fair. As Roy got in the Scirocco Jack was grinning, waiting to tell him, "It's too bad we can't stay and watch. Some guy's gonna come along and take off with that Chrysler. Be driving down the street and wonder what in the hell that noise is, coming from the trunk. Like somebody pounding to get out. Or he hears a voice calling to him like it's from far away, 'Help, señor, help.' "

Roy said, "Delaney, you're a weird fucker, you know it?"

Jack didn't say anything. He felt pretty good, the way things were going.

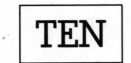

TEN

They parked at a cab stand on Bienville. Roy, who would never get over having been a cop, said it was all right; he knew the cabbies and if they didn't like it, fuck 'em. The St. Louis Hotel was right across the street.

Jack sat at a table in the big center courtyard, ordered vodka and a scotch when the waiter finally appeared. He asked the waiter if it was a slow night. The waiter said it seemed to be. Where was everybody? The waiter said they must be out having a good time.

Out on Bourbon Street bumping into each other, the whole bunch of them aimless, probably thinking, this is it, huh? The street a midway of skin shows and tacky novelty shops. The poor guys at Preservation Hall and the other joints playing that canned Dixieland, doing "When the

Saints" over and over for the tourists in the doorways. There was some good music around, if Al Hirt was in town or you found a group with Bill Huntington playing his standup bass or Ellis Marsalis somewhere. His boy Wynton had left town with his horn to play for the world.

It didn't matter, there was enough to see and you could always eat. Maybe it was because he lived here he didn't understand why anyone would bother with Bourbon Street. If he came to town from somewhere else he'd sit right here and watch the lights in the fountain as he sipped his drink, soothed, in the shade of magnolias and japonicas at night, the whole courtyard all the way up bathed in a pale orange glow.

If he came from out of town he would look at the upper floors, at the white porch railings that ran all the way around the four sides and see doors to guest rooms and dark shutters decorating the windows, the hallways up there open to the courtyard. He would sit here as he was sitting now and decide you wouldn't necessarily be seen going into somebody else's room, but it could give you a funny feeling, being exposed like that, standing with your back to this whole place.

The fundraiser was in 501, top floor, the suite in the alcove there, right off the elevator. The desk clerk said he was out.

Roy was checking to see if he knew any of the help. If he didn't it would be the only hotel in the Quarter. Roy said it was good to have a lot of friends. Especially if they owed you. He used to have a girl friend who lived on Bienville up just past Arnaud's, a call girl named Nola Roy said did a better lunch business than the restaurant. He said she was a pretty thing and sweet as could be till her life closed in on her. That was the trouble with broads. On the one hand they made the best snitches, they were born to be informants, especially whores. But on the other hand they became emotional and didn't know when to shut up.

"Now that I know that," Roy had said, "what the fuck am I gonna do with it here?" Telling Jack the story after they met at Angola and became friends.

"This was a sweet kid I'm talking about. Didn't look atall like a whore. She was demure, had this little tiny voice. 'Oh, Roy, I didn't have you as my friend I'd be smacked out twenty-four hours a day.' "

"That's all you were?"

"Hey, friends can go to bed, can't they? Two people misunderstood at home. My old woman, Rosemary, all she did was bitch that I was never home. You see her, you'd know why. And Nola was married to a guy was a half-assed bookmaker. You probably knew him, Dickie Duschene, sometime they call him Dudu, had a place upstairs on Dauphine. He's making book and she's hooking, so they didn't have what you call a home life. The deal was, I'd stop by and Nola'd tell me her troubles, or anything she might've heard would be of interest to me. You know, stuff she picked up on the street or from Dickie. And my part of the deal, I'd look out for her and wouldn't hassle 'em none, let 'em go about their business. One day I'm over there she's sniffling and nervous like she's strung out or somebody died. I ask her, 'What's wrong, precious?' Nola pulls a trash bag out of the closet has thirty grand in it, all fifties and hundreds. I tell her, 'My, you been working your cute little tail off, haven't you?' She says Dickie gave it to her but she's afraid to keep it in the apartment. She gets a john every once in a while will go through her things. She says some freak's liable to rip her off, so would I keep it for her. She says the money's from Dickie's bookmaking and card games in that joint he had, place on Dauphine looked like it was boarded up. Okay, but something doesn't smell right. He's gonna let her keep thirty grand in a room guys walk in and out of you don't know? I said, 'Hey, Nola, bullshit.' She says he did, honest. But then tells me a little more. She found out Dickie was going out on her with this nurse at Charity and Nola had a fit. Started breaking things over at his place, so he gave her the thirty grand to calm her down. Only it worked the other way, made her nervous.''

"He gave her thirty, the guy must've had a lot more."

"That's right, and the guy didn't run that big of a book. But I take the money home and hide it in a good place, 'cause now I have this tremendous idea. Put the money to work, as the occasion arises, in my continuing fight against crime. Like using a confiscated car on surveillance? Use some of the scratch to pay off informants. Get these assholes tripping over each other to tell me stuff.''

"Don't they lie to you?"

"Sure they do, it's their nature. You got to jam a snitch, get him against the wall. Fella's dealing against a third fall, he tells you where this other fella's gonna be with a load of smack on him, only he ain't there. So you tell the guy, 'He ain't there the next time, asshole, you gonna get triple-billed and go on up to 'Gola.' Now the word's on the street I'm paying off, shit, I got 'em lined up like I'm hearing confession. Listen, I'd get phone calls in the middle of the night, which Rosemary would answer on account of her sour fucking disposition kept her awake. And if it was a broad on the phone that was cool, 'cause then Rosemary wouldn't even look at me for about a week. I got mostly shuck, but not all.''

"You have kids, Roy?"

"My babies are grown up and gone, two fine girls, but they come to see me." Meaning, to Angola.

"Go on with the story."

"Talking about snitches . . . there was a case I was working on, a Wells Fargo stickup in Jackson, Mississippi, where some of the money was showing up in New Orleans. The feds already had a lead on four local guys they're watching. But the feds don't have any police experience, they use computers, and a computer isn't worth shit on the street, to get information. You have to get down there in the sewer with the assholes and talk to 'em man to man. One of my ace informants tells me to see a guy at Charity in there with a gunshot wound he says was from a hunting accident. The feds ask him if he hunts with ninety-grain .38s from a Smith and Wesson service revolver. See, they know one of the guys in the Wells Fargo heist was shot on the way out. This guy in the hospital, his wound is through and through, but he doesn't know that. See, they don't have a slug, they're just trying to bullshit him. The day I go see the guy, first thing in the morning, I'm too late. During the night some guy walked in his room, put a pillow over his face, and shot him five times through the pillow. Leaves the gun and walks out. The guy in the next bed saw the whole thing. The nurse tells me they have to change his sheets every time somebody walks in the room now he doesn't know. I think, hey, this nurse is a cool broad. I begin to wonder about her and a couple days later I meet her for a drink, place there on Gravier, when she gets off her shift. I'm employing now what's called the swag approach to police work, a Scientific Wild-Ass Guess. We sit down, order Manhattans, the drinks arrive, and I say, 'Say, how's your friend Dickie Duschene?' She just about chokes on her cherry, can't fucking believe it. The cool nurse is no longer cool. We make a deal and by the time she's on her fourth Manhattan I've been apprised of the fact the guy that got whacked in the hospital expected it, saw it coming while, in the meantime, he was falling in love with the nurse and telling her where he stashed a hundred and fifty big ones, in a locker at the airport. She didn't know what to do with it, so she gave it to her boyfriend, Dickie, for safekeeping. You see what's coming? Honest to Christ. Dickie gives Nola thirty grand to keep peace in the family. She gives it to me and I'm using part of the take from the same fucking heist I'm investigating."

"That's an amazing story."

"I'm not done yet. I see where I am, I'm right in the middle of all this shit and I gotta get out, fast. But the cool nurse who's no longer cool goes immediately to the feds, who've been talking to her anyway, and now the fucking daisy chain comes around again. Dickie talks. Nola screams she didn't do nothing, she gave it to the police, *me.* The feds and cops both come to the house. They ask, where's the money? I'm in deep shit if I admit anything. Nobody's gonna believe I used some of it only to pay snitches. Those administrative assholes don't understand the value of snitches. They want to get me anyway 'cause I never told 'em dick what I was doing and that infringed on their management position. So I say, 'What money?' "

"Play dumb."

"Sure, but you know what they did? They take Rosemary aside and question her. I haven't told her *nothing* about the money, so I figure I'm home. But then, Jesus, they tell her about my relationship with Nola, dirty bastards, that it was Nola gave me the money. Rosemary says, 'Oh, is that right?' They tell her it was thirty grand. It could've been thirty cents, it wouldn't a made any difference. Rosemary opens up her sewing box and takes out a handful of money straps *I* had taken off the dough each time I got some to pay a snitch and threw the paper straps in the wastebasket. And each time I did, Rosemary dipped in and got it out. Then waited for the right time to stick it in my nose. Finding out about Nola was the time. They trace the bank straps to the Wells Fargo heist, I'm brought up on accessory charges, possession of stolen currency, shit, I'm convicted and draw ten to twenty-five. Rosemary, at the sentencing, she has tears in her eyes. A woman from the TV news asks her how she feels. Rosemary wipes her eyes and says, 'Thirteen years married to that son of a bitch he barely spoke a word to me. Let's see how he likes it when nobody speaks to *him.*' Meaning in here," Roy told Jack Delaney at Angola. "A cop trying to make it in the joint."

Roy appeared, coming past the illuminated fountain. He sat down across from Jack, took a drink of his scotch, then hunched over, his arms laid on the table.

"You have a fire key for this place?"

Jack shook his head, comfortable in the patio chair. "This wasn't a hotel when I was working. I don't recall what it was; I think they made it into one. It's nice, huh? Cozy."

"You don't have a key, how you plan to get in the man's room?"

"Maybe we won't have to."

"Then what do we need a burglar for?" Roy said. "What's your part in this deal?"

"You afraid you're gonna do all the work?"

"I have so far."

Was he being serious? Jack wasn't sure. He got out a cigarette and scratched a hotel match to light it. Roy's tone was always the same unless he was talking to traffic or a lavatory door, so it was hard to tell. But was he serious at this moment or not?

"I'm gonna follow the guy," Jack said, "and learn all about him. Where he banks, where he eats his supper. . . . If I have to go in his room I'll find a way, so don't worry about it. Okay?"

Roy said, "I'm not worried. I already found you a way." He sipped his drink, not taking his eyes from Jack, then put on a grin as he said, "You starting to feel some strain?"

It told Jack, yes, Roy had been serious a moment ago and now he was letting up, turning it around. Roy was a friend, but Roy had to be handled with a pair of Leo's rubber gloves, carefully.

Jack said, "You found somebody working here you know," and watched Roy put a little more into his grin.

"Guess who."

"Man or woman?"

"Man."

"Black or white?"

"Dark brown. Give you a hint—great big nigger."

"I know him?"

"There was a time he might've killed you, if it weren't for me."

Roy was maintaining his importance. Jack said, "It surprises me I even knew how to take a leak before I met you, Roy. This was up at the farm you're talking about. Lemme think. . . . The time I was watching TV and the hogs came in the room and switched the channel." He saw Roy nod. One of his first nights in Big Stripe. The lights went off in the dormitory at ten-thirty, but TV could stay on, in the bare room with folding chairs, till twelve.

That same day, just before they blew the yard at six and everybody had to be somewhere, the black con had approached him making a kissing sound, said, "Hey, bitch, I think you my style, yeah," made that kissing sound again and Jack hit him in his puckered mouth, half turned and threw the punch with a lot of body in it. He took the guy by surprise and decked him the same way he used to do it when he was fifteen and sixteen at the river beach and it was for fun, not a matter of staying free, out of some guy's bunk after lights out. He had heard guys with each other in the dark, Jesus, and couldn't believe it. Right after he hit the guy and a crowd began to close in, Roy had walked up and said, "You willing to fight anybody wants you as their galboy?" Jack had all his adrenaline there handy and said, "You want to find out?" Roy said, "You need me, Delaney." Knowing his name already. "There are seventy-one of them and eighteen of us." Meaning blacks and whites in the dorm. "If you don't care to be part of a mixed marriage then tell them you're Roy Hick's round-the-way. You understand? You're my home-boy, friend from civilian life. It'll save you breaking your hands or dying, one."

Now at the table in the hotel courtyard Roy said, "You were watching 'Lifestyles of the Rich and Famous' and the three hogs come in and switched it to 'Bugs Bunny' or some fucking thing."

Jack said, " 'Lifestyles of the Rich and Famous,' the burglar's dream program, wasn't on the air yet. I was watching a movie and I'll tell you what it was, it was *The Big Bounce*, a terrible movie, but Lee Grant was in it and I was in love with her at the time. Woman has a wonderful nose. And the hogs, they came in and switched it to 'Love Boat,' which I couldn't stand to watch. So I got up and switched it back."

135

"That's when I came in," Roy said. "And who was it switched it back to the 'Love Boat'?"

"Biggest black guy I ever saw—up until the Superbowl and the Refrigerator was playing with the Bears. You mean to tell me Little One is working here at the hotel?"

"He's a waiter," Roy said. "I just saw him, pushing a table into the elevator. Little One, that night, he switched the TV back and you didn't know what to do."

"You talking about? I would've switched it back soon as Little One sat down. You walk in, look at me. You go, 'What're you watching this shit for?' I *wasn't* watching it, I was watching the movie."

"He'd a killed you."

"He might've tried."

"I told him, 'Little One, sit down.' You remember? I told him, 'You behave, or I won't let you join the Dale Carnegie Club.' Shit, I was on the executive committee and Little One knew it. He was dying to get in the club 'cause you know the man liked to talk. But they wouldn't let him in account of he was such a mean asshole."

"I remember you tried to get me to join."

"You should've. Dale Carnegie changed Little One's life. They even let him in the Angola Jaycees."

"You mention the fundraiser to him?"

"Sure I did. He knows him. Says the man's running up a bill you wouldn't believe, but doesn't tip for shit."

"I wonder when he's coming back."

"That desk clerk's got his head up his ass—the man never left. He's sitting right in there, in the cocktail lounge." Roy nodded. "That door over in the corner. The dining room and the bar."

Jack didn't move. "Little One said he's in there?"

"Last time he saw him."

"Were you gonna tell me or keep it to yourself?"

"I just told you, didn't I?" Roy leaned back in his chair as he said, "Jack, if it ain't fun, it ain't worth doing. I thought we were of a mind on that."

Jack felt off-balance, awkward, but didn't believe it showed. He drew on the cigarette, blew a thin stream of smoke, and said, "I forgot. Make it look easy."

"Like we played the two guys in the car. Nothing to it."

"He's in the bar, uh?"

"I don't think you should stick your head in there, let him see you," Roy said. "That might not be too funny, would it? We could have us another beverage, wait for him to come out. There's no way he'd recognize you in this shitty light. Though you might move your chair back a speck, get behind the tree more."

Jack said, "That's an idea."

Roy grinned at him. "I thought you'd like it."

They had fresh drinks in front of them when Jack saw Roy look up and open his eyes with some expectation. Jack bent his head back as far as it would go as the black trousers and white jacket appeared next to him at the table. He said, "Little One, is that you up there?"

Little One said, "Mr. Jack Delaney, it's a pleasure to see you, but we better skip shaking hands. The man's coming out this minute and I don't know you gentlemen from any other convict dudes come in here." He walked off toward the lobby.

Roy said, "That must be him now."

Jack looked over his shoulder, surprised to see two figures, Mutt and Jeff: the colonel wearing that same tan suit and black tie, moving with the same confident, lazy stride, talking with easy gestures, using his hands a lot.

Jack said, "The short one."

Roy said, "I know that. But who's the gringo?"

Yeah, guy about fifty in a dark suit, dress shirt but no tie, dark-rimmed glasses, thin sandy hair. Little One held the door open, glanced back, and then followed them into the lobby.

There was a silence at the table until finally Jack said, "Maybe he's a contributor, an oilman."

Roy said, "Uh-unh, he's the law. I can't tell what branch of government, but you can put it down in your book he's a fed."

ELEVEN

Tuesday morning Jack had to pick up a body at Hotel Dieu, an eighty-five-year-old woman who'd spent her last month there at the hospital, light as a feather lifting her onto the mortuary cot. Back at Mullen & Sons he wheeled the cot onto the floor lift, pushed the button, and watched it rise through the opening trapdoor in the ceiling to the second floor. Jack went up the back stairs, wheeled the cot off the lift and into the prep room, where Leo was filling the embalming machine with Permaglo.

"Some guy by the name of Tommy Cullen phoned. I told him you were out."

Jack said, "I'd like to talk to you after. I want to take some time off."

"How much time? Few days, a week?"

"I'm thinking of leaving here."

Leo was lifting the body onto the prep table. He looked up from his bent-over position, the old lady in his arms. "What're you talking about? You're gonna walk out on me?"

"Leo, there young guys dying to be morticians. You can get help, easy."

"After I got you out of prison?"

"You helped and I appreciate it, but you didn't exactly get me out. I've been here three years now and you know I didn't ever plan to stay."

"What're you gonna do?"

"I'll look around."

He heard a phone ring, the one in his room, not the business number.

Leo said, "You're getting yourself into something, aren't you?"

Jack didn't have to answer that one. He hurried into his apartment, sat down in a sofa that had spent thirty years in a visitation room before coming up here, and picked up the phone.

Cullen's voice said, "Jack, they're gonna throw me out of here, say I have to leave. Soon as they get hold of Tommy Junior he has to come get me. They spoke to Mary Jo and she told 'em to call the prison 'cause she won't have me back in the house."

"What'd you do?"

"I didn't do *noth*ing. I don't know what's going on here."

"What'd they say?"

"Guy, one of the help, comes to my room this morning and tells me to pack up, I'm leaving. I said, 'What're you talking about I'm leaving?' He says Miz Hollenbeck sent him to tell me. That's the broad runs the place. I go to her office, I'm gonna find out what's going on. She jumps up, says, 'Don't you come in here. Stay where you are,' and says to her secretary, 'Evelyn, call Cedric.' That's the guy told me I had to pack. One of the colored guys that does the shit work there. I said, 'What is this? You didn't get the Medicaid check or what?' Miz Hollenbeck looks like she's afraid I'm gonna come over the desk at her, telling me stay right there, don't move."

Jack said, "Has this got anything to do with Anna Marie?"

"Well, sort of, yeah. But, see, at this point all she's telling me is that Tommy Junior signed the contract that says if there's any kind of improper conduct I have to leave, and they're trying to locate Tommy Junior. You know he's a house painter. Only he's had, well, kind of a drinking problem lately and he isn't always where he says he's gonna be. I think it's between the paint fumes and being married to Mary Jo causing it."

Jack said, "What'd you do to Anna Marie?"

There was a pause. "What do you mean, what'd I do to her? I never did nothing she didn't want me to."

"When was this, last night?" He heard the buzzer sound in the hall; it meant someone had entered downstairs.

"I had the colored guy, Cedric, pick me up a bottle of port wine; nice stuff, cost four dollars and I give Cedric a buck. I had a couple glasses and then later on I stopped by Anna Marie's room, see if she cared for a glass."

Jack lighted a cigarette with his hotel matches, listening, staring at a framed print on the wall over the refrigerator: two young ladies in a primeval forest playing on a swing in a time Jack could not imagine. There was nothing

141

in the room that belonged to him; he could pack one bag and be out of Mullen & Sons in five minutes.

"I mentioned she's got a very nice room of her own here. Anna Marie says well, if I think it's all right, looks up and down the hall, and I go in. Soon as I pour us a couple of glasses she gets the album out. Here's Robbie and here's Rusty and Laurie and Timmy, shows me her kids, her grandchildren, her great-grandchildren, and names every one of them. I said to her, 'Anna Marie, you can't be old enough to have grandchildren, huh, come on?' "

Jack said, "Cully, I don't know if I want to hear this."

"I meant it. She doesn't look her age. She only looks about seventy . . . seventy-two, maybe. The hell, I'm sixty-five. What's the difference? I said, 'Anna Marie, that's a swell-looking family and you are a good-looking woman.' We're sitting next to each other on these two chairs pushed together. I can see she liked that, what I said. So I lean over, give her a little kiss in the ear. She jumps, scared the shit out of me, and let out a yell. What happened, I kissed her hearing aid. I said, 'Anna Marie, you don't need that thing, take it off.' So she does. I give her another kiss and tell her, my, you're a good-looking woman and all this shit, you know, and I say, 'Why don't we go over and sit on the bed, be more comfortable.' Everything I say she says, 'What? What?' I put my arm around her, get her up, take her over to the bed. We're sitting there, you know, on the edge of the bed, she doesn't move or say a word. I mean she did not object once to anything I did."

Jack didn't want to ask, but something made him. "Like what?"

"Like kissing her. You know. Put my arm around her . . . I undid her robe, she's got a flannel nightgown on underneath. I kiss her some more. She just sits there. I'm

142

thinking, Jesus, it's been so long she doesn't remember what to do. But I'm in no hurry. You go twenty-seven years, Jack, without any quiff what's a few more minutes when it's right there? Right? But, I don't know, I'm thinking either it's been too long for her or she's frigid. I put my hand inside the robe . . .''

Jack felt himself tense.

"I touch one of her tits. No, first I had to find it. It wasn't where they usually are. I put my hand on it and Anna Marie became it was like she turned to stone, her eyes wide open, staring straight ahead. So I said the hell with it, this is not gonna be my night."

Jack felt himself relax.

"You didn't do anything."

"That's what I been telling you."

"Then why're they making you leave?" He saw Leo standing in the doorway, Leo with the same expression Jack pictured on Anna Marie's face when she turned to stone, and said, "Cully, hang on a second."

Leo said, "There's a man downstairs asking about the pickup you made Sunday at Carville."

"Who is he?"

"I don't know who he is, I said I was off Sunday but I'd see about it. I didn't know what to say."

"What's he look like?"

"He looks like—I don't know what he looks like. A normal, everyday person."

"Take it easy, Leo. Is the guy American or Latin?"

"He's American." Leo sounded surprised.

"Did he show you identification?"

"I didn't ask."

"All right, I'll take care of it."

"He's in the lounge. . . . You gonna talk to him?"

"Yeah, soon as I'm through here." Jack waited, his hand over the phone. He watched Leo shake his head before he walked away. Jack raised the phone to his face. "Cully, where were we? Yeah, why're they making you leave?"

"Remember I said she took off her hearing aid?"

"Yeah?"

"I put it in my robe while we're sitting there. When I left, I forgot to give it back, and this morning she tells Miz Hollenbeck I stole the fucking thing."

"That's all?"

"That's what I said to Miz Hollenbeck. You serious? The fuck do I want with a hearing aid? I can hear better'n you can and I'm twice your age. She didn't like that."

"You packed?"

"Not yet."

"Well, get ready, I'll pick you up."

"Jack? I don't think you can get laid here."

"No, I guess not."

"Jack? I don't want to stay in a funeral home."

Jack said, "Who does?"

The man waiting in the Mullen & Sons smoking lounge was the same man who had left the hotel with Dagoberto Godoy. Jack realized it coming along the hall, seeing the man from about the same distance as he did last night, the same heavy-framed glasses, the same dark suit, but now with a necktie. Up close the man was as Leo said, a normal, everyday person; not quite eye to eye with Jack, an inch or two shorter, but twenty-five pounds heavier in the buttoned suit coat.

Jack said, "Can I help you?"

The man cocked his head to one side, appraising him with a nice grin but a very steady look in those glasses. He said, "Are you asking if you're able to? I think you are, Jack. I might add, it would be in your best interest if you do."

Jack cocked his head at the same angle and stared back with his own faint grin, believing Roy was right, the guy was the law but not local, some government agency with initials; New Orleans cops might bullshit you, but would never act cute doing it. Jack also believed he could outwait and out-stare this guy, and he was right.

The guy put out his hand and said, "Wally Scales, I'm with the Immigration service."

Jack gave him a dead-fish handshake, a question in his eyes. "I never immigrated from anyplace. I've lived here all my life."

"Except for three years in there." Wally Scales had straightened his head but continued to grin. "Am I right, Jack?"

"You're referring, I believe," Jack said, "to when I was upstate that time?"

"Upstate, that's good. Well, you seem to have enjoyed a successful rehabilitation."

Jack put on a reasonably stupid grin for Wally Scales and slipped a little bit of West Feliciana Parish into his sound. "Well, I can't say it was enjoyable, but I come through it, yes sir."

"You have a good job here—you like it?"

"Yeah, I do. I work for my brother-in-law."

"I spoke to him"—Wally Scales began to frown—"asked about a removal you made at Carville Sunday and he seemed distressed by the question. Why would that be?"

"How'd he seem?"

"Apprehensive . . . nervous."

"Well, that's the way he is. Leo's a nervous type a person. He's a worry wart."

"But if he's in charge here he'd know about a removal."

"Yeah, he would."

"Unless the request came in Sunday morning and you handled it yourself and didn't tell him."

Jack waited. There was no question to answer.

"Is that what happened?"

"Was what happened?"

"They called and you went up to Carville?"

"They never called, least that I know of."

"They said they did."

"Well, I must've been on the toilet or someplace, 'cause I never heard the phone."

"They said you came and removed the body of one Amelita Sosa, deceased."

Jack shook his head. "No, sir, not me. Must've been some other funeral home and they got the name wrong. Sunday I was here all day. I washed the hearse. Hey, maybe that was it, I was outside a while."

Wally Scales cocked his head again, this time without the grin. "We could take a ride up there, Jack. Ask the sister if you're the one that came."

Jack said, "Well, if it's okay with Leo, I don't mind. I used to go up there when I was working for my Uncle Brother and Emile in the pipe organ business. I'd have to climb way way up there, you know, in the loft when they were tuning the organ."

Wally Scales said, "Jack, let me ask you a question. I want you to give me a straight, honest answer. All right?

146

Because I don't want to see you get in trouble and have to go back upstate." Wally Scales paused. "Are you putting me on?"

Jack frowned, then shook his head. "No, sir."

"You swear you did not go to Carville."

"I did with my Uncle Brother and Emile."

"I mean *Sunday.*"

"No, sir, I was right here."

Jack eased his eyes open a little wider so Wally Scales, staring hard, could see the truth in them. It was difficult not to grin at this asshole, but Jack managed.

Wally Scales looked past him, down the hall. He took a step away, turned around slowly to look out the window at the empty parking lot, and came back.

"Who's here besides you and your brother-in-law, Jack?"

"There's a dead woman upstairs."

"There is? What's her name?"

"I don't know what her name is. Some old woman."

"Will you show her to me?"

Jack felt it was safe to grin now, giving the guy a sly one as he said, "You like to look at 'em, too, huh? 'Specially when they're bare nekked. Yeah, Leo's up there hosing her out. You want to watch, come on."

Wally Scales kept staring with pretty much the same expression except for a tightening around his nose and mouth, like he'd bit into a green persimmon. He said, "Why don't I believe you, Jack?"

"She's up there, I'll show you."

"Maybe I should talk to your brother-in-law again."

Threatening him. "Sure, come on."

"Or I could talk to Lucy Nichols."

It was sneaky, but it wasn't a question, so Jack stared back at him with his bare trace of a grin, waiting. It was coming though.

"You know her, don't you?"

"Who's that?"

"You're gonna keep acting stupid, aren't you? Till I leave."

"Don't you want to see the dead woman?"

He watched the man shake his head and give up; maybe not caring that much, one way or the other. That was the feeling Jack had, along with relief.

He showed Wally Scales out and called Roy at the bar.

"You give your notice?"

"Yeah, but I can change my mind," Roy said, "depending on the numbers, how much the guy's put in the bank."

"How about Crispin Reyna and Franklin of God?"

"Who?"

"Franklin de Dios. You find out anything?"

"They're supposed to be with Immigration, looking for wetbacks. It's a fact, the radio cars over in the Second District were given a Code Five, they see that Chrysler parked on Audubon, leave it alone."

"But the two guys are from Florida."

"So? If they're federal they can go anywhere they want."

"Yeah, but they wouldn't rent a car. They'd get one from some office here. Wouldn't they?"

"It's more likely, yeah."

"Will you check it out?"

"I could."

"I don't want to put you out any, Roy, if you're busy there serving mankind."

"Fuck you."

"But if we're gonna play these guys we better know the names and numbers and how much they weigh. I don't want to get blindsided, Roy, get my fucking head taken off and I don't even see it coming. I'd like to know why the fundraiser brought in two guys from Florida who pack guns, wouldn't you?"

"Don't worry about it."

"What does that mean?"

"I'll take care of it."

"You still haven't told me anything."

"I'll check 'em out. Jesus Christ."

"You're in a shitty mood, Roy."

"So what else is new?"

"Find out about a guy named Wally Scales, also suppose to be with Immigration. He came by looking for the girl, Amelita, and you know who he is? The guy last night with the fundraiser."

"That one could be Immigration," Roy said. "Or he could be Internal Revenue or Treasury."

"Will you find out? Call me at Lucy's, I'm gonna go pick up Cullen now, take him over there."

"I'll tell you where you're going tonight," Roy said, "case you didn't know. You're gonna go to work for a change, take a look in the guy's room."

"Roy, you feeling out of sorts? Didn't get your period, or what?"

"I have to get out of this fucking place."

"Now you're talking."

He phoned Lucy and asked her if it was all right if he came over with Cullen. She said fine, any time. He asked her if a guy named Wally Scales had paid a visit.

"He phoned this morning, told me who he was. He said, 'I understand you were at Carville Sunday, to pick up the body of a deceased friend of yours.' I told him no, that wasn't true."

"Your first lie."

"Of any importance. I asked him where he got his information."

"What'd he say?"

"He said it didn't matter, he was sorry to bother me."

"Good. He was here, but I got the feeling he was just going through the motions. Didn't have his heart in it."

"But then he said, 'Next time you see your dad, give him my best.' "

TWELVE

"I'll try to tell you," Lucy said, "but I've tried before and when I hear myself, well, it's never exactly what I want to say. I guess because it's a gut feeling that brings you to the point of doing it. You make a choice. If you don't do it, you can list reasons why, all kinds of reasons. Or you can say, 'What, do you think I'm crazy?' But if you go ahead with it, if you *do* it . . . that's something else."

They were in the sun parlor of Lucy's mother's house, the banana-tree room in dim afternoon light, rain coming down outside. Lucy came away from the gray windows to sit down facing Jack and Cullen, both of them on the sofa.

"I became a nun because of a love story that took place eight centuries ago. Because of a man who was in love with love and because of a seventeen-year-old girl named Clare who, I'm convinced, was in love with the man. And I fell in love with the whole idea. I was nineteen, at a time when I could empathize with her, the poor little rich girl, not happy but not sure why. Her mother and dad arranging her marriage, planning her life. I was, well, I got caught up in what I believed was a mystical experience. I even thought, if I'd been around in the year 1210 I could have been that girl. I attend mass at the cathedral of San Rufino and hear a man named Francis speak quietly but with great passion about God's love and my life is changed. I put myself there. I could smell the candles, the incense, and imagine falling in love with the man in the brown Franciscan robe."

Cullen sat hunched on the edge of the sofa, hands folded on his knees. Jack could hear him breathing through his nose, both of them held by the mood, the quiet tone of Lucy's voice, Lucy sitting in sweater and jeans, gray light behind her, telling about a mystical experience.

"Five or six years earlier I might've left to join a commune." She looked right at Jack. "But by the time I was ready to make my run the flower children had gone home. I'm thankful for that, because I would have been running *from* rather than *to* something. What Clare did, under the influence of Francis and a wild, I mean extraordinary, combination of romantic and universal love, ran away and started an order of nuns, the Poor Clares. And it was Francis who performed the tonsure, cut off all her blond hair. He had spoken to her before, advised her, but never alone. I think because Clare was stunning, they say incredibly beautiful, and I really believe he saw more than just love of God in her eyes. His biographers say, oh, no, he was never tempted. But he had another friend in Rome, Jacqueline de Settesoli, he used to visit whenever he went to see the pope and there was never a hint of scandal with Jackie. Because I think she was mannish if not unattractive, so there was no problem. He even called her Brother Jacqueline. But Clare was something else. I have a feeling they would look at each other and there it was, in their eyes, without a word spoken."

It had begun with Cullen meeting Lucy and making casual conversation with a former nun, saying he'd thought about entering the seminary when he was fourteen, the one up on Carrollton Avenue, and Jack saying he did enter it; they were living across the street and he went over there with his mother and sister during a hurricane alert when he was two years old. Then Cullen had come right out and asked her, "Why would a good-looking girl like you . . ."

"You know that before he acquired that gentle Saint Francis image, with the birds flocking around him, he was from a fairly wealthy family and ran with the swingers. But when he gave it up he went all the way. Stripped himself naked in the town square, in Assisi, and gave all his clothes to beggars. Everyone thought he was crazy; they called him *pazzo,* madman, and threw rocks at him. But he got their attention. Maybe he was in a state of metaphysical delirium, divine intoxication, I don't think it matters. He preached unconditional love, love of God through love of man, love without limits, without the language of theology, and he touched people. . . . He kissed the sores on a leper's face."

Cullen said, "Jesus Christ."

"That's right, in his name," Lucy said and looked at Jack and, for a moment, seemed to smile. "He took money out of his dad's business, you might even say he stole it, because a voice said to him, 'Francis, repair my house.' He offered the money to a priest, to rebuild his church that was falling down, but the priest wouldn't take it. Maybe because he was afraid of the dad. So Francis returned the money. But the church, San Damiano, became the first convent of the Poor Clares."

Cullen said, "He really kissed a leper?"

"He bathed a leper who cursed God, blamed him for his condition, and the man was healed."

Jack said, "You believe that?"

Lucy looked at him. "Why not? He said he couldn't stand the sight of lepers, but that God led him among them. 'And what had seemed bitter turned to sweetness.' " She paused. " 'And then, soon after, I left the world.' "

There was a silence in the room.

Jack felt the back of his neck tingle. He watched her cross her legs and saw the sandal hanging loose on her toe. She didn't seem to be the least bit self-conscious. She could sit here in her mother's house and talk about a mystical experience, about going back eight centuries and feeling herself there, knowing what it was like. . . . He saw her look at Cullen.

"He washed a leper. But do you know what the Saint Francis experts argue about? Whether he did it before or after he received the stigmata. It would seem to have happened after. But if it did, how could he wash the leper and pick clean the man's scabs with his bloody hands bandaged?"

Cullen said, "You lost me."

"That's what happens," Lucy said. "We lose sight of the act of love in what he did and get carried away questioning details. They say he had the stigmata, the wounds of Christ, that he bled from his hands, his feet and his side. But whether he had the stigmata or not, would it change who he was? He didn't need his hands to touch people."

Cullen said, "He touched you and you joined the nuns."

"I got out of myself, the role I was playing as the little rich girl, to find myself. It comes with being touched and then touching others."

Jack said, "That's *good*," narrowing his eyes and nodding, wanting her to know he understood. Maybe he did. There was this Jack Delaney and there was Jack Delaney the fashion model, the poser. . . . He stopped there, surprised by the clarity of this inward look, and brought up something he'd been thinking about. "You mentioned the other day he did time."

That straightened Cullen. "He did?"

"When he was still in his teens," Lucy said, "Assisi was at war with another city. There was a battle—well, a skirmish, and Francis was taken prisoner and spent a year in a dungeon."

"The hole," Jack said. "I've seen more than one come out in their white coveralls saved, born again."

"So not much has changed," Lucy said. "He was ill the rest of his life. Tuberculosis of the bone, malaria, conjunctivitis, dropsy. They don't call it that anymore. What is it? . . . But his poor health didn't seem to matter because he was never *in* himself."

She paused and Jack could see her concentrating, wanting to tell about this man who'd changed her life in a way they would understand.

"He was childlike. He attracted young people especially because he was never pretentious, theologically preachy. He accepted people the way they were, even the rich, and never criticized . . . which is something I have to work on. What he was saying is, if you need nothing, you have everything. . . ."

Cullen stirred, moved his hand over his face.

"The first step in finding yourself is not to be hung up on *things*. And when I was nineteen it all seemed very simple."

Cullen said, "Excuse me, but you have a powder room I could use?"

Jack said, "Back in the real world after twenty-seven years." He waited while Lucy walked Cullen to the hall and pointed the way. When she came back he said, "What about Clare? Did he ever see her again?"

"She would invite him to San Damiano, but he always refused to go, until near the end."

"Didn't trust himself."

"He told his Franciscans if they were ever tempted by carnal desires, find an ice-cold stream and jump in."

"What'd they do in the summer?"

Lucy smiled. "I don't know. . . . I used to picture a bunch of guys in brown robes running through the snow, diving into a river. . . ."

Jack said, "Clare went all the way, became a saint. But you decided not to go for it, huh?"

She said, "If you're aware of going for it, Jack, you don't have a chance."

"I was kidding."

She said, "Were you?" and kept looking at him.

Now he didn't know what to say and had to think of something. "You were in, what, nine years?"

"Eleven, altogether."

That would make her thirty. "Well, you must've decided something. You came out."

"Into the world. It's changed a lot."

"Yeah, but you stepped right back in. You know what the ladies are wearing better than most ladies."

"That part's easy, you get it out of a magazine. But it's only a cover, Jack, while I change into something else."

"You don't mean clothes."

"No, it's more like changing your skin, your identity."

"Are we talking about another mystical experience?"

"I don't know."

"What do you think you're going to turn into?"

"I don't know that either."

She kept looking at him, looking at him in a strange way. Or else it was the mood, the quiet, the rain, faint daylight showing in the windows of the room. But he could feel something.

"You're different every time I see you."

She said, "So are you."

"Why did you leave?"

"I was burnt out."

"What does that mean?"

"I was touching without feeling."

"You were taking care of people that need you."

"There are always people who need you. They're everywhere you look."

"I thought you left because of Amelita."

"That was a reason to leave when I did. But the time was coming. . . . I finished one life when I became a Sister of Saint Francis and I finished that one when I left Nicaragua."

"Are you sure?"

She nodded. "I need to be used."

He never knew what she was going to say.

"I need to lose myself in something."

"You don't think this deal we're into, walk off with five million, is gonna require any concentration?"

"Yes, but what's my part? I'm not doing anything."

"You're the brains."

Her reaction came slowly, a look of mild surprise. "You see this as a game."

"It isn't like going to the office."

"You sort of shrug at the idea. But you're willing to do it. Why?"

"Money."

"No, you were willing right away, before you knew we were going to keep it. Remember? You said we'd be doing something for mankind. Were you serious?"

"I don't know. . . ."

"Are you ever serious?"

"Sure, I am. It's just, I don't see that many things to be serious *about.*"

She began to grin, across the coffee table from him in the dim afternoon light, and it surprised him. She said, "Jack, I love you. You know why?"

He felt that tingle again on the back of his neck.

"You remind me of someone."

The tingling stopped.

"What we do is serious, our motive. But how we go about it is something else, isn't it? How we look at it, our attitude."

"How we look back on it a year from now," Jack said, "and think it was pretty funny. If it works, and if we're not looking back on it from the joint. You have to be optimistic, assume you're gonna make it. And you think of it as a game, because then it's not as scary."

He could make out lights in her eyes, her lips parted, Lucy beginning to smile at him again. He wanted to ask her who he reminded her of, but Cullen came back in, followed by the housekeeper.

Dolores said, "Phone for Mr. Delaney."

Roy's voice said, "Crispin Antonio Reyna was convicted in Florida, 1982, of uttering fraudulent checks and did nine months in South Dade FCI."

"What's uttering mean?"

"Like hanging paper, only a higher-class way of doing it. He was brought up another time, falsified his 4473 making a multiple gun purchase, also Dade County. Trying to buy five dozen model 92s Berettas he said were for a gun club. The indictment fell through. The feds tried to get him for running dope from Florida to Baton Rouge, said he was selling it to the students up at LSU. They couldn't make that one stick either. Crispin Antonio's originally a Cuban. His family moved to Nicaragua in '59, he was an officer in the National Guard and came here in '79, to Miami. Franklin de Dios, it says his nationality is Miskito Indian, born in Musawas, Nicaragua. Came to Miami a year ago and was a major suspect in a triple homicide, but was never brought to trial."

"They don't sound like they're with Immigration," Jack said.

"Except Second District radio cars were told to leave 'em be. They were assumed to be working as federal agents."

"Assumed to be—what kind?"

"Call Wally Scales and ask him. His number's 226–5989."

"Roy, what is he?"

"He's the fucking CIA, Jack. I want to know what side we're supposed to be on, the good guys or the bad guys."

THIRTEEN

There was no way to miss Little One, even at night, the size of him coming along Bienville from the hotel, toward Royal, where Jack was waiting near the corner. Little One put out his hand and palmed Jack the room key. He said, "That fucking Roy. Okay, now we even. Tell him that."

"We appreciate it."

"You better 'preciate it. Leave the key under the chifforobe, where the maid can find it. See, like the man dropped it. The man's mostly drunk, having a good time. He won't know."

"I may have to go back in."

"Come on, Jack." Little One twisting his head, in pain. "You see how far out my neck is right now?"

"I'm not gonna take anything. The guy won't even know I was there. In and out, take me ten minutes."

"Yeah, you slick, like all those boys at 'Gola use to think of themselves, cool dudes. I remember correctly, Jack, was up there you and I met, wasn't it?"

"I did something pretty dumb one time," Jack said. "I should've known better. This is different. One more time, that's it."

"Yeah, like the Count say, 'One more once,' huh? Only that was 'April in Paris' and this is April in N'Awlins, man, gets hot and sticky."

"I'm not back in business, anything like that."

"Just want to check the man out."

"That's all. Take a look around."

"Man with the Cuban skin and five-hundred-dollar suits. Sweep his room, see if he's got a badge or any bugs 'fore you start to deal."

"Nothing like that."

"Jack, when you get back up to the farm, give my best to Smoke and Too Good, and that cute little rascal Minne Mo, if he still there. Lemme think who else . . ."

Jack walked through the empty lobby and across one end of the garden courtyard to the cocktail lounge, cream-colored in soft lights, elegant, and not a soul here. The Oriental barman came to life and poured Jack a vodka.

If he were back working his trade he would have looked in, turned around, and walked out to find a big downtown hotel full of noise, full of tourists and people with name tags drinking and having fun in the bar. He'd become someone else as he felt the glow, breathed the scent of girls in cocktail dresses, girls scouting their own

game while Jack looked for ladies wearing respectable dia-
monds, husbands who brought billfolds out of their jackets
or folds of currency in silver slips. He'd take a few days to
sort them out, then ride up in the elevator with a likely pair,
get off a floor below the button they punch and run up the
stairs to watch them going into their suite. An hour later
he'd try their door to see if they put on the chain. The next
day he'd slip into those rooms while they were snapping
pictures in Jackson Square; go through the drawers, their
suitcases and bathroom kits, look in their shoes, feel
through clothes hanging in the closet. He'd look at the
door chain then. If they used it he'd remove the chain and
replace it with one he'd brought along that had three or
four more links in it. The couple would slip the chain on
that night and never notice the difference. He'd come along
later, open the door with his fire key, and be able to reach
in and slip off the chain. Then hook it up again on the way
out, if it was a better-than-average score and he was feeling
good. Or else he could cut it going in.

Do all that, get away with it, and he couldn't tell anyone about it.

He'd hear salesmen bullshitting the girls, trying to
impress them with how many computers they'd sold, and
he'd sit there at the bar or reach for something like, "Didn't
you and I do a modeling shoot last year?" Or he'd tell them
he was learning English and put on a half-assed French
accent.

He tried it on Helene the first time he saw her in the
bar at the Roosevelt, knocked out by her profile, her bare
legs crossed beneath a short green skirt, told her he was
from Paree, and Helene said, "Is that by any chance near
Morgan City?"

She told him it wasn't a bad approach, it was different,

but how far could he take it? Or was his life so boring he had to pretend he was someone else?

He told her, without the French accent, she had the most beautiful nose and brown eyes—he threw in the eyes —he had ever seen and that his life, his profession, was far from boring.

"What do you do?"

"See if you can guess."

"Do you live here?"

"Yeah."

"Do you have a lot of money?"

"Enough."

"You sell dope."

"I don't sell anything."

"You buy things."

"No."

"You steal things."

"Right."

She hesitated. "What do you steal?"

"Guess."

"Cars?"

"No."

"Jewels."

"Right."

She said, "Sure you do." She said, "Really? Come on." She said, "What do you do with them, the jewels?"

"I sell 'em to a guy for about a quarter of what they're worth."

She said, "I don't know whether to believe you or not," with a different tone now, softer, hesitant.

Jack turned half around on his stool, looked over the room, and came back to Helene. "What're you doing to-morrow?"

"I work. For a lawyer."

"Stop by here during your lunch hour. I'm in 610."

"What if I'm not hungry?"

"You see the lady in the blue net?"

"Chiffon."

"The guy has on a tux."

"What about her?"

"You see the ring she's wearing?"

It was about one-fifteen the next day, the hotel room silent except for faint street sounds, when Helene turned her head on the pillow and said, "Jacques, I think I'm falling in love with you."

Buddy Jeannette had told him, "Always look nice and always ride the elevator. You run into somebody on the stairs they gonna remember you, 'cause you don't see nobody on the stairs as a rule. But a elevator, man, you so close to people they don't see you."

So Jack rode an empty elevator up to the fifth floor of the St. Louis Hotel in his navy-blue work suit, got off, and there was 501 in the elevator alcove, out of sight from the courtyard below. He stepped over to the door and knocked three times, waited, giving the man plenty of time if he was in there, then used the key to enter the suite.

The fundraiser had left lights on, even the one in the bathroom. Little One told Roy he had checked on the man at seven, phoned to see if he could pick up the room-service table and there was no answer; but the man and two other Latinos were there at five-thirty when Little One said he brought up the champagne and booze and snacks, and a couple white girls had come in while he was there that looked like whores.

The party mess was in the sitting room, bottles and

glasses and a tray with a few canapés left on it, tiny sandwiches, deviled eggs, and a bowl of melted ice and shrimp
tails. There were shrimp tails in ashtrays, napkins on the
floor, wet spots on the red carpeting . . . several envelopes
on the desk addressed to Col. Dagoberto Godoy, c/o the
St. Louis Hotel, postmarked Tegucigalpa, Honduras. The
letters were typed in Spanish. Jack saw himself in the mirror
over the sofa as he crossed to the phone on the end table.
He remembered letters from his dad with the Honduras
postmark; he had soaked off the stamps and saved them.
There was nothing by the phone; a few shrimp tails.

This was like an afternoon scouting trip, not even close
to what the real thing felt like, going in when you knew the
people were there in the dark, hearing their breathing and
more different kinds of snoring sounds than anyone could
imagine.

He'd said to Helene, "Did you know women snore as
much as men? I've made a study. Women aren't as loud, but
they're more original. Some of 'em go, 'chit . . . chit,' like a
little sneeze. Some of 'em go, 'pissssss,' on the exhale."
Helene said, "You fascinate me," shining her brown eyes at
him, chin resting on her hand with the blue stone, the
sapphire. He had told her she was the only person in the
world, outside of Buddy Jeannette, who knew what he did.
She liked that; she hunched her shoulders. He told her he
knew he was going to tell her; as soon as they started talking
that night he knew it. She said she knew right away there was
something different about him, mysterious. She said, "It's
real scary, huh? Doing that." He said, sometimes, when it
was quiet, he would imagine the man and woman lying there
listening and that was really scary. She said, "That's why you
do it, huh? 'Cause it's scary." He said he didn't think too
much about *why* he did it. But he did think, every once in a

while, that maybe if he'd gone to Vietnam he wouldn't be doing it. Strange? He was turned down when he took his physical, he had mono; then after that was just never called. He told her that sometimes after he left the room with his flight bag and would be standing there waiting for an elevator, that was scarier than being in the room. The best part was when he got to his own room and closed the door, or when he walked out of the hotel, if he wasn't staying there. Jesus, the relief. Helene said, "Like it doesn't have anything to do with robbing people." He said, well, there had to be something in it for you; you weren't gonna put your ass on the line just for thrills. That was part of it, though. *Doing* it. Yeah, because he never thought of it as . . . you know, just a robbery. Did that make sense? Helene said, "I want to go with you. Once, that's all. Please?"

It took a few weeks to let himself be talked into it. Then spent the next thirty-five months wondering how he could have been so fucking dumb. When he told Roy, Roy said, "Jesus, you deserve to be in here. Take a fall just on stupidity alone."

They went into a suite at 3:00 A.M. and weren't even across the room before Helene bumped into something and giggled, Jesus Christ, and a voice said from the bedroom, "Who's in there?" and a light came on and they ran down the stairs from the fifteenth floor, no elevator ride this trip, and hotel security was waiting in the lobby. Jack opened his eyes wide and said, "What's this about?" Looked puzzled as he said, "You have the wrong party." Put on a pissed-off look as he said, "We're *staying* in this hotel." The guy in the bathrobe said, "Yeah, I'm pretty sure that's them." Jack told hotel security they were going to hear from his lawyer. Only the lawyer they heard from was Helene's, the guy she worked for, a lawyer who specialized in divorces and didn't know shit about plea bargaining on a criminal justice level. But that's what he did, stuck his nose in and offered them a deal when he didn't have to: immunity for Helene if she'd put Jack Delaney in that hotel room and the cops and the district attorney could've kissed him. They got a search warrant and found his fire keys and an alligator attaché case with the initials RDB he'd picked up months before, stuck in his closet, and forgot he had. They tried to hit him with thirty burglaries over the past two years; so Jack and his Broad Street lawyer made their own plea deal. Okay, he'd give them the thirty and they could close the files in exchange for one Unlawful Entry, look at five years, and be out in three if he was a good boy. Helene said, "Jack? I'm awful sorry."

There were wet towels on the floor in the bathroom, two pair of Jockey briefs, both bright red; five $100 bills rolled tightly together and a 35-millimeter film container of cocaine in the fundraiser's shaving kit. His bed was unmade, thrashed apart it looked like, pillows and spread on the floor. There were at least a dozen pair of Jockeys, all that bright red, in the dresser; a Beretta automatic tucked away beneath the shirts.

The good stuff was on the desk in the bedroom, by the phone. Bank deposit slips, a stack of them in different pastel shades. . . . Wait. Some of them were withdrawal receipts. Here was the same amount deposited, withdrawn, and deposited again on different dates . . . and realized there were four or five different Whitney and Hibernia branch banks involved. The guy wasn't putting everything into one account. Jack copied the figures, with plus and minus signs, on a hotel memo pad.

On another memo pad was a name and telephone

number. *Alvin Cromwell (601) 682–2423.* Jack copied this, too, wondering about the Mississippi area code. In a file folder were a dozen or more sheets stapled together that listed names of individuals and companies, most of the addresses in New Orleans, Lafayette, and Morgan City. R. W. Nichols, Nichols Enterprises, was one of the names that had a check mark after it. There were a lot of check marks. . . . And a sheet of stationery in the file folder that Jack picked up and began to read, because at the top of the sheet was printed *The White House, Washington, D.C.*

It was a letter to the fundraiser from . . . Jesus Christ, Ronald Reagan. It said:

Dear Colonel Godoy:

To assist you in delivering your message of freedom to all my good friends in Louisiana, I have written to each one personally to verify your credentials as a true representative of the Nicaraguan people, and to help affirm your determination to win a big one for democracy. Because I know you have the "stuff" heroes are made of, I have a hunch that modesty might not permit you to describe, personally, the extreme importance of your leadership role in this fight to the death with the Marxists who now have a stranglehold on your beloved country.

I have requested my friends in the Pelican State to give you a generous leg up, that you may ride to victory over communism. I have asked them to help you carry the fight through their support, and come to realize in their hearts, *no es pesado, es mí hermano.*

And there, under "Sincerely," was the president's signature.

Amazing. He wrote the way he spoke. Or he spoke the way one of his aides, who believed all this or could do it out of either side of his mouth or with either hand, spoke or wrote. They all sounded the same, presidents; presidents of anything. But look at that, his autograph. Jack wet a finger with his tongue, touched "Ronald Reagan" and saw it smudge, but not much.

He began to read the letter again, bent over the desk, got as far as "win a big one for democracy," and heard the TV set in the sitting room go on.

Voices. A man and woman talking almost at the same time, snapping one-liners at each other, fast, without letup, the voices hyper, irritating. What was the show? A guy and a girl private eyes . . .

He pictured the sitting room. From the bedroom doorway the door out was close on the left, within ten feet. The TV set was to the right in there, in the corner past the desk. He listened. There were no voices other than the nonstop television voices. Maybe it was the maid. Turned on the TV while she cleaned up. Jack said, Sure, it's the maid. And walked around the bed to the doorway and looked into the sitting room.

It wasn't the maid.

It wasn't a Nicaraguan either. It was a guy in profile with slicked-back dark hair, seedy-looking in an old gray tweed sport coat that reminded Jack of Lucy's soup kitchen and told him the guy didn't belong here. The guy stood within a few feet of the TV set looking down at the lady private eye and her partner snarling at each other in fun, acting wacky. The guy in the herringbone sport coat chuckled, rubbed one of his eyes.

In that moment Jack would bet ten bucks the guy had

served time; twenty bucks he wasn't with the Nicaraguans. Except that he seemed to know where he was.

So Jack stepped over to the dresser and dug out the fundraiser's pistol, the same model Beretta as the ones they'd picked up last night. He didn't check to see if it was loaded; he wasn't going to shoot the guy. He wouldn't mind popping the TV set, the annoying sounds, but not the guy. For some reason he felt sorry for him. Jack moved into the doorway again and stood with the Beretta down at his side. The guy appeared to be in his forties; all dressed up in the ratty sport coat, dark pants that dragged on the floor and nearly covered his worn-out tan shoes. A commercial came on before he looked around.

Paused and said, "Oh, my. I have the wrong room, don't I?"

Buddy Jeannette had said he *bet* he had the wrong room. This guy's line was close enough and either way it took an awful lot of poise. "Oh, I have the wrong room ..." The guy crossing to the door now in his raggedy outfit, trying to pull it off. Look at that. Jack watched the guy hesitate, his hand on the knob, then look over his shoulder with a frown, a question on his face.

He said, "Or do I? Or might we both have the wrong room." With an accent from some British isle.

What was it, Irish?

Jack said, "Step away from the door and turn around."

The man opened his arms wide to show a belly beneath the awful tie. "Please yourself, but trust me, I don't go about your city armed."

It was Irish. Jack said, "Take off your coat."

"I'm happy to oblige you." He pulled it off to show a soiled and wrinkled white shirt, a red-and-gray patterned tie, and dropped the coat on the floor as he did a turn all the way around to face Jack again. "There. Tell me you're not a cop, please. It's all I ask."

"Do I look like a cop?" He watched the man's expression relax, begin to smile.

"Not now you don't, no. You have a sense of play about you, a soft quality to your voice. It indicates to me you're a man of reason, not a dumb brute, and I say this from experience. The last copper I spoke to was in Belfast, an RUC thug what he was. He asked me my name, I answered him in Irish. The fucker said, 'Speak the Queen's English,' and beat me with a stick. I'll show you the marks."

Jack said, "What's your name?"

And drew a smile. "You say it different to what he did. First I'm beaten, then lifted for disorderly behavior. My name's Jerry Boylan. Will you tell me yours?"

Jack was waiting to tell him. From the moment the man opened his mouth Jack could feel something between them, because the man was familiar to him. Not as someone he knew, but someone from an old photograph brought to life: snapshots from a family picnic at Bayou Barataria in the 1920s, before he was born; the women wearing straw hats their faces peeked out of, dresses that looked like slips; but it was the men he remembered now, the men with slick-combed hair like Jerry Boylan's, the men posing in white shirts without collars, their Irish Channel mugs grinning at the camera on a sunny day, his dad's dad or an uncle holding Spanish moss to his face to make a beard. This one, Jerry Boylan, could be one of them now, come to life in the St. Louis Hotel.

He said, "Jack Delaney."

And saw the familiar slit-mouth grin from the photographs, eyes beaming for a moment, then turned to low as the man said, "How serious a Delaney are you? Where you come from?"

"I think Kilkenny, my dad's grandfather."

"Of course you do," Boylan said. "Castlecomer in North Kilkenny. There was a Ben Delaney played horn in the Castlecomer Brass Band. . . . Oh, but wait now, it could be Ballylinan. Sure, Michael Delaney was from there, my God, second in command of the North Kilkenny Brigade, IRA from 1918 to '21, before the truce, when they were giving the crown bloody hell. Made land mines out of iron skillets packed with gelignite. Before plastique and pipe bombs"—his voice drifting—"and rocket launchers you can stick under your coat . . ."

"How do you know that?"

"I'm from there. Swan, a stop in the road, if you've heard of it."

"I mean what happened a long time ago. How do you know about a Delaney and that IRA stuff?"

"How do I *know*? It's my fucking *life*. Ask me where I've been the past month, since I wasn't dodging Brit patrols and getting the stick from the bloody peelers." Boylan frowned. "You know what I'm talking about? The Belfast coppers, Jack, the Royal Ulster Constabulary. Their idea of great crack is cornering one such as myself, alone. But you say that IRA stuff a long time ago, like you don't know any of this. It still *is*, Jack, more than ever. My God, don't you read the newspapers?"

The man played his voice like a hi-fi system, adjusting up and down, treble to bass. Now he was silent, at rest, his gaze wandering to the coffee table, the bottles and glasses, the tray of picked-over canapés. Jack watched him cross the room to bend over the tray and poke at the dainty sandwiches before choosing one.

Look at him.

Unconcerned, turning to watch television as the voices shrilled and he stuck a sandwich in his mouth, sucked two fingers, and wiped them on his coat.

The guy thinking they were buddies now, like they might've marched together last month in the Saint Patrick's Day parade. It was one thing for Jack to feel a tie, reminded of Delaneys that had come before, but this guy was presuming way too much. Jack walked over to the TV set, the annoying voices still competing, and shut them off.

Boylan, bent over the tray again, looked up. "What're you doing there?"

"Sit down, on the sofa."

Boylan popped half a deviled egg in his mouth. "I do, I'll fall asleep sure. It's half nine, the man could be coming back any time."

Jack crossed to him raising the Beretta and put it in his face. Boylan cocked his head, still bent over, and opened his eyes and Jack could see the deviled egg in his mouth as he stopped chewing and stared.

"Sure, Jack, I'd be happy to."

He lowered the gun to feel it against his leg. "You've done time, haven't you?" Watching the man step around the coffee table to ease himself carefully into the chintz-covered sofa.

Boylan sighed. "Long Kesh. Where we smeared our shit on the walls and the lads in H-Block woke up the world with their hunger strike. The bloody Maze, some call it."

"What were you in for?"

"Talking in church," Boylan said. "To a bastard that touted on me. They came in the night as they do, knocked my old woman's teeth out breaking in the bloody door, found a revolver in the dirty wash, and that was my sin. I got five Hail Marys and five years in the Kesh." Boylan bent over, took his time choosing another canapé. "How is it we know our own kind, Jack? What was your sin? Don't tell me you're only a burglar. Come in here in your proper attire all lavender-scented. What would you steal, his shirts? Christ, but he's got enough of them."

"You've been here before," Jack said.

"Now and again." Boylan eased forward, placing his hands on his knees. "We're going to chat, we might go down the way. Watch the naked ladies dance and have a jar. Would that be to your liking?"

"You're a long way from home, aren't you?"

"You prefer to test my nerves. Keep me on the hook till I tell you what I'm up to. See who outlasts the other, before the nasty colonel returns. Oh, I'd love to know your game, Jack, before I say." A squint narrowed his eyes and he nodded. "I would like to believe our politics are near enough the same. . . ." And now his eyes opened with hope. "Have you seen me before, Jack? Heard me speak at a Holy Name Communion breakfast?"

Jack said, "Will you cut the shit and tell me what you're doing here?"

Boylan blew his breath out in a sigh. "All right, I'll take the risk and put it flat to you. The man from Nicaragua is here for guns. You know that?"

Jack nodded.

"Well, so am I."

Jack said, "Only he's going to buy his." And let it hang and saw the Irishman's sly smile forming.

Boylan said in a soft voice, "Oh, but our minds run in harness, don't they, Jack?"

FOURTEEN

They were in the upstairs dining room, seated near the wall of glass that looked out on the palmetto garden, the green foliage illuminated with pinpoints of light. Dick Nichols said, "Like having Christmas all year round, huh?" as he turned back to his dinner guests, the colonel and his silent friend from Miami.

Dagoberto Godoy said, *"Feliz Navidad,"* in a flat tone, not sounding too merry. "By nex' Christmas I want to be in Managua, but I don't think is going to happen."

Dick Nichols looked at Crispin Reyna across from him, over the place settings of crystal—see if he could get him to open his mouth. "Why is that? You boys aren't doing so good?" The guy from Miami shrugged, but didn't change his cool-sour expression or say anything; which could mean he either didn't know or didn't give a shit. So Dick Nichols turned to the colonel. "What's the problem, Dagaberta? I thought you had your war good as won."

"You read in the news we have seventeen thousand freedom fighters," Dagoberto said. "We have maybe fourteen thousand. The Communists have sixty thousand, more than that in reserve, and all those *chicos plasticos* in Managua, the kids with no work, nothing to do, they can put in the army when they want. They have helicopter gunships, the Mi-24 from the Soviets. We need ground-to-air missiles, the SA-7, many of them. But most of all we need to have those flying monsters of our own, the gunships."

Dick Nichols said, "Now you're talking about a big-ticket item." He looked up, almost caught the eye of a good-looking woman at the next table, but the headwaiter got in the way, coming over. Dick Nichols said, "Hey, Robert, I think we could manage three more of these. Tell you what, make 'em doubles and we'll save you a trip. Huh? How'd that be?"

"Chivas, Mr. Nichols?"

"You bet, Robert. Listen, what you do, stop by every twelve and a half minutes and see how we're doing." Deadpan, waiting for Robert to give him his haughty-waiter smile. "Is that a deal?"

Robert said, "Yes, sir, Mr. Nichols, my pleasure," giving him just a flick of a smile, not looking at the Nicaraguans.

Dick Nichols was drinking scotch with them because they seemed to favor it. He drank scotch or bourbon with people in the business, drank beer with Cajun fishing guides, and chased whiskey with beer sitting with drillers over in Morgan City. It was how you learned things. Drink and grin, egg them on some and listen. He told Dagoberto and his buddy from Miami, dying to call him Crispy, that raising the capital to buy a helicopter was one thing, then you had to service the son of a bitch. An engine overhaul'd run you a hundred and twenty-five thousand or more. Hell, get a bullet in your fuel-control system, it's like your carburetor, you're talking forty-five Gs to replace it, and that's just your four-seater model. He told Dagoberto he was talking big bucks to maintain a fleet. Was he going to raise enough to finance a real war or not?

Dagoberto said, "You want me to tell you the cost of making war? To pay each freedom fighter twenty-three dollars a month before we buy one bullet? A wealthy friend of yours, rich beyond measure, gives me a check for five thousand. I look at it. . . . Do you know what it will buy? It will buy rice for a few weeks and maybe twenty thousand rounds of AK-47 ammunition. You want me to tell you what it is to buy from the Israelis? Arrange a drop shipment to Honduras and all the ones in between you have to pay?"

Dick Nichols said, "Not if it's gonna depress you, Dagaberta." That woman at the next table had a pretty face but picked at her dinner and didn't appear to have much juice in her: the kind would rather go to a club meeting than slip out for a nooner. He said, "Hey, you boys slowing up?" And watched them get busy with their drinks. Couple of macho banana pickers. "I had a geologist look at a piece of land one time, he said, 'Mr. Nichols, you hit oil on this property I'll drink it.' Shortsighted son of a bitch didn't look deep enough." Dick Nichols's gaze slid over to the colonel idly rearranging his silverware. "But I have never forced a man to drink anything he didn't want." He looked up at the headwaiter and said, "Robert, you're just in time." Waited for the headwaiter to serve them and leave, then turned to the colonel and said, "Dagaberta, my little girl tells me you like to kill people. Is that right?"

The colonel stopped fooling with his silverware and tried to give Dick Nichols a calm, steady look. "Your daughter saw war as a civilian. Naturally she didn' understand it. In war the purpose is to kill the enemy."

"She says you killed women and children."

"And you didn't when you bombed cities in your wars? It happens."

"I didn't know you people had an air force."

"I mean is the same thing. In guerrilla war you hit and run, hit and run. Without jails you don't take prisoners. But you can't let them go free, uh? Or tomorrow they try to kill *you.*"

Dick Nichols said, "There's killing and there's cold-blooded murder, two different things."

"And there is assassination, with a thin line between them in war," Dagoberto said. "Listen, your own government, the CIA, they instruct us on the selective use of violence to neutralize people against us. What does that mean, neutralize? Your own President Reagan tells us it means, 'Well, you jus' say to the fellow who sitting there in the office, you not in the office anymore.' Isn't that beautiful, he think is so easy. I wish your president was at Ocotal with us. I see one of my men so afraid he can't move, he's shitting his pants, pressing himself to a wall. I say to him, 'Come on, man, let's go.' But he won't move and there are others behind us watching this. I take his gun, the magazine is still full. 'Man,' I yell at him, 'you haven't fired a single shot.' Good grief, what kind of example is this man? I neutralized him with his own gun and neutralized several of the enemy after we tore down the Sandinista flag and set it on fire. What I'm saying to you, Dick, the only thing neutral is the gun. It doesn't care who it kills."

"How old was the man you shot?"

"Old enough to die for freedom."

"Whose freedom?" Dick Nichols said. "My daughter says we're on the wrong side in Nicaragua and have been for seventy-five years."

Dagoberto said, "Twenty-first June, 1979, the ABC journalist was killed by a Guardsman in Managua and everyone in the entire fucking world saw it on film. That should never have happen, but it did and is the reason some people don't like us. Ninth July the Sandinistas took León. Estelí on sixteenth July, the same day they overran the garrison at Jinotepe. I was looking at an M-16 in my face, refusing to close my eyes, and Somoza is flying to Miami with his family and his chiefs of staff and the coffins of his father and his brother. Leaving us to die."

Dick Nichols watched the Nicaraguan glance at his friend from Miami.

"Just as he left the family of Crispin to die, on their coffee estate, taking the Guards away from there. Anastasio Somoza Debayle, the Supreme Ruler and Commander of the Guard, Inspired and Illustrious Leader, Savior of the Republic. . . . Do you want some more of his titles? How do you think of son of a fucking whore who left us to die?"

Dick Nichols watched him.

Boy, a little Chivas could stir the man up. Dick Nichols watched him raise his drink, throw his head back to take a macho gulp, and knock over a couple of empty wine glasses putting the drink down again. While his buddy remained impassive. Maybe he was stoned. But now Crispin's dead expression belonged to a man born of coffee money and had everything handed to him. Dick Nichols would bet Crispy had swung with a sizable amount, now invested in some Miami venture. Wasn't that interesting?

It got even more interesting when Dagoberto said, "I

returned to Nicaragua to fight the war. But I'll tell you something, Dick, you can understand. You say the business of America is business. . . ."

"I did?"

"You know it if you don't say it. Okay, is the same with me. What I do is not in the name of nationalism or Somocismo, an allegiance to a dead man. What I do is a matter of economics. I want what you want. And what's good for you, Dick, is good for me."

Wally Scales followed Dagoberto into the Men's room, watched the way the colonel weaved standing at the urinal and had to flatten one hand against the wall to steady himself. Close behind him, Wally Scales said, "You feel somebody breathing down your neck? . . . Hey, watch where you're aiming."

"What are you doing here?"

"I've come with intelligence of grave importance." Wally Scales stepped up to the next urinal, not liking the colonel's glazed look one bit. "You okay?"

"I feel better when I do this. Oh, man." The colonel shivered, jerking his shoulders.

"You find out about your girl friend?"

"The hell with her. I'm not going to worry about the leprosy."

"I wouldn't. I'd worry more about raging social diseases, if you're gonna entertain French Quarter whores. Or I'd worry about a guy breathing Bushmill down my neck. That's what they drink over in Ireland. They love it, booze and Guinness stout, that dark stuff. You smell either one in your room you know he's been in there again. Well, we were in his room, too; he's staying in your hotel. Found his burglar tools but no gun—unless he packs it. Though I doubt that, being a visitor with an iffy passport. You don't know what I'm talking about, do you? Shake it but don't break it. Hey, you're pissing on your shoes. . . . There you go. Now wash your hands."

The little Nicaraguan, with his glassy eyes and gigolo mustache, zipped up and pushed off the wall to the washbasin.

Wally Scales said, "You don't know it but you have an IRA agent on your ass, a Provo living in the same hotel. Checked in through New Orleans Immigration from Shannon by way of Managua, the provisional IRA's great circle route; stop off to visit with comrades, the Micks now sleeping with the Latin Marxists. Why not? Jerry Boylan would take Khaddafi in his mouth for a rocket launcher. Five years in Long Kesh, the Ulster slam, flies down to the tropics for R and R and what have you, and now makes his appearance in New Orleans. Ask him, he'll tell you to address Holy Name Societies, raise a few quid for the Sinn Fein and the unification of bloody Ireland. But he follows you all over and goes in your room when you're out to dinner. Now, what do you suppose he wants, outside of all the freedom dollars you're raising?"

Dagoberto splashed his face with water, rubbed it hard with a towel, but didn't look much better than before.

"This guy is *irlandés*?"

"*Irlandés negro*—black Irish and full of bullshit. You can hear him across the room telling stories to bartenders. It's his cover. No one with that big a mouth could be an agent."

"What will you do with him?"

Wally Scales said, "Not what will *I* do with him. I have three weeks coming I'm gonna spend at Hilton Head, get out of this goddamn humidity and not do a thing but feel proud of myself, how I'm playing a vital role in the manifest destiny of my country. That have a ring to it? In any given situation I can exercise a flexible response, up to a point. But something like this, I think it comes under your taking up arms against an oppressive government and its agents. I have nothing to lose but a little self-esteem if you fuck up; and I can handle that, it's a temporary loss. You, on the other hand, stand to blow your mission and lose everything."

Dagoberto listened, squinting, till he threw the towel in the basin and fire came into his bloodshot eyes.

"Goddamn, you say something to me, say it!"

"His name's Gerald Boylan and he's in 305."

"You want me to neutralize him?"

Wally Scales put his hand on Dagoberto's shoulder. "Did you hear me say that? No, that would be unacceptable for me to say that. You must've heard somebody else say it."

Clovis, Dick Nichols's driver, walked away from the white stretch limo to where the dude in the dark suit was standing across the street by the edge of the cemetery. The dude had stood by the black Chrysler Fifth Avenue without moving and finally had gone over by the cemetery entrance and stood there without moving, up the street from the restaurant. The dude was good at standing without moving. Clovis said, "How you doing?"

The dude nodded at him; sort of nodded. Close up he looked like a light-skinned brother with a little Chinese or something in him. Strange-looking dude, Chink with nappy hair.

"Gets tiresome, huh?"

The dude didn't say if he thought it was tiresome or

not, standing here like a cemetery statue. Clovis turned to the restaurant, a big old mansion of a place with striped awnings in front and neon lights up around the roof.

"Place look like a boat to you? . . . Oh, is that right? Yeah, it looks like a boat to me, uh-huh." Clovis turned to the dude and said, "My name's Clovis. I believe the man you work for, one of those two guys or both that got out of that Chrysler, are with the man I work for." Clovis waited a moment, looking at the dude standing like death at the iron-grilled entrance to where dead people lay. "You speakah English? You don't, it's cool. But if you speakah English, then I want to know what you have up your ass prevents you from opening your fucking mouth. You understand what I'm saying to you?"

Franklin de Dios smiled.

Clovis said, "Well, hey, shit. The man come to life."

Franklin de Dios nodded and said, "I learn English from the time I was born, but I don't use it much or hear it until last year. The people I work for don't use it."

"You from Nicaragua."

"Yes, from there. I learn Spanish, but I learn English first, at home and also at the school."

"Wait now. You telling me you from down there, but you didn't learn Spanish when you a baby?"

"No, they make us learn it. I'm Miskito. You understand? Indian. The Sandinistas make us learn Spanish, but I learn English first."

"No shit, you Indian, huh?"

"No shit."

"Say something in Indian."

"*N'ksaa.*"

"What's that mean?"

"How you doing?"

"Yeah." Clovis grinned. "No shit, you a real Indian."

"No shit."

"Man, why didn't you talk to me when I said hi and all that shit what I said before?"

"I don't know who you are."

"I *told* you who I was. You bashful, what? Man, I look at you close I thought you were a brother. You know what I'm saying? I thought you were black."

"Yes, one part of me. The rest Miskito."

"How 'bout the man you work for? He Indian too?"

"No, he was from Cuba, but now is Nicaraguan. Also the other one is Nicaraguan, the colonel. We both fought against the Sandinistas, but not together. I don't know why he don't like them. I don't like them because they come to my home, Musawas, and kill some people, kill the animals, the cows, with machine guns, and made us leave. They burned all the Miskito villages and made us go to *asentamientos*—you know like they say a concentration camp?"

"Man, that's bad."

"So, some of us go to Honduras, go to a place—you know Rus Rus?"

"No, I don't believe I do."

"But it's not good there. So I join the war. You know the CIA?"

"Yeah, CIA, sure."

"They gave us guns, show us how to fight the Sandinistas. Nice guns, they shoot good. But I don't like it in the war, so I go to Miami, Florida."

"Yeah, shit, if you don't like the war. How'd you work that?"

"You fly there by the airline. Tell them you going back, but you don't."

Clovis said, "Uh-huh." Thinking, but how did a Nicaraguan Indian know enough to do that?

"But when I go to Miami, I don't like it so much. They have war there too, but a different kind. They arrest me one time, want to deport me."

A car came along the street toward the restaurant and Clovis saw the Indian's face in the headlights. Then it was dark again by the cemetery, but he had seen enough of the man's face to know the man was talking to him straight on like he wanted to talk, not to show he was cool.

"So they try to deport you."

"Yes, but the guy I work for spoke to somebody—I don't know. They said it was okay and then we come here. . . . I like this place. Some of it is like the city in Honduras, where they have the airport. Not like Miami. I could live here. But you need money, what it cost to eat."

"You need it anywhere," Clovis said. "I was wondering, you kill anybody in the war?"

"I kill some."

"Yeah? Close that you could see 'em?"

"Some close."

"With a gun?"

"Yes, of course, with a gun."

"I never had that experience." Clovis looked off at the restaurant. "So you just drive for the man?"

Franklin de Dios hesitated.

"Or you have to do anything around the house. You know what I'm saying? Clean the garage, drive the kids, anything like that?"

"He don't have a garage or any kids. He has women."

"I know what you mean. But what it is, you drive and wait, huh? Wait and then drive some more."

Franklin de Dios said, "I drive, but I don't wait so much. I go with him. . . . Or sometime I go alone."

There was a silence. Clovis had a question all ready. Go where alone? What'd that mean?

But then the Indian said, "You like the man you work for?"

Clovis said, "He's okay. He's full of shit, but he can't help it. The man's got so much money nobody can say no to him."

And there he was, like coming out on cue, Mr. Nichols waving at him, and that was the end of the visit with the Indian.

The man sat in the front seat most of the time, the rest of the limo stretched out empty behind them, unless he was working, talking on the phone.

Clovis said, "That's an Indian drives for one of the gentlemen you were with. A Miskita. I try to talk to him, he don't say a word, like he's a wooden Indian. But then, see, he does, he becomes friendly. I said to him, 'How come you wouldn't say nothing before when I'm talking to you?' He said, well, he didn't know me, was the reason. No, what he said was, 'I don't know who you are.' I said, 'Man, I *told* you who I am.' You understand what I'm saying, Mr. Nichols? Why'd he change his mind like that?"

"He said he didn't know you."

"That's right. 'I don't know who you are.' "

"It sounds to me like he was being polite," Dick Nichols said. "He didn't want *you* to know who *he* was."

"Yeah, but he told me all about himself."

"Like what?"

"Like being in the war and killing guys. Like he went to Miami . . ."

"What's he do now?"

"He drives for one of those Nicaraguan fellas."

"What does the Nicaraguan fella do?"

"He never said."

"So what did you really find out?"

Clovis kept his mouth shut and held tight to the steering wheel. Pretty soon the man's head would nod and he'd sleep all the way to Lafayette, dreaming of how smart he was. The man looked at things from way up where he was, on the boss level, too far away to feel things down on earth that didn't feel right.

It was quiet for some time, the interstate stretching ahead of them in the high light beams.

Close in the dark of the car the man's voice said, "How did the Indian get to Miami?"

Clovis grinned. Because the man could surprise you. He said, "Mr. Nichols, now you asking a good question."

FIFTEEN

One in the afternoon, Jack and Lucy were in the Quarter walking along Toulouse toward the river, stepping around groups of tourists, Jack trying to explain Jerry Boylan to her. "I didn't know what to do with him. We had to get out of there, so I took him to Roy's bar."

"For a second opinion," Lucy said.

"Yesterday was Roy's last day. I was suppose to meet him anyway, after I did the colonel's room. . . . I saw Cullen this morning, gave him all the figures."

"He said he was going to meet you. Something about checking the bank accounts."

"Yeah, make a ten-buck deposit, see if they're still active. Or whatever else he can find out. Cullen was a little nervous, after twenty-seven years. He give you any trouble?"

"He spends most of his time in the kitchen, with Dolores. He hasn't had a decent meal in all those years."

"That isn't the only thing he hasn't had. Tell Dolores, he makes a move, hit him with a skillet."

"I like him. I think he's nice."

"You like everybody." He smiled at her.

But she was looking at a stained plaster Mother and Child, Mary with her foot on the snake, the Sacred Heart, statues filmed with dust in a dim store window. Walking past she said, "All that made it easier to believe, didn't it? They wrapped you in ritual, solemnity."

He said, "I'll tell you about it sometime."

And now saw her smile: composed, Sister Lucy this afternoon in a simple blue-cotton blouse and khaki skirt, to meet Jerry Boylan as a nun from Nicaragua and not distract him with another story. He had told Jack he was in Managua last month. Lucy would see.

"So I took Boylan to the International—you know it's a nude showbar. Exotic dancers from around the world, Shreveport and East Texas. We walked in, Roy was with Jimmy Linahan, the guy that owns the place. Roy's drinking, Jimmy's pouring, trying to get him to stay. He's offering him more money, a cut of the bar business. . . . We came over to the table, Jimmy's telling Roy he was made in heaven for this kind of work. He said God had given him a special gift to deal with tourists and drunks."

"When am I going to meet him?"

"Later on, probably this evening. So we sit down. You could see Boylan and Jimmy Linahan were gonna get along. Linahan is kind of a professional Irishman anyway, you know, and here was the real thing. He hung on every word Boylan said, ate it up. Boylan started telling about the world-famous pubs of Dublin and Roy would interrupt him. 'Famous for what? The drunks?' Here's Roy half in the bag, mean look in his eyes. Boylan says, 'What else you go there for but to get fluthered.' He mentioned Mulligan's, I remember, and the Bailey, pubs he said were world-famous because of Joyce. Roy *might* know who James Joyce is, I'm not sure, but it wouldn't matter. You mention books to Roy and he thinks you're trying to act superior. As soon as Boylan started talking you could see Roy was gonna go after him. Roy looks at me, he says, 'I'm getting out of here before I catch that new kind of AIDS.' Boylan says, 'What kind is that?' Roy says, 'Hearing AIDS. You get it from listening to assholes.' "

Lucy said, "Right in front of him?"

"Right *to* him. Then he looks at me. 'Where'd you find this guy?' I said, 'Roy, you won't believe it when I tell you.' Roy goes, 'I don't believe anything about him *now,* including that bullshit brogue he's putting on for us.' "

"What did Boylan say?"

"Boylan rolls with stuff like that. He tells you about pubs in Dublin, believe it. But anything else, I don't know, maybe you can cut in half. Except when he tells you he's done time. I knew that as soon as I looked at him."

"How?"

"It's something you know if you've been there." They were approaching the entrance to Ralph & Kacoo's. Jack paused, taking Lucy's arm. "He doesn't know what we're doing, but he'll slip around on you trying to find out."

"I'll be sweet and innocent," Lucy said.

"The question is, can we use him? See what you think."

* * *

Jerry Boylan ate his oysters with lemon; he'd loosen the meat, then raise the shell to his mouth, let the oyster slide in, and as he began to chew, shove a hushpuppie into his mouth and take a sip of beer. Jack and Lucy watched, finished with oysters and crab cakes, Lucy stirring her iced tea, both of them fascinated by the man's ritual: through two dozen oysters, chewing, sipping, talking, tongue moving around in his mouth. . . . He said to Lucy, "Sister, you're testing me, aren't you? Wanting to know why I went to Nicaragua but timid to ask. There was a cousin of mine entered the nunnery and took the name Virginella. I said to her"—Boylan frowning—"'Why on earth would you want to be known as a *little* virgin? Girl,' I said, 'if you're going to be a virgin think of yourself as a big one, a world-class virgin.' But do you see the paradox, Sister? One vow is an impediment to the other. Humility prevents her proclaiming her virginity." French bread with a pat of butter resting on it disappeared into his mouth.

Jack said, "Can I ask you a question?"

"Please."

"What were you doing in Managua?"

"Come right to it, uh, Jack? Sure, I'll tell you." Boylan sat back with his glass mug of beer. "It was on Easter Sunday, barely a month past, I was at Milltown Cemetery. On the Falls Road out of Belfast toward Antrim, is where it is." He looked from Jack to Lucy. "I'm there for the seventieth anniversary observance of the 1916 Rising. There in the biting cold and rain to honor our dead. . . ."

Jack said, "And that's what you were doing in Managua?"

"Ask what you like, you don't have a pistol in your hand this time," Boylan said, and smiled. "Oh, you're a cute hoor, Jack, but ridden with flaws and impatience, if I

194

judge you right. Don't know what to make of me or the present turn of events, so you bring this lovely sister to have a look, uh? But then your insecurity causes you to interrupt, just as I'm about to tell how I met the Nicaraguans." He turned to Lucy again. "It may appear, Sister, I'm coming round about, fond of rhetoric, which is often the mark of a revolutionary; but I'll spare you catchphrases. What you're waiting to learn is what Sandinistas were doing in Ireland on a cold Easter Sunday."

"Or at any time," Lucy said.

"If you hear we deal with terrorists, it's a lie. This group from Nicaragua are musicians that go by the name Heroes and Martyrs: revolutionaries who'd fought their battles and *won* and came to tell us about it in song, in their ballads. Well, a man fighting for his own cause is going to be moved, inspired. I wanted to know more. So I arranged to travel back with the Heroes and Martyrs to Nicaragua. It would give me the chance, also, to visit an older brother I hadn't laid eyes on in nearly ten years. A humble Jesuit priest who serves his flock in the village of León."

Jack stared at Boylan sipping his beer, wiping the back of his hand across his mouth. There was no way to stay ahead of this guy. He could come at you from any direction. First with a cousin who was a nun, now a brother who was a priest.

But then Lucy said, "I wouldn't exactly call León a village."

Jack jumped in. "And I've never met a Jesuit who was especially humble."

It was brief satisfaction. Boylan, unmoved, said, "Everything is relative. Towns, the clergy, even revolutionaries, depending from where you view them. Now the *contras* are the rebels and I think to myself, Isn't that a lovely name for the gougers, bloody killers of innocent people? Then I learn that people who live in comfort are paying for their atrocities."

He was wearing the same shapeless herringbone jacket, the same red-and-gray patterned tie, probably the same shirt . . . looking at Jack now, his slicked-back hair shining in the restaurant's overhead lights.

"Have you seen innocent people murdered, Jack, as the sister and I have? Do you know what it's like?" Boylan eased back again as he turned to Lucy. "The first time, Sister, it will be twelve years ago next month. I was sitting in Mulligan's having a pint when I heard the bomb explode, that hard terrible irredeemable bang. . . . I remember it today as I remember, too vividly, what I saw in Talbot Street as I turned the corner and heard the screams in the smoke that hung like a bloody fog."

Jack's gaze edged past Boylan's grave expression. His eyes returned as the man continued, then moved off again . . . and held.

"There was something else, too, the smell of it, now implanted in my nostrils forever. Not the smell of death you hear spoken of, but the stench of people's insides lying on the pavement. I saw a woman sitting against a lamppost staring at me, or at nothing, both her legs blown off."

Jack got up from the table.

"Haven't the stomach for it, uh, Jack?"

"I'll be right back."

"You have to see it. Like me and the sister here. . . . Isn't that right, Sister?"

Jack followed an aisle toward the rear of this big roomful of people busy with lunch, nodding to waiters he knew as he came to a table against the far wall.

Helene sat with a cup of coffee, dishes cleared, her

head bent over an open book, frizz-permed red hair jutting
out to both sides.

"What're you reading?"

Her brown eyes came up reflecting light and there was
the nose that fascinated him, the tender, delicate nostrils.
Helene closed the book with one finger in it and glanced
at the cover before looking up again, now with a different
expression, almost sly, a girl with a secret.

"Self-Love and Sexuality."

"Is it any good?"

"Not bad. It says if you don't like yourself you won't
have fun in bed. Or you have to like yourself first, before
you can love anybody else."

"If you don't like yourself . . . Why wouldn't you? I
mean since you're all you have."

"I don't know, Jack. There must be some people who
don't."

"You think people that are assholes realize it? No, they
think they're fine. But even if it's possible not to like yourself, you go to bed with somebody—what're you doing in
there, analyzing yourself?"

"I'm glad you straightened me out on that," Helene
said. "What're you up to?"

"I'm not working at the funeral home anymore." Helene waited and he said, "I'll find something."

Her eyes held on him, still waiting. In the open top of
her blouse he could see freckles he used to trace with a
finger, making up constellations, getting down to her twin
suns and from there to the center of her universe. Something between two people who liked themselves and maybe
had loved each other and were remembering it now—both
of them, if he could believe her eyes.

"That's a pretty girl you're with."

"I didn't think you saw us."

"When I came in."

"She used to be a nun."

"Really? What is she now?"

"She's looking."

"I guess everybody is. I spend half my life being interviewed. I end up typing memos for some weenie, I'm not even sure what he does. Offices are full of people doing things that, if they didn't, it wouldn't make any difference. Or the company's making some dumb thing nobody needs and they act like they're serving humanity, the higher-ups." She said, "I've been thinking about you, Jack, since we ran into each other. Well, even before that. . . . I miss you."

It was something the way she could get different looks in those brown eyes, from sparkly to sad to a kind of soulful light, one right after another, her eyes working him over, softening him up.

"But you still blame me, don't you?"

"I never did. It was that showboat lawyer you worked for."

"That's what you *say.* No matter what else, Jack, you're polite." She kept the soulful light burning low as she said, "Would you call me sometime?"

He smiled. It was all right to let himself be softened up as long as—there, telling him by her smile—she realized he knew what she was doing. Helene was fun. He said, yes, he'd call her.

And walked back to the table.

Lucy looked up. Boylan was still talking, telling her there was more to revolution than storming the palace, putting your boots up on the king's table, drinking his wine. He paused, glancing at Jack as he sat down. "You all right?"

"I'm fine."

Then turned to Lucy again, saying, "That's the glory part. Then comes the work of changing attitudes steeped in tatty, worn-out traditions. With your permission, Sister, consider a people raised to believe it's all right with just cause to blow a woman's legs off, but a mortal sin to spread them."

Lucy said, "You haven't stormed the palace yet."

Boylan sat back and, for the first time, seemed tired. "It will come."

"You'll keep trying."

"It's become a ritualized game, Sister. I play it or what? . . . Sweep rubbish and empty bins." For several moments he stared at the table in silence, finally looked up and said, "Jack, I'll visit the lavat'ry if you'll point the direction."

"By the front entrance."

He watched Boylan push up with an effort and walk off. Then turned to Lucy, her quiet expression. She was staring at him and it surprised him.

"Well, what do you think?"

"You had a gun last night. Boylan said, 'You don't have a pistol in your hand this time.' "

"Yeah, I had to find out who he was."

"You carried a gun with you?"

"No, it was the colonel's. I put it back." Jack paused. "But when we do it, we're not just gonna ask the guy for his money and he hands it to us. You understand, we'll have to have guns. There's no other way to do it."

She seemed to think about it before saying, very quietly, "No, there isn't, is there?"

Franklin de Dios, standing inside the entrance of the restaurant, watched Boylan push through the door to the Men's room.

He had followed Boylan here from the hotel, watched him sit down at a table, and watched the man and woman he remembered from the funeral coach at the gasoline station in St. Gabriel come in and sit with him at the table. The man in the dark suit he remembered well, talking to him in the funeral place, the man offering him beer. He had wondered if this was the same man that night, one of the police, who put them in the trunk of the car and left them until two more police in uniforms let them out, listened with patience to Crispin and then told him to have a nice evening. But how could this one be a police the same night? No—except he had a feeling he was one of those first two police, who were like the police of Miami, Florida. Or, as Crispin now believed, those first two weren't police at all. Then the one could be the man from the funeral place. He had said to Crispin he didn't understand any of this, who was who. Crispin had said to him, "You don't have to think or know everything. Do what you're told."

Okay. But he would continue to think.

Franklin de Dios unbuttoned his jacket as he walked toward the Men's room in Ralph & Kacoo's.

Lucy was hunched over the table. She said, "When you robbed hotel rooms, did you carry a gun?"

Jack was about to get up, his hands on the edge of the table. "Never, ever. Somebody happened to wake up, you don't think I was gonna shoot 'em."

She was nodding, thoughtful. "But this is different. We'll need guns."

"It's a much higher-class criminal offense, armed robbery. If you want to look at it that way. And if you'll excuse me, I'm going to the bathroom."

He saw her startled expression as he got up.

She said, "We're not planning a robbery, Jack." Sounding honestly surprised.

"What do you call it?"

"We're not bandits."

"Tell me what we are. When I come back."

Franklin de Dios walked up behind Jerry Boylan standing at the urinal. He extended the Beretta to place the muzzle in the center of the gray herringbone tweed, pushed it in to feel the man's spine, the man's head turning to look over his shoulder, the man saying, "What? . . ." and shot him. As the man's body jerked and then became loose and began to sag against the urinal, Franklin de Dios raised the pistol to the base of the man's skull, placed the muzzle in that hollow spot, and shot him again and stepped away now, turning away, with no desire to look at the wall smeared red or the man falling dead to the floor.

Franklin de Dios worked the Beretta into the waist of his pants close to his left hip, buttoned his jacket and pulled it down straight. He could hear a ringing in his ears but no sounds from beyond the door, in the restaurant. In the war they searched the ones they killed, if there was time; find a few cordobas if they were lucky. This one could have money or not, it was hard to tell from his appearance; but there wasn't time to see. Crispin had said to kill him because "He wants to steal money that's for your people, the *contras.*" Franklin de Dios had said, "They're not my people." And Crispin had said, "Do it or we'll send you back." There was no way to leave the war.

He said to himself, Now walk.

He pulled open the door. He stepped out of the Men's room. He saw the man in the dark suit from the funeral home coming toward him, the man's eyes on him. So he touched the front of his jacket to unbutton it and the man from the funeral home stopped, two strides from him.

Franklin de Dios said, "How you doing?" The man didn't answer him or move. So Franklin de Dios walked away from the man, out of the restaurant to join the tourists on their way to see Jackson Square and the Cabildo and the St. Louis Cathedral.

SIXTEEN

Jack introduced Roy Hicks, expecting some kind of reaction from Lucy. Finally, the man she was so anxious to meet. But she seemed to hold back, cautious, quieter than times before. A different Lucy this evening—with Boylan shot dead that afternoon. Boylan had touched her.

All four of them were quiet at first.

Jack watched Roy sit down with a drink and in silence, without comment, look over the sun parlor; he'd save his remarks for later. Cullen eased into a deep-cushioned chair, stretched his legs over a matching ottoman, and picked up a magazine. *Vogue.* He'd told Jack the maid had left. No, not because of him. Gone to Algiers for the rest of the week, to visit her sister.

Jack placed his drink and a sherry for Lucy on the

coffee table and sat down with her on the sofa. He put his hand over hers and asked her if she was okay. He could feel Roy watching. She nodded, smoking a cigarette, staying within herself. He could feel Roy waiting to take charge, ask questions, become once again a cop interrogating witnesses.

Jack said, "I looked in, that's all. I didn't go in all the way."

"But you were the first one."

"I was standing there holding the door open, a waiter went in past me. He took one look and turned around."

"He say anything to you?"

"Not to me. But people were coming over and I heard him say, 'Don't go in there. A man's been killed.' "

"How'd he know Boylan was dead if he went in and turned right around?"

"I guess all the blood."

"What else did he say?"

"I didn't hang around to hear any more. We left."

"You talk to anybody?"

"Not a soul."

"The waiter know you?"

"I don't think so, not that particular one."

"You hope not."

"Nobody was interested in *me*, I'll tell you." Jack picked up his drink. He'd need another one in about two and a half minutes.

Roy sat facing them across the coffee table. In front of Lucy, on the table, were pages torn from news magazines, a pad of writing paper, a pen, several letters in envelopes, and the glass of sherry, untouched. Roy said to Lucy, "You hear the shots?"

She shook her head.

Jack heard her say no; it was almost a whisper. He said to Roy, "By the time I got back to the table people were standing up, everybody looking toward the front. We got up, we walked out. No one paid any attention to us."

Roy said, "You could pick the guy out of a show-up? This Nicaraguan?"

"I told you who it was. Franklin de Dios, the one suppose to be an Indian but looks like a colored guy."

"What I'm getting at," Roy said, "he could pick you out, too. Isn't that right? You were fairly close?"

"Of course he could pick me out. He *knows* me, for Christ sake. We talked, at the funeral home. I asked him what he carried the gun for. Well, now I know. He said, if he has to use it, and the guy wasn't kidding. He'd know you, Roy, from the other night, the way you pulled him out of the car. Man, I'm telling you, this guy . . . He came out of the Men's, as soon as he saw me he made a move like he was gonna put his hand inside his coat. We stood there . . . You know what he said? He said, 'How you doing?' "

Cullen looked up from his magazine. "The guy said that? No kidding."

"Then he walked out. By the time we got outside he was gone. Not that we were looking for him."

Roy said, "He came there to do Boylan, so he must've made the three of you at the table, before. Have you thought, if Boylan hadn't gone to the can the guy might've come over to the table?" Roy said, "I want to know if you feel you should identify the guy. For your own protection. But once you become a star witness this deal here is out the window. You understand that? Homicide gets you into it they'll bring her in, too." Roy was looking at Lucy now.

When she didn't say anything he asked her directly, "You feel you should go to the police?"

Lucy said, "No, I don't."

"Since you know Boylan? Since you know the nigger Indin and the nigger Indin knows you?"

Lucy was lighting another cigarette. She stared at him, then shook her head.

Roy stared back at her and Jack said to him, "Roy, what're you doing?"

"Don't worry about what I'm doing," Roy said. "What's the Indin doing? Has he run? I don't think so. You can place him at the scene, but not with a smoking gun. The Indin could say he walked in, Boylan was laying there dead as another guy ran out nobody saw but him. Okay, they did Boylan 'cause they knew who he was and what he was after. They'd have no idea you're after it, too. But you're getting in their way and they may want to take you out of it. You understand? Now I'd like to know if she has a problem with that. She does, we can forget the whole thing."

Lucy said, "You want to know if I have a problem?"

The phone rang. One that Lucy had brought in and plugged into a jack on the front wall of the room, away from where they were seated. She got up and walked around the sofa.

Jack hunched closer to the coffee table, looking at Roy. He waited until the ringing stopped and knew she had picked up the phone.

"Roy? . . . When I went back to the table to get her . . . Cully, listen to this. I said, 'We have to get out of here.' That's all. She didn't say a word. Everybody's looking toward the Men's room—what's going on? She got up, didn't say a word till we're outside, in fact till we're walking up Chartres toward Canal and I told her what happened. She said, 'Who was it?' And didn't say another word after that till we were in the car. You want to know if she can handle this? Roy, she's seen more people shot and killed than you have—people in her hospital hacked to death with machetes, people she was taking care of . . ."

He saw Roy look up. Lucy came around to the front of the sofa and sat down again.

"That was my mother. She can't decide whether to go with Claude Montana or de la Renta. I said, 'That's a tough one, Mom. Let me think about it and call you back.' "

Jack kept his eyes on Roy. Do you get it, you dick? You see it? He could tell Roy wanted to say something, stay in control, not wanting to be outclassed by some girl who used to be a nun. Roy took a big sip of his drink, rattled the ice, and took another sip, giving himself time. Jack said to Lucy, "I guess everybody's got problems, huh?" And looked at Roy again. "How about you, Roy?"

Roy said, "You mean outside of how we're gonna pull this off? Outside of they know who you are, but I still don't know who in the hell *they* are, or what side we're on?"

Lucy leaned over the coffee table, began to go through her papers and clippings as Cullen said, "The money don't care, Roy, what side it's on. You want to know how much the colonel's got so far?"

Roy said, "I want to know, for my own information, which are the good guys and which are the bad guys."

Lucy pushed the pile of pages torn from magazines toward Roy. "Read the quote from the *contra*'s chief military strategist, Enrique Bermúdez. 'We've learned the hard way that good guys do not win wars.' Alfonso Robelo, another of their leaders, says, Well, atrocities always occur in a civil war. Look at the photo in there of a man lying in a grave, alive, his eyes open, while a *contra* rams a knife into his throat. Look at it." She opened one of the letters then. "From a sister I worked with in Nicaragua. Listen to this." Her eyes moved down the page, stopped. " 'The *contras* ambushed a truck with thirty people going to pick coffee. Those who weren't killed by grenades were shot or burned alive on the truck. Including a five-year-old boy and four women. . . . And we are to give thanks they're fighting for democracy, fighting the antireligious Communists. . . . They kill coffee pickers, telephone line workers, farmers on cooperatives. Who pays them? It comes from our government. Now I hear it's from private corporations in the U.S. There is so much death. I have never seen so much death in my life.' " Lucy continued to read in silence. When she looked up from the page she said to Roy, "Would you like to hear more? Concepcion Sanchez was four months pregnant. They put a gun in her mouth and shot her, then used a bayonet to slice open her stomach. Paco Sevilla was tortured in front of his wife and seven children. They cut off his ears and tongue and made him eat them. They cut off his penis and finally they killed him. . . . More?"

Roy said, "So if these dudes are fighting the Communists, then there aren't any good guys. They're both dirty."

"If that satisfies you," Lucy said, "fine. We'll count you in."

She was lighting a cigarette when the phone rang.

Roy waited until Lucy got up and went to answer it. "Tell you the truth, I don't see you doing it without me. Shit, a cat burglar and an old-time bank robber." He pushed up out of his chair and looked over at the bar. "I may as well help myself, huh?"

"You're running the show," Jack said, "I guess you can do what you want."

Roy said, "If I didn't, who would? You?" He walked over to the bar.

Cullen said, "Jesus, they cut the guy's yang off." He looked across the room toward Lucy, on the phone, then held up *Vogue,* open, and said, "Hey, Jack?"

He turned and was looking at five bathing-suit models in a fashion spread, a full-color shot, coming out of the surf smiling, having a wonderful time.

"Which one would you pick?"

"For what?"

"You mean for what? To go to bed with."

"Cully, you're out, you don't have to do that anymore."

"I think the dark-haired one. Jesus."

Roy said, "Lemme see." Cullen turned the magazine toward him. Roy said, "None of 'em. They don't have enough tit between 'em to make one good set." Roy sat down with his drink. "But old Cully now, he'd fuck a chicken if one flew in the window."

Jack glanced over his shoulder at Lucy, across the room. When he turned back Roy was staring at him.

"You nervous, Jack? She can't hear me. . . . You chase her upstairs yet, show her what she's been missing? . . . Not saying, huh? You want her, I won't mess you up. She's not my type."

Jack said, "Thanks, Roy," got up and went over to the bar. Lucy was about twenty feet away, leaning against the wall in her jeans and a black sweater, smoking her cigarette, concentrating, saying a few words into the phone, Lucy in profile against the green banana leaves. Jack watched her move her hand through her short, dark hair.

Roy waited for him to come back with his drink. "I

spoke to Homicide, told 'em I'd heard about it. They have a victim was shot through the spine and the back of the head while thirty-seven people were having their lunch and they didn't learn a goddamn thing. Hey, but I got you something." Roy brought a notebook out of the inside pocket of his corduroy jacket. He said, "Alvin Cromwell," leafing through pages.

Jack took one of Lucy's cigarettes, his first one this evening. Alvin Cromwell was the name he'd copied off the memo pad in the fundraiser's bedroom. Phone number with a Mississippi area code.

"Here it is. Cromwell Men's Wear and Sporting Goods. Gulfport. Tell me why a Nicaraguan would go to Gulfport to buy his clothes."

Jack said, "Why would anybody?"

"There you are. I got you the name, you go on over and find out who the guy is."

"Maybe Alvin sells guns."

"That could be."

"Or he has a lot of money and he hates communism."

Jack half turned as Lucy appeared. He watched her pick up the sherry and take a good sip. "That was my dad. He had dinner with the colonel last night." She took another sip and sat down on the edge of the sofa, placing the glass on the coffee table.

Jack watched her. Composed, staying inside herself, hard to reach. He said, "What happened?"

"Nothing, yet. It's what might happen. My dad said if he could stop payment on his check he probably would. He thinks it's quite possible the colonel's going to run off with all the money. And then he said—this is good—'Of course, it's still a tax deduction.' He said even though it's just a feeling he has, he's going to tell his friends who haven't contributed yet to think twice about it. He said it's only a hunch. . . . But my dad got rich playing his hunches."

Jack said, "Is that why he called you?"

"He wanted to tell me I'm probably right about the guy and he shouldn't have given him a dime. Then covers himself by saying the colonel does have credentials, a letter from the president, and the fund's legitimate. They have an account, he said, at Hibernia."

"At Hibernia and Whitney," Cullen said, "four different branches, so far."

Roy said, "Honey, how much did your dad give this guy?"

"Sixty-five thousand."

Roy said, "Jesus Christ, I work two years to make that."

Or even three, Jack was thinking, as Lucy said, "The colonel starts out, he suggests at least a hundred thousand. Then, if he has to come down, he tells about the woman in Austin, Texas, who gave sixty-five thousand and they named a helicopter after her. Lady Ellen. Well, a big oilman from Louisiana should be able to match that, at least."

Jack said, "It's like playing blackjack against a woman dealer. We'll have to give this some thought. But if it's true, it might even be better. You know it? This guy Bertie, if he's honest he could have the CIA or even the military fly the money down there. But if he's gonna sneak off with it, that's something else. He's on his own. Or, as far as we know, it's Bertie and the other two guys." He thought about it a moment. "It would even make sense why he brought in the guy from Miami, what's his name? Crispin Antonio Reyna, if you see what I'm getting at. The guy was into dope, has a sheet . . ." He looked at Roy. "What was it, kiting checks?"

"Uttering fraudulent checks," Roy said. "Did nine

months. Then was brought up on transporting narcotics from Florida to here, but that one fell through."

"And the guy that killed Boylan," Jack said, "Franklin de Dios, who didn't look like any Franklin of God, I'll tell you, coming out of that Men's room. He was picked up on a homicide in Miami, a triple."

"He was a major suspect, but never brought to trial," Roy said. "So you have your doper and you have your shooter."

"You see it?" Jack said. "Where the money could be going, associating with guys like that? Right to Miami, fly or drive, either way. You look at it like that"—turning to Lucy—"your dad's hunch makes a lot of sense."

Roy said, "I better check, see if Alvin Cromwell's got a sheet."

"Or a plane," Jack said, "or a boat."

Lucy was looking at him. "You know who he is?"

"Alvin has a men's store in Gulfport. I'll drive over," he said to Roy, "after you check him out."

Cullen said, "Jack, you're gonna have to go back in the guy's room, too."

"For what?"

"Why's he have the money in four different branches? I wondered about that," Cullen said. "Well, one advantage, if it's in smaller amounts he can get it out quicker. Along with what you're talking about. Say he wants to leave in a hurry. What you want to find out, Jack, if he's moving it around, has any new receipts."

"What difference does it make, he moves it from Hibernia to Whitney?" He didn't like the idea of going back in there.

"You're the one brought up Miami," Cullen said.

"What if they don't put the dough in a suitcase but have it transferred there, bank to bank?"

"Not if they're gonna use it illegally."

"Jack, these guys own banks—guys in the dope business. You have to go in there and take a look. Also check the guy's list, how many names are crossed off. If Lucy's dad tells his friends not to kick in then maybe this's it, what the guy's raised so far and there won't be no more."

"Tomorrow," Jack said. He didn't like the idea one bit.

"What I don't understand," Cullen said, "we're sitting here working on a score. . . . This's the first time I've ever done it and nobody's asked the big question, the most important one of all."

"How much does he have?" Lucy said.

"There, finally." Cullen gave her a smile. "I'll tell you right now, the way it's going the guy's never gonna make his five."

Roy said, "I never expected he would."

"Or even come close," Cullen said. "I'm talking about what he has right now is two million two."

There was a silence before Roy said, "What's wrong with that?"

Jack said, "Not a thing," and looked at Lucy.

Lucy said nothing.

She reached under the lamp shade to turn off the light, but then paused and looked at Jack, on the sofa. "I'd better wait till they get back."

"You want to go up, I'll let them in."

Roy and Cullen had left to get something to eat, Cullen with a craving for fat-boiled shrimp after twenty-seven years of catfish. They'd find a place open on Magazine, come right back and cruise the street, take a walk around the grounds. It was Roy's idea. He said they'd better all three of them stay here. Watch out for Nicaraguans and a nigger Indin sneaking around in the night.

"You won't know where to sleep."

"I can stretch out right here's fine."

"There're seven bedrooms upstairs," Lucy said, "not counting servants' quarters, in this huge house. My mother wouldn't think of moving. She has a cleaning woman come in every day, the gardener twice a week. I asked Dolores what she does all day. She said, 'Mostly I look after the house.' I said, 'What does my mother do?' She said, 'Your mother gets herself ready to go out.' "

He watched her pick up her glass and walk over to the bar, slim in her Calvins and black sweater. A different Lucy. But what was it? Something in her eyes. Or something gone from her eyes.

"How's your drink?"

"I've had enough," Jack said. "Thanks."

She poured sherry. "Did you notice the Carnival pictures in the hall? That's my mom."

"She looks awfully young to be your mother."

"Ball gowns don't change that much." Lucy turned with her glass of sherry. "Those pictures were taken about thirty years ago. Mom was Queen of Comus and has never gotten over it. She adorns herself and goes out to be seen. My dad makes money and surrounds himself with possessions. A five-hundred-thousand dollar live oak he's holding prisoner. He once possessed my mother."

The new Lucy leaning hip-cocked against the bar in her black cashmere and Calvins. He could ask her how she'd paid for them . . .

"Come sit down and tell me what's wrong."

She took her time about it. Sat on the edge of the sofa, sipped her wine, placed the glass on the table before easing back. She was close now but staring off. That was all right, he could look at her profile, the nose and dark lashes, the lower lip he'd like to bite, and wonder about her still, if she'd ever gone to bed with anyone. . . . No lipstick on, not a touch of makeup this evening.

She said, "I don't care for your friend Roy."

"Is that what's bothering you?"

"No, it doesn't matter. But I'm curious, how he can be a friend of yours."

"I don't know. . . . I guess he's not a very likable person. . . ." Jack paused. *Lik*able person—the guy was out of the Stone Age. "He's hard to get along with, he's narrow-minded, has a terrible disposition . . . I don't know, now that you mention it."

"You talk about him, you sound like you're proud of him."

"No, I think it's amazement more than anything else. You know, that he's the way he is. I don't see him that much."

"But you like him."

"I wouldn't go so far as to say I *like* him. I accept him. Isn't that what you're supposed to do?"

She turned to look at him.

"I don't make excuses for him," Jack said. "I don't criticize him, either. I wouldn't dare."

She said, "Do you trust him?"

Jack took a moment. "Roy says he's gonna do something, you can put your money on it. He's the kind of guy you want on your side, whether you like him or not."

She said, "Because the same kind of guys are on the other side. There's no difference, is there?"

He put his hand on her arm, gripped it to feel flesh and bone beneath the soft wool. He said, "I'm an ex-con, you know that. Roy's an ex-con who used to be a cop. He's a mean, miserable guy, but he kept me pure for three years. Cullen's an ex-con who used to rob banks. What are you? Right now at this moment, what are you?"

She was facing him and her eyes held, but she didn't answer.

"Have you changed your skin yet?"

He gave her time, moving in slowly, closed his eyes as he kissed her and she stayed with him, moving her mouth to fit his mouth, knowing what she was doing. He saw her eyes beneath dark lashes, saw them come open, saw her lips slightly parted.

"You're not a nun anymore."

"No."

He kissed her again the same way, gently, with a tender feeling.

"You've become something else."

She said, "A new identity," and seemed almost to smile, still looking at him. Then touched him, put her hand on his leg as she got up. She said, "I want to show you something," and walked out of the room.

He lighted one of her cigarettes.

She was different. . . . Or maybe she had changed back. Because now, as he thought about it, she seemed more like the one he thought of as Sister Lucy, the way she was last Sunday in the hearse, telling him about Nicaragua, getting into it and making him feel it. Or the way she was that evening when he realized he was being set up and liked it —shit, *loved* it—and said, "You're wondering if I might be able to help you," and she looked at him with those quiet eyes and said, "It crossed my mind." She was like that Lucy again. Into something, feeling it.

But she wasn't making *him* feel it. Not now.

He thought, Maybe you're the one that's different. Become something else. And she's the same girl who ran off to take care of lepers.

He believed he might have another vodka, one more, get ready for whatever. But then heard her behind him and looked around to see her in the lamplight holding something against her leg. She sank to her knees almost in front of him, watching him, and placed a nickel-plated revolver on the coffee table.

She said, "Now I'm part of this."

He kept quiet, looking at the gun. It would have to be her dad's. A .38 with a two-inch barrel. He wondered if it was loaded. He looked at Lucy.

Staring at him.

She said, "I learned something from Jerry Boylan. Or some of him rubbed off on me. Not anything he said, but the fact of the man, what he was, and the fact of the way he died."

"Did you like him?"

She paused. "Yes, I liked him."

"Did you trust him?"

"No, but that's part of it. Why should he want to help us? He had his own cause, and that's what I learned from him. You have to take sides, Jack. You can't stand outside and reach in for what you want. You have to commit to something. You and I were talking about what we are. Remember? In the restaurant. While Jerry Boylan was being murdered for what he was."

"Do you want to know why he died?" Jack said. "Because he didn't look behind him. That's the fact of Jerry Boylan. He wasn't careful."

"But he was there because he believed in something. And it wasn't just the money."

"What did he tell us? If he wasn't doing this he'd be sweeping rubbish. And if I weren't here I'd be picking up dead bodies. You'd be giving lepers their medicine and Roy would be making drinks for tourists. . . . But if we're not in it for the score, what are we? How do you see us?"

"We don't need a label, Jack, or initials like the IRA." Sitting back on her legs, looking up at him. "Or the FDN, the *contras*. It's enough to say we're against that, what they stand for."

He looked at the revolver. "And pack a gun."

She said, "There's a big difference between packing a gun and taking up arms in a political, counterrevolutionary cause, and those aren't just words, it's the fact of it." She paused and said, "What happened to doing something for mankind? Remember? You said it yourself. That's what this is all about."

"It sounds good, anyway."

"It's *true.*"

"But would you kill for it, Lucy?"

SEVENTEEN

Little One came out of the hotel kitchen to the back hall where Jack was using the pay phone, Little One saying he had a bone to pick with him, saying his good nature was being taken advantage of. Jack raised the palm of his hand to Little One while he said into the phone, "If you could come right away I'd appreciate it."

Helene's voice said, "You'd appreciate it? You're not talking about just a drink, are you?"

"We can have dinner after, if you haven't eaten."

"After what? You call up at—what time is it?—almost eight-thirty, and ask me if I've eaten yet."

"Have you?"

"I'm not hungry. I had a big lunch."

"I was gonna call you earlier, but I had to go to Gulf-port."

"This guy takes me to Arnaud's," Helene's voice said, "for a job interview. By the time we're having our coffee he's telling me how important compatability is and we should stop off at the Royal Sonesta after, continue the interview in a relaxed atmosphere. Which means if I go to bed with the guy I get an office with drapes, carpeting, and a word processor. I said, Gee, what I've always wanted, a word processor."

"You get the job?"

"Listen, I was tempted. I have to be out of my apartment in ten days or else buy it; they're turning the building into a condo. I'm thirty-two years old and I don't have a job or a place to live."

He felt sorry for her feeling sorry for herself, the poor girl. She wasn't thirty-two, she was thirty-five, at least, married once before he met her, married again for about a year while he was in prison. What had either of them learned?

"I'll meet you in the bar. And wear a dress, okay? . . . Helene?"

"You sound different. You're the same, but there's something, I don't know what it is, different."

"It's been a long time," Jack said. He told her to hurry and hung up.

Little One, waiting, said, "Now then."

"I didn't leave the key because I have to use it again. I told you I might. Remember?"

"And I said to you we was even, I don't owe Roy nothing and I don't need no unexpected shit coming down on my life."

"Nothing's gonna happen. There's no way, I promise."

Little One said, "There's no way you going in the man's room, neither, long as he's in there."

"I have to work on that. . . . He have his dinner sent up?"

"Bottle cold wine was all, some shrimp. Man love his shrimp. Say he's waiting on his car."

"He's being picked up?"

"No, the man bought a new car, brand new *Mer*cedes. Told me he give 'em cash for it and they had to deliver it to him tonight or no deal. Man likes to talk about himself like that."

"He say he was leaving?"

"Uh-unh, but it look like it."

"How about the other two guys?"

"Haven't seen 'em. They not staying here, they come by's all."

"Can you find out if the colonel's checking out?"

"You don't think they would look at me strange at the desk? How'm I suppose to ask 'em that?"

Jack said, "I wouldn't think a Dale Carnegie graduate'd have any trouble at all."

Little One served them drinks in the hotel courtyard, looking over Helene in her black dress with the little thin straps, giving Jack a look then but not saying anything. He walked off.

And Helene said, "You're out of your mind."

He was thinking this would be the place to begin an evening, let the soft glow and the sound of the fountain and a few drinks set the mood. . . . But he said, "All I'm asking you to do is get him out of the room for ten minutes."

"What do I do, pull him out by his hair?"

"You could, he's a little guy."

"The little guys are the worst; they're more physical."

"You go up to 501." Jack's eyes raised. "The top railing, that's the fifth floor. See the alcove right by the elevator? That's his suite. You knock on the door. He opens it. You say, 'Oh, gee, I'm sorry. I have the wrong room.' "

Helene said, " 'Oh, gee, I'm sorry?' "

" 'I have the wrong room.' "

"You're practically in the tree. Why don't you pull your chair out so I can see you?"

"I'm okay."

She said, "You're hiding, aren't you?" Picked up her scotch and water and continued to stare at him. "What're you into, Jack?"

"I'll tell you later."

"You said you quit."

"I did. This's something else. Okay. You say, 'Sorry,' you turn and walk away."

"You're not doing it for fun. I can tell."

"You start to walk away, take a couple steps, you turn around . . . You listening?"

"I turn around."

"You say, 'Oh, if another girl comes, it's a friend of mine. I told her I'd meet her, but I guess I have the wrong room.' You understand? Then you say, 'I'll watch for her downstairs. But if I happen to miss her, would you tell her I'm down in the courtyard? Or else I'll be in the bar.' "

"Do I have to say it word for word, Jack, or can I ad lib?"

"Any way you want, as long as you understand what you're doing. You can't just walk away. You have to let him know where you'll be, so he'll come looking for you."

"What if he doesn't?"

"He will."

"But what if he doesn't?"

222

"You make him want to. The way you look . . . I don't mean you roll your eyes, anything like that."

"Flash my tongue?"

"You know what to do. You have guys coming on to you all the time."

"But I don't do anything."

"Come on, you could be in the movies, all the different looks you turn on."

"The guy's a Latin?"

"From Nicaragua."

"Is he cute?"

"He's a doll, looks like a waiter at Antoine's. . . . Wears red Jockeys."

"How do you know?"

"He comes down, you're at this table. He offers to buy you a drink, you say, 'Oh, no thank you."

"Why would I say that?"

"*Why?* You don't know this guy. But he'll keep after you and finally you say okay, one. You chat about this and that, how're things in Nicaragua. . . . Oh, try to get into talking about cars. Find out if he just bought a Mercedes, yeah, and how long he's staying, when he's checking out. Mention Miami if you can, see what he says."

"I thought I was just suppose to keep him busy."

"Well, you'll be talking to the guy. You're not gonna do card tricks, are you?"

"I could do a tap routine. On the table."

"I only need ten, fifteen minutes. Or till you see me up there. I'll stand by the rail for a minute. You tell the guy you have to leave or go to the can, whatever you want, and I'll meet you across the street at the Sonesta, in the bar. . . . Okay?"

"But what if he doesn't come down?"

"I can't believe it's you saying that," Jack said. "With your looks, those big brown eyes . . ."

"My nose. You always liked my nose."

"I love it, I love your nose."

"You like my hair like this?"

"It's you." It was. Her frizzed red hair was beginning to look good to him. "Helene, there's nothing I can think of that could keep the guy from coming after you."

She said, "Yeah, I guess."

Colonel Dagoberto Godoy opened the door wearing his red Jockeys and a scowl that changed at once.

As Helene said, "Oh, I'm sorry. Gee, I have the wrong room," and began turning away.

The colonel reached out and took hold of her arm in a grip that startled her and pulled her around to face him again. "You don't have the wrong room. This is the room you want. You come to see a man, didn't you?"

Helene said, "I happen to be staying in this hotel." Cool, but not quite haughty. "I see now that I got off the elevator on the wrong floor. If you'll be kind enough to let go of my arm and behave yourself, I won't have to report this to the manager."

She could, Helene was thinking, knee him in the crotch. Take some of the spunk out of the arrogant little asshole. But that wouldn't get her a drink, would it?

She let the colonel tell her, "Oh, please, you must forgive me. You must let me show you how I'm a real nice guy . . ."

Jack stepped from the elevator to the hall railing and looked down into the courtyard. Helene was seated at the table again. The colonel stood over her talking, bowing over her, taking her hand, kissing it—Jesus Christ—holding onto her hand as he sat down, talking a mile a minute.

He turned and walked back past the elevator to 501, listened at the door, and then used the key to go in.

There was the bottle of wine Little One had delivered, open in a silver bucket. A bowl of melted ice and shrimp tails. Shrimp tails in ashtrays. Letters on the desk by the TV set, the same letters he saw the last time he was here.

Two packages of clean laundry on the bed. That could mean something. The light on in the bathroom. Towels on the floor. A bottle of cologne with the top off, on the wash-basin. Next to it a blow-dryer, the cord plugged into the wall. He didn't want to be here.

He didn't want to be here the other night when he came. But this time the urge to hurry up and get out was stronger, the feeling more intense that he was crazy to be doing this. He was too old to be doing this. He wasn't the same person. He could feel it walking over to the dresser, his body telling him he shouldn't be here. He felt slow. He had felt alive going into all those other rooms, to score but also to be doing it, to be in there—look at him—getting away with it. But that didn't make any sense at all now.

It was a show-off thing to do you could only do in front of people who were asleep.

He opened the colonel's shirt drawer, slipped his hand beneath folds of soft silk, and felt the pistol and two extra magazines. He brought them out, closed his hand around the grip of the Beretta, feeling the solid heft of it as he walked over to the desk. The pink copy of a car dealer bill of sale lay next to the bank deposit and withdrawal receipts.

Helene had to pick up her scotch and water with her left hand. The colonel, hunched over the table in his black silk jacket, wouldn't let go of her right hand. He held it in both of his, the one with the diamond on top. He looked like a gangster in the movies. Or a record promoter, hard rock. Except when he spoke.

"I'll tell you something from long experience. I have never seen a woman so attractive as you in my life."

"Oh, I don't believe that," Helene said. "You're exaggerating. Aren't you?"

"I have had associations with very beautiful women. One of them was going to be in the Senorita Universo. You know of that? To choose the most beautiful woman in the world. But she got sick."

"I was homecoming queen at Fortier," Helene said, "my senior year. I probably could've been Sugar Bowl Queen one time, but I didn't try very hard. You know, why bother? You get in those big pageants I hear it's just politics. You know, who you go to bed with, and I'm not that kind. I have too much self-respect."

"Politics, yes, of course. My whole life I devote to the government of my country. Yes, I was in Washington, I know your president very well. He wrote a letter to me I like to show you. He sign it Ronald Reagan, the president. Listen, I'll get it to show you."

"No, that's okay, Dagoberda. What do you like to be called, Dago?"

"No, I prefer with my friends, Bertie."

"That's cute. I like that, Birdy."

"No, not Birdy, like a bird. Bertie. Ber-tie."

"That's cute, too."

"I think you the cute one. Listen, you visiting, uh? From where?"

"Miami."

"No. Is that true? You from Miami?"

"Have you ever been there?"

"Sure, I been there. I'm going back there, too, pretty soon."

"Are you? When?"

"You from Miami. You know what this is, how you come to my room and we meet? Is destiny. It was going to happen and we don't know it. See, and there is nothing we can do to stop it."

"It's weird," Helene said. "When're you going?"

"You have to give me your phone number and your address, for when I go there."

"Why don't you give me your number instead?"

"I don't know it yet." He looked up, straightened, letting go of her hand. "Ah, but now I can get it for you, good." And called out, "Crispin!"

Helene turned enough to see two men coming over from the lobby, both Latins in mod-cut suits with pointy shoulders. The one coming ahead of the other, hands in his pockets, had on sunglasses. Now the colonel was saying, "Crispin, this beautiful lady is from Miami. Elene, Crispin, my associate, is also from there. Crispin, sit with us, have a drink."

Helene said, "Listen, you guys, I'm gonna have to run in about two minutes."

Now the colonel was shaking his head, telling her he wouldn't hear of it. She watched him snap his fingers, once, at the other Latin guy, who'd hung back holding his hands in front of him, but came toward them now as the colonel told him something in Spanish that sounded like an order and tossed his room key in the air for the guy to catch. There, do it. Then turned back to her smiling, Bertie again.

"He's going to get the letter from President Reagan so I can show you."

"You don't have to do that," Helene said. "I really wish you wouldn't."

But the colonel was snapping his fingers now at the giant black waiter and the one named Crispin turned his sunglasses on her to ask, "Where you live in Miami?"

Jack went through the deposit and withdrawal receipts, saw nothing that looked like a transfer to a Miami bank, saw one new account that had been opened and copied all the figures down again, just to be sure. Several more names had been checked on the colonel's prospect list, others crossed out. He came to the letter on White House stationery and began reading it again, wanting to memorize his favorite parts: the one where our president tells the colonel to "win a big one for democracy," and the one where he mentions "my friends in the Pelican State." Jesus Christ, the Pelican State. That closing, in Spanish, Jack had figured out to mean "he isn't heavy, he's . . ."

In the silence, concentrating, he heard the sounds coming from the other room. The key in the lock. Someone coming in, trying to, pushing on the door but having trouble with it. Trying again now. Jack picked up the Beretta from the desk. He moved around to the other side of the bed, by the window, eased down against the wall behind the headboard and hump of pillows and didn't like it, the feeling of being cornered here. He'd rather be standing and thought of the closet with its sliding doors, closed now. They made a noise when you pushed them open. He'd have to move past the bedroom door to get to the closet. He'd have to hurry. Now he didn't want to move.

Then did it all at once. Got up as he began to crawl, crossed toward the closet, looking into the sitting room and saw the door knob jiggle, saw it turn. He kept going, past the closet into the bathroom, turned off the light, eased the door half closed, and stepped behind it, against the tiled wall. He held the Beretta upright, almost touching the side of his face, listening.

It was quiet now.

It was dark in front of him, a crack of light along the inside edge of the door, next to him. He waited. He heard nothing until the door moved.

The door moved toward him. The bathroom light came on. The door moved away from him, closed, and he was looking at a head of dark hair, nappy, thick, above the sharp angles of the man's suit coat, the shoulders hunching over the washbasin. Above the man's head was his own reflection in the mirror. He watched himself bring the Beretta down from his face to extend it, almost touching the man splashing cologne into his hand. The Nicaraguan Indian with the weird name, rubbing his hands together, raising them to his face as his head came up. Now Franklin de Dios was in the mirror with Jack, the Indian who looked like a Creole. He stared, his fingers pressed to his pointy cheekbones, at the half face above his own. He brought his hands down, starting to turn.

Jack put the Beretta into the groove at the base of the Indian's skull, into his hair, and that kept him looking straight ahead.

At first Jack bent his knees a little, trying to stay directly behind the Indian, trying to hide. But, shit, he had seen the Indian's eyes. The Indian knew who he was. So he stood straight to play it straight, not having any idea what he was going to do other than try to fake it somehow, try to get this guy who'd killed Boylan more scared than he was. Shit. But even holding the gun against the guy's head he didn't feel in control. He wasn't sure if the guy would do what he told him.

"Put your hands on the mirror."

The Indian obeyed, leaned over the sink and placed his palms flat. He looked into the mirror again, past his own reflection, and seemed resigned. Jack reached around in front of him, ran his hand along the Indian's belt and then up under his arms and felt perspiration but no gun. He felt his coat pockets. He stooped and ran his hand down one leg and started down the other when the Indian moved, tried to turn. Jack jammed the Beretta into the crack of the guy's ass and heard a grunt as the guy's hips jerked against the sink and he went up on his toes. Taking control was not as hard as it looked.

There was an ankle holster on the Indian's right leg holding a two-inch .38 revolver. Jack slipped it into his coat pocket as he came up. Now they were looking at each other again in the mirror. Staring at each other: the Indian's expression, Jack's too, mildly curious, nothing more. Nothing to show Jack wondering what he was going to do with the guy so he could get out of here. It would be easier to shoot him than hit him over the head with two pounds of metal. How hard would he have to hit him? Shit, it could kill him, the Indian with the weird name, fracture his skull. Jack had hit guys before they hit him; it was the way to do it if it was going to happen. He could get mad, charge himself up in two seconds, all of a sudden have the desire, that aggressive urge to hit, and would hear himself letting go as he went in and hit, a sound that packed energy and was more than a grunt. He could turn the guy around and belt him and he could break his fucking hand, too. He hadn't hit anybody in five years, at least.

Franklin de Dios said, "How you doing?"

Jack heard him. The weird-looking Indian was right there in front of him. He *saw* him say it. The same way he said it coming out of the Men's room.

But Jack said, "What?"

"I wonder if you are a cop."

Jack kept looking at him.

"But I don't think so. Man, now I don't know who you are. You drive that coach. . . . Will you tell me something? That girl was in there, wasn't she?"

Jack didn't answer. The guy spoke with an accent, but without strain or any kind of emotion. The guy sounded as if he really wanted to know. It didn't make sense.

"See, they never told me what that girl did, why they wanted to have her. . . . If you not going to tell me, it don't matter. You going to shoot me, uh?"

"You just do what you're told, is that it?"

"They say you have to take orders."

"You don't seem to have any trouble with it. Shoot Boylan in the back, nothing to it."

"Who is Boy-lon?"

"You mean you kill a guy, you don't even know his name?"

Now the Indian's face showed surprise, a glimmer of it, and then gone.

"After, maybe, yes, you can know who you kill. If you have time to look in the man's pockets for food or for money."

"For *food*?"

"Yes, and you see his name sometime. The guys that have army IDs. But what difference does it make? He don't know you either. He could be looking in your pockets if you not lucky that day."

"What're you talking about?"

"You going to kill me—do you know my name?"

Jack said, "You're a weird fucking guy, Franklin," and saw that glimmer of surprise again on the face in the mirror. "Take off all your clothes and get in the shower."

Franklin de Dios nodded, moving toward the tub as he took off his coat. "Shoot me in there so there won't be no blood." He stepped out of his pants and they were looking at each other directly for the first time.

"We tie their hands behind them, make them kneel. They do that, too, the Sandinistas. I think everybody does it that way."

"You're talking about the *war*. Killing prisoners."

"Yes, of course. Tha's what you do." The Indian's shirt came off to show a muscular torso, green-striped boxer shorts. He looked over again. "Tell me how you know my name."

Jack said, "Listen, I'm gonna step out for a minute. Turn the water on and get in. I'll be right back."

"I have to take my shoes off."

"They get wet, what difference does it make?"

"Yes, you right. We always make them take their shoes off. But nobody is going to need these shoes. Unless, do you want them?"

"Will you get in the fucking shower?"

Jack stepped out of the bathroom, closed the door and waited. In a few moments he heard the shower go on. He pictured Franklin de Dios in there in his green drawers adjusting the faucets, not too hot, not too cold. . . . Jesus, the guy accepting it, waiting to die.

The next ten seconds he spent at the dresser, opening the drawer, shoving the Beretta and the extra magazines under the guy's shirts, then closing the drawer and walking off and then returning to the dresser—because it didn't make sense to put the guy's gun back, the guy was going to know he was here—and wasted another ten seconds thinking about it, Christ, hearing that shower going. He told himself, forget the fucking gun; started out again, stopped, dropped the key on the floor, and kicked it under the bed.

No more going into hotel rooms, never again.

EIGHTEEN

"**A**ll I could think of was, no more of this shit. I have to get out of here. I did look over the rail. You were still there."

"Yeah, stuck with those guys. This creep asking me about Miami. Have I ever been to the Mutiny, Neon Leon's? He wants to know what *bars* I go to, if I ever get over to Key Biscayne. Where's Key Biscayne? I was in Miami once in my life, when I was eighteen."

They were in Jack's Scirocco parked at the foot of Toulouse, the river close by in the dark, beyond the cement dock and the silhouette of a dredge against the night sky.

"That was my last time. Ever," Jack said. "I'm not even sure if I'll ever stay at a hotel again." He started the car. "We better go to your place."

"No. It's too depressing . . . It's sort of a mess."

"Tell me what the guy said, when he came back."

"He didn't say anything. So I assumed, well, at least you didn't get caught. You were either gone by then or hiding under the bed or in the closet . . ."

"You didn't see me leave?"

"How could I? They're looking right at me."

"The guy must've said *some*thing. The Indian. That's what he is, a Miskito Indian."

"He handed Bertie the letter and Bertie started yelling at him in Spanish, I guess for taking so long."

"What letter?"

"From the President, Reagan. First he read it out loud and then I had to read it. . . . I didn't understand the last line. It was in Spanish."

"Was the guy, when he came back, did he look wet?"

"Wet? Why would he be wet?"

"He didn't say anything at all?"

"Nothing, not a word, he just stood there. Bertie yelled at him and then the other guy got into it."

"Crispin?"

"Cris*peen*. Those little arrogant guys love to yell. I did look up at the top floor when they were yelling. I knew you were okay, but where were you? The colonel, he started touching me then, running his hand up my arm, telling me what a wonderful time we're gonna have. Jack, I had to get out of there. I said, 'I'm sorry, Bertie, but I can't go out with you.' He said, 'But why?' I said, 'Cause you're too fucking short,' and left."

Turning out of the lot toward Canal Street Jack said, "Did the guy's hair look wet?"

They had a drink at Mandina's while he told her about the Indian, Franklin de Dios, coming into the room. Then he had to tell her about the colonel raising funds, that much. He'd tell her the rest in a quiet place. They left the car at Mandina's and walked. She asked him where they were going; he said, wait.

When they came to Mullen & Sons Helene said, "Oh, no, uh-unh. I'm not going in there at night. Are you kidding?" She looked up at the gray turreted shape in the streetlight and said, "It used to be someone's home, didn't it?"

She stood in the lighted front hall, not moving, while Jack looked in the visitation rooms. He came back to her shaking his head, took her arm as they moved toward the stairway and she said it again, "Oh, no, uh-unh."

"If I'm not here and there's a body, Leo gets somebody in. You know what I'm talking about? He calls a security service and they send a guy over."

"Jack, I don't want to see a dead person."

They were in the upstairs hall. "There aren't any here. I'll show you." He reached into a doorway and turned on the light. "This's the embalming room. If there was a body it'd be laying on that table."

"Oh, my God," Helene said. She didn't move. "What's that thing?"

"That's the embalming machine."

"*Porti*-Boy? Oh, my God. . . . How does it work?"

"Come on." He turned the light off and took her down the hall to his apartment.

"What's this?"

"Where I've been living the past three years."

"Gee, it's nice, Jack. Who's your decorator?"

He said, "Helene, I was in a bathroom with a guy that thought I was gonna kill him. Try to imagine something like that. He didn't cry, he didn't say please don't. . . . It was the same guy yesterday at the restaurant. You were *there.*"

"I must've left just before."

"Well, it was the same guy. He's standing there in the bathroom, he thinks I'm gonna shoot him, and he asks me if I want his shoes. Can you tell me what kind of a guy would say that?"

Helene didn't answer. She watched him get a bottle of vodka from the refrigerator that stood in the barely furnished room; she sat with him in the old sofa that used to be downstairs and didn't say anything, not a word, until he had told her everything that had happened from the trip to Carville on Sunday until this Tuesday evening at the St. Louis Hotel.

She said, "I think you've left out a few things."

"I might've, I don't know."

Helene sat curled in the sofa, facing him. "You stayed at her house last night?"

"All three of us did."

"Yeah . . ."

"I told you, the guy saw us in the restaurant and he knows where she lives. We thought he might come around."

"But he didn't."

"No. Then I run into him again, tonight. He knows who I am. This's the third or fourth time he's seen me, we're getting to know each other. But he didn't tell the colonel or Crispin, Cris*peen.* He could've told them later, but—no, he catches me in the *room?* Shit, he'd have told them right away. But he didn't. . . . Why?"

"Where did you sleep?"

"What?"

"Last night, at her house. Where did you sleep?"

"In a bed, where do you think? That house, there nine, ten bedrooms upstairs."

"Who with?"

"Roy and Cullen had a room and I had a room. . . . What, you think I sneaked in her room during the night?"

"She could've come to yours."

Jack took his time. "As a matter of fact, she did. She wanted to talk."

"She get in bed with you?"

"She sat on the edge. You know, on the side."

"Hey, Jack? Bullshit."

"It isn't like what you think. She's a dedicated person."

"You mean dedicated people don't get it on?"

"I mean I really don't know, since this's my first experience with people who give a shit about anything outside of themselves."

"She probably calls it going all the way."

"Helene, she's not like a nun that teaches third grade, she spent nine years taking care of lepers. Now she's got a gun. I asked her if she'd be willing to use it. She said it isn't something you plan. But if she'd had a gun when the colonel murdered the lepers there's no doubt in her mind she would've tried to kill him. Even knowing his men would shoot her on the spot."

"Maybe," Helene said, "she wants to be a martyr. I mean a real one, go straight to heaven."

"You think you're kidding, she might go for that."

"I wasn't kidding."

"But she isn't a fanatic. She might sound a little strange sometimes, but she knows what's going on, she's very aware of things. She says you have to take sides, make a commitment, and then, I don't know, whatever happens happens. Like the guy in the bathroom, the Indian. He's on the other side. He's willing to kill, but he's also willing to die for whatever it is he believes in. He sees it coming and accepts it, Jesus, didn't kick or scream or anything."

Helene handed him her empty glass. "Why are you telling me all this, Jack? Why haven't you called Lucy or one of your buddies?"

"I'll see 'em tomorrow."

"I think you want to hear yourself," Helene said. "Hear what it sounds like out loud."

"Maybe."

"You're not telling it to impress me. Like the first time, when we met and you were dying to tell somebody about your secret life. This is a lot different."

"You bet it is. These guys are awake."

"But you're in it for more than the money, or the excitement."

"I don't know. . . ." Jack got up, went to the refrigerator with their glasses, poured a couple more ice-cold vodkas, and then stood there, holding them. "On the news this evening, I look up, there was Tom Brokaw asking Richard Nixon, for Christ sake, what he thought about our giving the *contras* a hundred million dollars. Asking Nixon, who used to have this gang of burglars working for him and didn't do one fucking day of time. Nixon says, sure, they need our help. Brokaw says, but couldn't that lead to our military involvement down there? Nixon says, no, it will prevent having to send our young men later. And Brokaw says, 'Thank you, Mr. President.' He doesn't say, 'Are you out of your fucking mind? Why would we send *our young men*?

You want to go, go ahead. And take all those asshole advis-
ers in the White House with you.' No, Brokaw says, 'Thank
you, Mr. President.' "

"What else's he gonna say?"

"I know, but I got mad. Asking that fucking crook his
opinion. He didn't even do trash time in a country-club
joint."

Helene said, "You know what I think?"

"What?"

"I think you've taken sides."

Jack opened his eyes to a sight that, fantasized, could
carry a convict through the day and into the night: Helene
coming out of the bathroom in just her tiny little panties.
He told her she better get back in bed, quick, before she
caught cold.

"You're suppose to pick somebody up at ten?"

"Cullen. We're going to Gulfport."

"I thought you went yesterday."

"We did, but the guy wasn't there. Here." He raised
the sheet.

"It's twenty to." She began doing a twisting exercise,
feet apart, hands on her hips, her breasts a half beat behind
her shoulders. "You realize we didn't make love? We fell
asleep? I don't believe it. I think you're getting old, Jack."

"I'm ready—you're the one got up."

"Do you know that's the first time we ever slept together and didn't?"

"I think you're right."

"We may as well be married."

"There's a kitchenette down the hall, next to the embalming room . . ."

"Oh, God, this place."

"If you want to put some coffee on."

Jack took a shower and put on a work shirt and cotton pants, picked up his jacket, and walked down the hall. The kitchenette was dark. He saw the doors to the prep room open, the light on, then saw Helene as he heard Leo's voice.

"No, that's arterial, the Permaglo, it takes the place of the blood. What I'm injecting now, through the trocar, is cavity fluid. It's a chemical you use to firm up the organs."

Leo had a body on the embalming table. A man, it looked like. Helene was standing at the head of the table in her black dress, watching.

"You want to shoot some inside the mouth, too, so you don't have any sag."

"It's fascinating," Helene said.

"See this? It's a trocar button."

"Oh, to fill in the hole."

"Right, so you don't have to suture it as you do incisions and lacerations. Then you cover 'em with a special wax we use."

Jack said, "I don't suppose anybody made coffee."

"Hey, there he is," Leo said. "I was just showing your friend here how we prepare the deceased."

"This's Helene, Leo."

"Yeah, we met."

"If nobody made coffee," Jack said, "I have to leave."

Helene said, "Oh, nuts. I wanted to see how you do the cosmetics."

"Stick around," Leo said. "I can drop you off later. Sure, no problem."

"I'm going to Gulfport," Jack said. He walked off. Helene was asking, what're those? And Leo was telling her eye caps, you slip 'em under the lids.

People were acting weird. Everyone he met.

Or it's you, Jack thought. The way you see them.

Franklin de Dios, watching Lucy Nichols's house, saw the old car arrive: the light-colored one he believed was a type of Volkswagen and needed repair, something to make it quiet. He knew whose car it was.

It turned into the driveway. Thirty-five minutes passed. Now the dark-blue Mercedes sedan, two people in it, came out of the driveway and turned toward St. Charles. Franklin de Dios was parked on a beautiful street named Prytania, near the corner where it joined Audubon. He gave the Mercedes the head start of a block before he got after it: up to Claiborne Avenue and then to the interstate, number 10, going toward the east . . . going far out of the city and across the lake on a beautiful day, following the Mercedes in the rented black Chrysler Fifth Avenue. If he could buy any car he wanted it might be one like this. Or the Cadillac he drove for Crispin Reyna in Florida. He had never driven a Mercedes. He had driven a truck and an armored troop carrier after he had learned to drive in 1981. A man who worked for Mr. Wally Scales in Honduras had taught him to drive and said in front of him to Mr. Wally Scales he was a natural-born driver with a respect for the machine, not like those others who became crazy behind the wheel and destroyed whatever they drove.

Mr. Wally Scales had said to forget about Lucy Nichols, but the colonel had insisted. Watch her house. If the car leaves, follow it.

Crossing the state line at this moment into Mississippi.

Franklin had lost confidence in Mr. Wally Scales, in his ability to see into people; but he did trust him and could talk to him. He could not talk to Colonel Godoy or Crispin

Reyna. The reason was simple. They didn't listen when he said something to them. He was beneath their social class, far beneath them with his mixed black and Indian blood.

But it was Mr. Wally Scales, the CIA man, who had brought him to Miami; they were in a way friends, or they could be friends. Mr. Wally Scales listened when he said something to him. He listened this morning when Franklin de Dios told him he no longer trusted the word of the colonel or Crispin Reyna. Mr. Wally Scales said, "Why is that, Franklin?"

"They talk always of Miami, Florida, but not the war."

"Oh, is that right?" Mr. Wally Scales said, trying to act as though he was concerned. "Well, then you better keep an eye on them."

See? He was kind and he listened, but didn't have feelings that told him about people. Or he didn't care.

When Franklin de Dios asked him about Lucy Nichols, the CIA man said, "Oh, she's a peace marcher. One of those bleeding-heart types. Had it in for the colonel, so she got his girl friend out of town most likely. No big deal."

When he asked about the guy at the funeral place, Mr. Wally Scales said, "Jack Delaney? She must've suckered him, that's all. Used him. Hard-up ex-con with no brains."

That was when Franklin de Dios realized he could trust the CIA man as a friend but not rely on his judgment. He decided not to ask any more questions or tell Wally about meeting the guy with no brains five times in the past week.

Maybe the sixth time coming up.

The guy, Jack Delaney, and another guy were in the car he was following, the dark-blue Mercedes turning off the highway now at the second exit sign to Gulfport.

Anything else he wanted to know, he would have to talk to the funeral guy himself.

Ask him why he didn't kill you.

Ask him what he was doing.

Ask him what side he was on.

He followed the Mercedes for five miles. As the road became the main street, Twenty-fifth Avenue, four lanes wide and with a tall building down there against the sky, Franklin de Dios was wondering if he was certain about the sides. If there were more than two sides. If he was on the side he thought he was on or on a different side. He was getting a feeling, more and more, that he was alone.

NINETEEN

The sign over the sidewalk said CROMWELL'S, straight up and down. Across the lower part and much smaller it said *Men's Wear * Sporting Goods * Military Surplus New and Used.*

Alvin Cromwell asked Jack and Cullen as they looked around, "You fellas want a suit of clothes? You need some resort wear? Tell me how I can fix you up."

Jack kept looking around as they moved toward the back of the store. They seemed to be the only customers. For something to say he asked if they carried Hollandia Sportswear, the outfits with the little tulips on them.

Alvin Cromwell had to stop and think. "I have these shirts with different little animals on 'em. Let's see . . ." He had a beard and looked like a weight lifter in his black T-shirt with white lettering that said *Never mind the dog,*

Beware of owner. He seemed like a nice guy though. He told Jack, "No, I don't think I have any with tulips."

"You sure have guns. I'll say that."

"You know guns?"

Cullen said, "I bet I can still strip an M-1 in the dark and put it back together."

It surprised Jack, but he was looking off toward the guns now, racks of them across the knotty-pine wall in the rear of the store: rifles, shotguns, and what appeared to be submachine guns, all with red tags attached to them.

To get there they walked past pipe racks of camouflage fatigues, jackets and trousers ON SALE! *Reduced from $29.95 to $24.95.* There were new and used Genuine USAF flight jackets. Ranger vests, *Good-looking and functional.* Camouflage T-shirts for kids, stiff-brim drill instructor hats, Ranger boonie hats and combat caps, holsters, binoculars, canteens, knives, and bayonets with sawtooth blades . . .

As they approached the knotty-pine shelves and racks, Alvin Cromwell said, "If you men have been to war or know your assault weapons, this here ought to turn you on."

"I was with the First Cav in the big one," Cullen said, "WW Two. The first time in the history of the First was when we got off our horses and took an island in the Admiralty group, Los Negros."

Jack looked at him. This was the first he knew of Cullen being in the army. Now Alvin Cromwell was shaking Cullen's hand. So Jack said, "I wanted to go to Nam in the worst way but, damn it, I got turned down." Alvin Cromwell nodded, but didn't shake his hand. He said, "You the two fellas in here yesterday asking for me?"

"We happened by," Jack said. "My friend here misplaced his car keys. We stopped back wondering if it might've been here."

Alvin Cromwell said, "Guys from Alcohol, Tobacco and Firearms are always losing something in here too and come looking around. I point out to 'em I deal only in legal sport and recreational weapons, semiautomatic at best."

Jack said, "If you think we're government we'll leave right now and sue you for slander. We're just looking, is all, and don't even know what we're looking at."

Alvin Cromwell said, "There's no harm in that. What you see up there, left to right . . . There's your Ruger Mini-14, your Uzi, your Tech-9. Next, your H and K 91, fires the 672 NATO round or a 308 Winchester. You recognize your Thompson? Popular with World War Two guys willing to pay the price. Next, your handy-dandy AR-15 Armalite. With a conversion kit you can turn it into an M-16, if that's what you want. I'll tell you, in Nam it had the attrition rate of about a C-ration can. We got 'em, everybody thought, oh, man, this here's a gas on full automatic. But see, it was the gas, tapped at the front sight and sent to the rear to run the gun, that fucked it up. The mechanism'd get filled with debris and then she'd malfunction on you. So what we had to do then was kill us a VC and appropriate his AK-47 'cause, man, that's a gun, second only to your FN-FAL, made by the Belgians. I don't know how they know how to do it, but shit, they're good. That FN-FAL. The Brits use it, and just about anybody else can get their hands on it, like those crazy assholes over in Lebanon. We've managed some for the *contras,* but not a lot."

"Down in Nicaragua," Jack said.

"Yeah, shit. Man, they need all the help they can get. The *contras* don't cut it, man, we're gonna be down there."

"You think so?"

"I already been," Alvin Cromwell said. "I'll tell you what made me go. I'd think of Nam I could cry of embarrassment how we let those little suckers run us out. I came back I didn't know which way to turn. I tried the Klan, but they're a bunch of negative thinkers is all. You name it, niggers, Jews, Catholics, they're against it. I told 'em, 'Don't you know what the only evil in the whole world is we have to stop? It's commonism.' I hate Commonists, always have. But hate doesn't do you a bit of good less you can direct it. It was through a gun-club convention I joined the CVP, the Civilian Volunteer Program, and got a new lease on life. What we do is assist the freedom fighters down there. Take them in supplies, food and gear, see, and train them in field tactics. Over in Vietnam I was a gunner on a Cobra—got blown out of the sky during Tet and I was six months in the hospital getting my legs to work again. Anyway, I went down there . . . Listen, I've spent over twenty-five hundred of my own money showing Miskito Indians how to fire an M-60 machine gun, a piss-poor weapon but all we got. I've taken them into Nicaragua from Honduras on what we call, quote, a practical application exercise, if you know what I mean. But don't ever say I told you that. Like I've never mentioned the CIA in this deal, have I? Well, seven weeks with the Miskitos I lost thirty pounds eating beans and rice, what they had of it. But, man, I come home feeling gooood. I know what's shaking and what it's gonna take for us to win down there. See, it's way different than over in Nam. It's the bad guys have the firepower and the fucking gunships."

Jack said, "You were with the Indians."

"Yes, sir, and learned I wasn't twenty-one no more. Those people have got a hard life, what the Sandinistas done to 'em."

"They kind of a strange people?"

"They're *good* people. Been there minding their own business since before Columbus till the Sandinistas come along and fucked 'em over. You know what Commonists remind me of? Hard-nosed as they are and can't see past it? The Klan. I think one's as bad as the other."

"You ever going back?"

Alvin Cromwell looked out toward the front of his empty store. "My wife don't want me to. I told her, honey, there's way more for me to do there'n here. I got two ladies and a fella working for me now I don't even need. They're having their lunch. I tell 'em, take as long as you want. Go on home and have a nap afterwards. My daddy always went home, had his noon dinner and a nap. But times are changing, huh?" He looked toward the front again, then at Cullen, then at Jack. "I'll tell you something if you don't breathe a word. I have a chance to go down there this weekend and, shit, I'm gonna take it. Do some good in the world."

Jack hesitated. "You fly down?"

"Too expensive. We got a load of gear and supplies and there's a fleet of banana boats that puts in right here. They'll take any cargo you got rather than go dead-head."

Jack said, "It sounds like you lead an exciting life."

Alvin Cromwell said, "When I'm not here I do."

When they were outside, squinting in the sunlight, Jack said, "Jesus Christ, you believe that guy?"

Cullen surprised him. "Jack, you haven't been to war, so don't say anything, okay?"

"What's that got to do with it?"

"If you don't believe there're people like Alvin Cromwell then you're dumb, that's all. They're the kind of guys become regular army and are right there when the time

251

comes we have to fight a war. They're the ones save our ass."

"What're you getting mad for?"

" 'Cause you think you're smart. You think a guy like that's square that believes in his country and is willing to lay down his life for it. Where were you during Vietnam?"

"I tried to get in, I told you."

"Bullshit."

"I didn't go to Canada or burn my draft card. I got called and they turned me down."

"And you were glad."

"Well, of course I was. Cully, what's the matter with you? All I said was, do you believe him?"

"I know what you said."

They reached the Mercedes parked on the street, opened the doors, and stood there to let the air circulate inside. Jack looked at Cullen, across the sun glare laying hot on the roof.

"I didn't know you were in the army. You never mentioned it before today."

Cullen didn't say anything. He was studying the buildings across the street, his gaze inching along.

"Were you in the whole time?"

"Three and a half years," Cullen said, looking up the street now, past the few cars angle-parked along the blocks of storefronts. He turned then, slowly, to look toward the port area, the small-craft harbor and commercial fishing piers. He said with wonder in his voice, "Je-sus Christ."

"What's the matter?"

"The first bank I ever walked in and robbed, all by myself, was right here in Gulfport."

"Is that right?"

"But it's gone. I don't see it."

"That big new building we passed coming in, that's a bank."

"Naw, this was an old bank."

Jack moved out toward the street, shading his eyes with his hand. "Look up there, Cully, this side of the new building. The Hancock Bank."

Now Cullen came out to the rear end of the car. He said, "Oh, my Lord, that's it. We passed right by it."

Jack turned to the car, his gaze taking in the wide expanse of Twenty-fifth Avenue. He stopped and looked down that way again: at the man standing in the street about fifty feet away, at the rear end of a black car parked on the same side of the street. It took Jack a moment to realize it was the Creole-looking Indian, staring back at him.

"Yeah, that's it all right," Cullen said. "I remember those pillars in front."

Franklin de Dios, in a dark suit and white shirt, his coat open; he stood there without moving, looking this way.

Jack said, "Cully, let's go."

They got in the car and backed out. There he was through the windshield now. The guy hadn't moved. He turned as they drove past, watching them. Turned all the way. There he was in the rearview mirror, still watching.

Jack said, "Cully?"

Cullen said, "I think back now, the best time of my life was when I was in the service."

They drove down to the port area and turned right looking at empty semitrailers parked in the yard of the banana truck depot and drove past the Standard Fruit pier and then the small-craft and shrimp boat harbor. Pretty soon they were looking at the clean white sand that stretched along the Gulf of Mexico and Jack began to glance at his rearview mirror: from the mirror to a windsurfer in the gulf, a blue-and-orange sail skimming along out there, and back to the mirror.

Cullen saying, "I saw fellas that were my buddies get killed on that island. Shit, it was only about seven miles long, I don't know what we needed it for, little piss-ass island. But we were all in that war together. There was a feeling there I've never experienced again, 'cause we knew we were *doing* something, I mean that was important. It didn't matter how big that fucking island was, not at all."

"We're into something now," Jack said.

"I have my doubts it'll ever come off. But you know what? I don't even think I care."

"I mean right now we've got something to think about. There's a tail on us."

"A cop? You haven't done nothing."

"Not a cop, the Indian. The one . . . you know."

Cullen said, "Yeah?" But didn't seem interested enough to turn around and look. He asked though, "What're you gonna do about it?"

"We'll get just the other side of Pass Christian . . ." Jack paused, looking at the mirror again.

"I used to admire those big homes along there," Cullen said. "I thought, yeah, boy, that'd be the place to live."

"Then I'm gonna punch it," Jack said, "get up to about a hundred and twenty miles an hour . . ."

"Around that curve?" Cullen said. "There's a big curve 'fore you come to the bay."

"Shit," Jack said, "you're right. Okay, I'm gonna get around the curve and then punch it. We're gonna fly across the bridge and then make a quick right on North Beach and lose his ass."

That's what they did.

TWENTY

Jack came to tree shade and rickety piers and coasted along the empty shore road: old frame houses under mossy oaks on one side, the worn cement steps of a seawall on the other—where they dropped crab nets into the shallow water. He saw the long plank walk reaching out into the bay. They were approaching the house that had weathered more than a hundred years of hurricanes. "Camille took off the front porch," he told Cullen, "left four feet of mud inside." He turned into the side street—noticing the name for the first time, Leopold—and parked at the back of the house behind Raejeanne's Chevette and some kind of sparkly blue car, brand new, that showed numbers instead of a name and the word *Turbo*. A woman was watching them from the back screened porch. Then another woman, a bigger shape in the dim area, moved past her to push open the screen door. His sister, Raejeanne. She said, "Who's that? Friend or enema?" Getting out of the car he heard her say, "Mama, it's Jack."

They stood on the back porch by the long dining table set for five, Jack introducing Cullen, Jack taking his mother in his arms, his mom frail and getting smaller, her quiet voice saying, "How's my fine big boy?" as he patted her and got a sound of keen interest in his voice to ask her how she'd been. "Just fine." Everything was just fine with her at seventy-five, her hair done in blond-gray waves, her glasses shining, wearing white earrings that matched her beads; but she was an old-timey seventy-five and now she seemed alarmed and he asked her what was wrong. She said, "We haven't set enough places at the table." He said, hey, tell me what you've been doing, how you've been. His mom said, "I been fine till last week, I was in bed a while with artha-ritis." Jack asked her, "Who's Arthur Itis?" She grinned, trying not to show her dentures, and said he sounded just like his dad, her Irishman. Close by Cullen was sniffing, making mmmmmm sounds as Raejeanne said they were having a mess of boiled shrimp and there was gumbo left over. She said, "We have company. Guess who's here, Jack?" He knew, when she said it that way. His mom didn't have to tell him, giving him a sad look as she said, "Maureen and her husband." Raejeanne said, "Let's fix you all a drink and go out on the porch." His mom said, "Maureen was asking about you. I told her you were work-ing hard as ever with Leo; Maureen said, Oh, that was nice. Her husband's with her, that doctor." Jack said, Harby. His mom said, "She's the sweetest girl. . . ." Raejeanne said Leo was gonna try to get away early. She said to Jack, "Leo mentioned you ran into Helene. You seeing her again?"

"He tell you everything he knows?"

"I hope so," Raejeanne said.

His mother said, "You ran into somebody in the car?"

They followed a linoleum hall to the front porch. Maureen and Harby Soulé came up out of their chairs, Maureen smiling, putting out her hand to Jack. "I don't know why but I knew it was you in that nice car." He held her familiar hand and kissed her on the cheek as Harby stood by in his starched seersucker suit and little bow tie and eyebrow-pencil mustache, Jack feeling the man should have menus under his arm—my God, but he did look like the colonel —Jack feeling alive, glad to be here, feeling confident. There was a Creole Indian who killed people turning through streets in Bay St. Louis right now, looking for him, as Raejeanne handed him a vodka collins with a cherry in it and his mom asked if he felt the breeze. She said there was always a nice breeze in the afternoon. She said, "Remember how you and Maureen loved to go sailing? They don't have that boat no more. Raejeanne, what happened to that sailboat Jack and Maureen use to love so much?"

"It sunk, Mama."

Maureen said, "How's work, Jack?"

He looked at her slender body in the neat blue sundress, her slender arms, her slender legs crossed, her strong hands holding the drink in her lap; one hand or the other that used to sooner or later grip his when they were lying in the hammock that hung folded against the wall behind him and he would draw his hand out of her clothes.

"The same. It doesn't change."

Harby said, "Least you don't have to buy malpractice insurance."

Jack said, "No, we never get a complaint." He said things here he never said anywhere else—Maureen watching him, knowing it. If one time he had not taken his hand out of her clothes and they had made love . . . He couldn't imagine her making love to Harby Soulé.

Harby saying he worked two months a year for the darn insurance company. Cullen asked him what he did. Harby said he was a urologist. Cullen frowned and Rae-jeanne said he was a pecker checker. Cullen said, Oh, was that right? He said he had a question but had better save it, huh?

If they had made love . . . they could be sitting here right now, except Harby wouldn't be here, or Cullen, and there wouldn't be a Creole Indian named Franklin de Dios cruising around, or Nicaraguans. . . . He still could have met Lucy Nichols.

"Have you ever heard of the Sisters of Saint Francis?"

"I'm not sure," Maureen said. "Why?"

"I met one. They take care of lepers."

Maureen said, "Oh," nodding.

"Could you imagine doing that?"

"I doubt it. Where did you meet her?"

"Carville. Have you ever been there?" He felt himself pressing and he wasn't sure why.

"I've never had a desire to go."

"It's quite a place. Looks more like a college campus than a hospital."

"Harby, you've been there, haven't you?"

"Where's that?"

"Carville."

"No, I've never been there. Several of my colleagues have though. Why?"

Colleagues, Jack thought. Harby Soulé the urologist has colleagues . . .

"Jack was just asking."

"Yeah, if he wants to go there," Harby said. "I can't imagine why, but I suppose I could arrange it."

The phone rang in the house. Raejeanne got up, left the porch.

"I think Jack's already been there," Maureen said. "You had to pick up a body?"

Jack said, "Yeah, last Sunday." Wanting to tell them, *But she was alive.* See, there's a Nicaraguan guy who wants to kill her, so we sneaked her out in a hearse and got stopped by another Nicaraguan who's really Cuban and a Miskito Indian who later on shot that guy you might've read about at Ralph & Kacoo's, thinking he's up here fighting the war that these guys are raising money so they can keep it going and we're trying to steal. Jesus Christ. Try to tell them even a little bit of that, just the first part . . .

His mom said, "I don't recall that boat ever sunk. That was such a nice boat. You use to sail it all over the bay, didn't you? You and Maureen."

Raejeanne appeared in the doorway. "That was Leo. He said go on and eat, he won't be able to make it till later on." She said, "Mama, you want to help me in the kitchen?"

Maureen wiggled to get up. "Tell me what I can do."

Jack watched her take his mother's arm, the three women going off to cook.

"Raejeanne, what'd Leo say?"

She turned to look at him. "I just told you. I guess a body came in."

"He had one come in this morning."

"Well, I guess he got another one. I hate to say it, but I hope so. We need new drapes desperately." She started to turn and looked back at him. "Hey, how come you're not helping him?"

"It's my day off."

259

She said, walking out, "Poor Leo, alone with his dead while we're having fun."

Jack stood up. He felt an urge to leave, right now, and looked at Cullen.

Cullen, arms on his knees, was leaning toward Harby Soulé. "You don't see the cordee much anymore, do you?"

Harby said, "The what?"

"The cordee. It's when your dick curls up in a knot. They say there's only one way to bust it loose. Guy told me one time he had it. He said what you do, the best way was to lay your dick on a windowsill, close your eyes, and slam the goddamn window on it. Guy said it hurts like a son of a bitch, but it's the only way to break it loose once you have that cordee."

Harby said, "I never *heard* of such a thing."

Cullen said, "No, it's a fact, you don't hear about it so much anymore. The guy that told me, it was when we were in the service during WW Two. But I don't know anybody at Angola had it and there was a bunch of guys there. I suppose they have drugs now do the job. They have drugs for near everything, they must have something for the cordee. I wonder if—no, they couldn't. I was wondering if women ever got some form of it. You treat women too, don't you?"

Harby said, "Well, of course I do."

"Boy, you must see a lot of pussy, huh? You won't believe it when I tell you I haven't seen the old hair pie in twenty-seven years. I'm ready, it's just—I 'magine you heard the saying that if you don't use it you lose it?"

The way Jack saw Harby, he looked like a man who'd been embalmed and they forgot to close his eyes and glue his mouth shut.

Cullen was telling him, see, he was about to get back into action after all these years, a friend was fixing him up; but now his prostrate was giving him trouble and he wondered if before they sat down to their dinner the doctor would check it out for him . . .

Jack, walking into the house with his glass, heard Cullen say, ". . . give it the old finger wave," but didn't hear what Harby thought about it. Jack was in the hall now that ran through the middle of the house. He stopped as Maureen came out of a bedroom, Maureen looking up as she snapped her white purse closed. It was dim and quiet here.

"How've you been, Maureen?"

"Fine." Perking up as she said it, throwing her shoulders back. She had fixed her makeup, done something to her eyes.

"You look great."

"Well, thank you."

"You haven't changed one bit."

"Really? Well, I have to confess we work at it. Harby and I jog four miles every morning, rain or shine, before he goes to Oschner."

"You and Harby? . . ."

"And we watch what we eat. You know, stay away from all those rich sauces. It's a kick, I've had to learn how to cook all over again. I don't dare use a roux. If you can imagine that, a New Orleans girl."

"It must be hard."

"We don't dare eat a bit of red meat, either. No more grillades, spaghetti and meatballs . . ." She gave him a faint smile. "You look good, Jack. Life treating you okay?"

He hesitated. "Yeah, I think it is." He caught a glimpse of Maureen and Harby in bed together, serious, doing it by the number, one two, one two . . .

Maureen wrinkled her nose, staring at him. "What're you smiling about?"

"I don't know. I guess I just feel like it."

"You haven't changed one bit yourself, you know it? You still seem kind a, well, *different.* If that's the word."

He said, "It's as good as any," still smiling a little.

They had evening sun in their eyes coming off the freeway. Cullen said, "The days are getting longer, but I'm not getting any younger. I hope to hell Roy lined me up with something."

Jack said, "You know the kind of women he knows?"

"You betcha I do."

"You could catch something awful."

"Who cares."

"Have to go see Harby. Did he check your prostate?"

"He said I'd have to come by his office with thirty-five dollars."

"Wait and have him check you for both things."

"Do you want me to tell you what I give a shit about at age sixty-five," Cullen said, "and what I don't give a shit about?"

Lucy had come out of the sun parlor to the edge of the flagstone patio. Wearing black again today. Her new habit, Jack thought, the revolutionary new Lucy playing her part; his gaze held on her slim figure, her hands shoved flat into the pockets of her jeans. He followed Cullen along a brick walk through the backyard garden, through branches and flower stems grown lush from spring rains. In the tall cover of the trees the patio appeared in dim detail, Lucy's face pale in the fading light, composed.

She said, "Roy called, twice. They went to five banks today and came out of each one with a canvas sack."

Cullen made a sound that was like a groan.

Jack heard it, still watching Lucy as they reached the steps of the patio. He saw she was tense, holding on, the hands in the pockets no more than a pose.

"Where are they now?"

"They went back to the hotel. He just called again a few minutes ago. He said they put the car in the Royal Sonesta garage, across the street . . ."

"The new one?"

"Yeah, they got it. A cream-colored Mercedes sedan. The 560 SEL, top of the line."

"I guess they can afford it."

"Roy said they took the bank sacks up to 501, ordered champagne, and have been there ever since. He'll call again in about an hour. He said, 'To report in.' "

"Where is he?"

"He's *there*. He got a room at the hotel, on the same floor as the colonel's. . . . How do you suppose he managed that?"

"I don't know," Jack said. "Maybe he was lucky. You never know about Roy, what he's gonna come up with. That's why we have him and hold him dear to our hearts."

Lucy didn't change her expression or say anything. Finally she turned and they followed her into the house.

TWENTY-ONE

Dagoberto Godoy and Crispin Reyna drank champagne with their shrimp and spoke to each other in Spanish, ignoring the CIA man, Wally Scales. They were commenting on the Ferdinand Marcos home movies showing on the television news. In this one, at a party, his wife, Imelda, was singing "Feelings" to the dictator as he bit into a slice of pizza. "He doesn't even stop eating," Dagoberto said, "while the cow sings. I hear she left thousands of dresses and pairs of shoes . . ." Crispin said, "He stole billions of dollars, maybe more." Dagoberto said, "Listen to me. She had so many pairs of shoes she could wear different ones every day for eight years without wearing the same pair twice. She had five hundred bras to hold up her great breasts, most of them black. Look," he said then, "there's Bong Bong, the son of Marcos, the one singing now. I think he's a queer." Crispin said, "That's George Hamilton singing." And Dagoberto said, "No, not him. The other one, with his face painted, the queer." Crispin said, "That fucking Marcos, he had big balls for a little gook." Dagoberto said, "He knew how to live. I hear he had more women than Somoza. Well, of course, being married to that cow. But, man, he knew how to live. Look at that." Crispin said, "Yes, and now he pisses in a machine for his kidneys." Dagoberto said, "You pay in the end sometimes. You have nothing to say about it, what happens to you. But until the end . . . Man, he knew how to live." Dagoberto took a drink of champagne with shrimp in his mouth, then looked across the room and said, "Please, Wally, have something to eat with us, our last evening."

Wally Scales stood looking at the television screen. He turned, shaking his head, and adjusted his glasses as he came over to the room-service table. He picked a shrimp from the platter resting in a bed of cracked ice.

"We possibly could've save Ferdinand's ass, but the man's time was up. Even the president had to swallow hard and admit it. But that fucking slope knew how to live, didn't he?"

"I was saying to Crispin," Dagoberto said, "yes, is fine to enjoy yourself if your people aren' starving. But to take what he did, all that money, and put it in this country is a shameful thing to do. Here . . . " He pulled a bottle of champagne from the bucket stand next to his chair and poured Wally Scales a glass. "I look at this table I think, yes, here I am also enjoying myself. Ah, but there is a difference. It could be my last meal of this kind. In a few days I'm in the mountains again eating C rations, fighting for freedom." He raised his glass. "Who knows but this could be the last champagne I drink in my life."

"You better have a few more then," Wally Scales said. "Do it up good your last night. Hey, but don't forget to pay your bill when you leave." He looked at the five canvas bank sacks lying on the sofa, three of them full, two folded empty. "What'd you say you scored, two and a half million?"

"No, Wally, two million, one hundred sixty-four thousand," Dagoberto said. "Enough maybe to buy one gunship. Unless we get one for half price. You know we offering Sandino pilots a million dollars to bring us an Mi-24."

"And you understand why you haven't had any takers, don't you? They know they'll get shot in the head."

"No, no, we wouldn' do that, Wally."

"I know where you could get about a half million M-16s cheap. The Filipina army, they got all kinds of weapon systems and shit." Wally Scales finished his champagne and looked at the bank sacks again. "You think it's safe to leave it there all night?"

"We're going to guard it," Dagoberto said, "with our lives." He raised the champagne bottle, offering it.

Wally Scales put his glass on the table. "Uh-unh, I have to go. But you're gonna call me tomorrow from Gulfport, right? Before you get on the boat. Call me on my secure line and then eat the piece of paper with the number on it." Wally Scales watched the colonel's expression change to a dumb stare and said, "I'm kidding, Bertie; little spook humor. Everybody knows what we're doing. Some of the local Nicaraguans, I might add, are pissed off you didn't call them to help out."

Dagoberto leaned his head toward Crispin. "I use who

I trust. Sure, there people here I use to know, but people can change their mind. Crispin, I know his family, I know is loyal."

"You trust Franklin?"

"Yes, of course. He does what we tell him."

"Well, he isn't too sure about you guys, the way you're acting."

"What, he told you this?"

"He said all you talk about is Miami, what a great town it is, full of blond-haired quiff."

"Franklin said that?"

"I'll tell you fellas two things. One, you got somebody watching you, boy I took a keen interest in and loves me like his white brother. You understand the implication there? Boy is dedicated, eats his rais and bins during the trabil and never complains. Two, I think you should know Franklin's lonely. I think the only reason he's got a hard-on for you guys is because you don't talk to him enough. You dig? Invite him up and give him some drinks, for Christ sake, it isn't your money. What do you say?"

Dagoberto shrugged. "Of course. Why not?"

Wally Scales started to turn, looked over at the television set, and paused. "You know what I think was most interesting about this whole Filipina show? I mean about the way they threw Marcos out? I thought of it yesterday when I was reading about that guy Jerry Boylan getting murdered in the Men's room—I mean assassinated; excuse me. Way back when his people, the Irish Republican Army, rebelled against the Brits in 1916—the Rising, they call it —they stormed and took the post office in Dublin. But when the Filipinas revolted against Marcos, what'd they take? The fucking TV station. Times have changed, gentlemen; we live in an age of instant electronic intelligence. If the video camera doesn't get you the computer will."

Now the Nicaraguan colonel and the Cuban Nicaraguan from Miami were again speaking in Spanish and drinking champagne but only picking at the shrimp. Dagoberto frowned at the television screen. He thought for a moment they were showing more home movies from the Malacanang Palace, but it was "Wheel of Fortune" that was on now.

Crispin said, "You think Franklin tells him things?"

"I think Wally made it up," Dagoberto said, "so we'll think the CIA is watching us. I should have told him it was an insult. I should have been offended, perhaps gone into a rage."

"Forget it," Crispin said. "Today in the newspaper a man writing about aid to the *contras* asked the question, will it go to anti-Communist patriots or to bank accounts in Miami? I say don't protest, give them something to think about."

"Tomorrow, I'll tell him I was insulted."

"You have only one thing to tell Wally tomorrow. 'I've been robbed!' With feeling. Practice it. 'The son of a whore took all the money!' Like that."

Dagoberto was thinking, staring at the window that framed in faint evening light a balcony of the Royal Sonesta Hotel across the street. "Tomorrow, Nacio will pick up a ticket at the airport issued in the name of Franklin de Dios." Thinking aloud now. "At 9:10 A.M. he boards the flight to Atlanta. There, he changes flights to go to Miami."

"Nacio doesn't resemble Franklin in the least."

"It's all right. Nacio calls us from Atlanta when he's certain the Miami flight is leaving. Just before."

"As long as you can trust him."

"Nacio was in the Guard, my aide until 1979, when he came here. He asks no questions. . . . All right. Franklin goes to the airport tomorrow at the same time to return the automobile . . ."

"He doesn't know Nacio," Crispin said, "if he were to see him?"

"There is no possibility they could know each other. Nacio is from Managua. All right. Franklin comes back to the hotel in a taxi and we leave in the new Mercedes. Yes," Dagoberto said, "yes, before Franklin goes to the airport I could call Wally and tell him he insulted me."

"You're crazy if you don't forget it," Crispin said. He was relaxed, his leg over the arm of his chair. "Listen, the only thing you tell him, Franklin was in this room guarding the money during the time we went downstairs for breakfast. We came back and he was gone and the money was gone. And the automobile, the Chrysler."

"I don't tell him Franklin returned it to the rental company at the airport."

"Mother of God," Crispin said. "You don't mention the airport, you say he took the money and the Chrysler, the trusted friend of the CIA man, it's marvelous, and we're going now to look for him."

"Wally will ask me where."

"You don't know where—you're frantic, man, excited. Now you're in your rage. You tell Wally you'll call him back."

"What if he alerts the police?"

"Let them look, too, we don't care. Then by the time you call him back, we will know your man Nacio has left Atlanta, uh? Almost to Miami. You tell Wally you called several airlines, but they wouldn't give you information about a Franklin de Dios, so you *demand* that he finds out and you'll call him later."

"A third time."

"Yes, you're very anxious."

"Where do I call from?"

"Wherever we are, I don't know. We've left here. I suppose we're in the state of Mississippi."

"I call him after we kill the Indian."

"Of course, after."

"All right, I call Wally the third time . . ."

"And he tells you Franklin went to Miami."

"What if he doesn't know it yet?"

"He will, don't worry. You say we're going there immediately, and hang up the telephone. Simple? That's all you have to do."

"Yes, but go back. We've killed the Indian—where did we hide his body?"

"Something new for you," Crispin said. "The way you do it, you leave the bodies."

"I want to know where."

"We'll see the place. In Mississippi, in a forest."

"I don't want blood in the car."

"If it becomes soiled, buy a new one."

"Man, it cost almost sixty thousand."

Crispin raised his glass, sipped champagne, letting a quiet settle.

"What is it about killing this one that sticks in your mind?"

"I don't care about the Indian. He means nothing to me."

"Then why are you annoyed?"

"I'm a soldier. This isn't like fighting in a war."

"Well, you won't be a soldier for long," Crispin said,

and then smiled. "You can look at this as beginning to learn a new business."

Dagoberto was silent for several moments.

"We'll need a shovel."

"For what?"

"To bury the Indian."

"We bury only his hands and his head. We don't need a shovel for that."

"We'll need an axe."

"We'll get one."

"Or a machete."

"I think the axe will be easier to find."

"That fucking Indian, reporting on us."

"You said you thought Wally made it up."

"Some of it. But I know that fucking Indian has been reporting on us. It's shameful, isn't it, that we can't trust anyone?"

Wally Scales came out of the hotel and walked straight across Bienville to Franklin de Dios, standing by the black Chrysler in his mod black suit, shirt buttoned but no tie: the Indian chauffeur, brought out of the wilds of the Rio Coco by way of Miami to a street in the French Quarter. Man, oh, man—and you'll never know, Wally Scales thought, what's in his head.

"Why don't we have us a farewell drink, amigo?"

"I have to be here."

"They may have company in, but I doubt they'll be going out on the town, all that loot there."

"They say I have to stay outside."

"Use the back door, huh? And wipe your feet."

"What?"

"Nothing. I'm just talking. You suppose to stay here all night?"

"They say to keep watch, that's all."

"For what?"

"I don't know what."

"They don't seem worried about anything, that I noticed. They seem worried to you?"

"They see only themselves."

There, just for a second, the Indian starting to show himself.

"Anything you want to tell me, Franklin?"

Wally Scales noticed a slight hesitation before the Indian shook his head.

"No strange or unusual occurrences? . . . Where'd you go today?"

"Follow the woman's car."

"Yeah? Where'd she go, anyplace special?"

"Just around."

"You can tell me anything you want, my friend, that might be bothering you." Wally Scales gave him time to unburden, but got nothing for it. He said in a quiet, confessional tone, "I imagine it was you had to take out that guy in the restaurant. In the Men's room."

Franklin said nothing.

"I'm sorry you had to do that. You understand he was a very dangerous individual. He would've tried to steal your money, I'm confident of that, and kill anybody in his way. We know for a fact he was in Managua. . . . Well, anyway . . . Okay, so you're all set? Ready for your ride on the banana boat?"

"I think it's time to go back now, yes. See my family."

"And fight your war?"

Franklin moved his shoulders in what might be a shrug, the man back inside himself.

"You want to stay, I can fix it."

"I want to go home."

"If that's what you want, Franklin, you can have it. You can have the goddamn bats flying in the window, the malaria, hepatitis, diarrhea—Somoza's revenge, the son of a bitch—and the bugs. All the bugs known to man and some more. I never saw bugs like that anywhere in my life. They're more like fucking animals than bugs. Two years I spent down there, my friend, and I ain't ever going back. Not for pay or at gun point. I listen to those two freedom fighters upstairs saying they could be eating their last three-hundred-dollar meal, it breaks my heart. The colonel talking out of both sides of his mouth . . ."

Wally Scales looked toward Bourbon Street at the passage of tourists, stared for several moments before his thoughts came back, and he said, "I'll tell you something, Franklin, since it isn't likely we'll ever meet again. I speak fairly good Spanish and can even understand most of what I hear, but I never let on. Act dumb and listen and you learn things. I hear the colonel, for instance, saying one thing in Español and something entirely different in English. Even his tone, going from one to the other, gives him away and he doesn't even realize it. I failed to learn any deep secrets, but I recognize the man's greed and I'll tell you straight, keep your eyes open. If they haven't included you in their conversation there might be more to it than common snobbery. The way those two cowboys enjoy the good life it's hard to imagine them ever again taking a dump in the woods. They're just liable to leave you standing on a street corner and disappear. If the dirty bastards ditch you, call me. I'm gonna give you a number in Hilton Head—that's in South Carolina. See, I can have you picked up and some-how get you back home. That's a promise. Or, on the other hand, they take you along, say back to Miami or someplace like that? Key Biscayne? I'd appreciate your letting me in on that, too. I don't give a shit about the money they scrounged—they didn't exactly get it from widows and or-phans. But I'd hate to think I've been used. Is that a deal? You'll call me?"

Franklin nodded.

"Did they show it to you, the money?"

Franklin shook his head.

"Five bank sacks up there—three of them, they say, full of American dollars." Wally Scales put on a frown and adjusted his glasses. "Wait a minute—are they dumb? I doubt they know the capital of Nebraska, but they're not foolhardy, are they? Leave two million bucks lying on the couch and go to bed? . . . If you were the colonel, Franklin, how would you safeguard it?"

"If I didn't sit on it," Franklin said, "with my gun?"

"Yeah, what's a better way?"

"Hide it?"

"I suppose you could, but where?"

Wally Scales let him think about it.

"Franklin, remember how we taught you how to rig a grenade? You open a door or a window shutter and *kapow.* . . . I believe the colonel neutralized a priest one time with such a device. Priest opened the trunk of his car and went to his reward. You know why I'm telling you this? Should you get curious, my friend, and since those two don't tell you anything, be damn careful what you open. You under-stand? Nod your head."

Franklin nodded.

"They tell me they have over two million bucks. How

275

many cordobas is that? Add a few zeroes and trade it on the black, shit, that'd buy you some bins and fried plantains, wouldn't it? If it wasn't going for weapons and ammo."

The Indian didn't blink or say a word.

"But that's where we are, Franklin, in the business of making silent war." Wally Scales glanced toward the corner again, hearing faint Dixieland now from somewhere on Bourbon Street. Looking at Franklin again, he said in his quieter tone, "I'm gonna tell you something else. For your ears only, okay? . . . I'm getting out of this fucking job. The man who hired me and worked his way up to deputy director, the highest-ranking pro in the company, handed in his resignation. He quit, fed up to his eyeballs with this kind of shit, and that's exactly what I'm gonna do. You know why?"

He waited for Franklin de Dios, staring at him with his dark and solemn Indian eyes, to shake his head.

" 'Cause no matter what we do or who we use, we're always so fucking right. You know what I'm saying?"

"You're tired of it," the Indian said.

"Oh, man, am I."

TWENTY-TWO

Lucy told him she lived all her life in this house until she went away and that it was wallpapered and redecorated every few years but always looked the same, except for the sun parlor. She said if you didn't go in the sun parlor it would be possible to live in this house through several generations and never change your attitude. She said you had to be careful living in New Orleans, in this climate, not to let moss grow on you; though it wasn't just the humidity that might do you in. She said she had no idea what her mother thought about; maybe she'd ask her sometime, approach her as a corporal work of mercy. She said for some reason she was beginning to understand her father more and see him for the first time as a man and not simply as her dad.

They stood in the main hall, in the doorway of the dark formal living room.

"I began to realize I don't know much at all about men. I've never imagined being one."

"I've never imagined being a girl," Jack said. He paused a moment and said, "No, I don't think it's possible."

"You don't seem aware of yourself."

"Well, I catch myself posing every once in a while."

"You're aware of it when you're not being yourself."

"I'm not sure what we're talking about."

"The only men I knew, until I went away, were the boys I knew and some of their fathers. All the boys drank a lot and had a sense of tragedy about them that was theatrical, overdone, when I think about it now. I suppose they wanted attention. They didn't have anything to be tragic about, so they got drunk and took having a good time very seriously. I didn't learn anything from them. I knew boys or fathers, but I didn't know men. Do you know what I mean? I didn't think of men, other than to lump them all together, until I met you and then began to watch you with Roy and Cullen. I've never been this close to men before, to see them distinctly *being* men."

"You've been watching me?"

"Yeah . . . I have. You know a lot of women, don't you? I'll bet you always have. The one you went to talk to in the restaurant . . . That was Helene, wasn't it?"

"How did you know?"

"You told me she had red hair."

"It's different though, than when I used to see her. I mean her hair. It's curly now. She had a perm."

"I noticed her when she came in, the way she looked

278

at you. . . . You told her about what we're doing, didn't you?"

"I had to tell her something, after she helped us out."

"Did you spend the night with her?"

He said, "As a matter of fact . . ." He said, "Yeah, I did. But we didn't do anything." Jesus Christ. He heard himself and couldn't believe it. Making himself sound guilty—with all the things he could have said.

"Do you trust her?"

"Yeah, I trust her, sure. I wouldn't have told her."

"Did you want her opinion? Was that it?"

"Well, maybe. I don't know."

"Do you want to get out of this? You can. All you have to do is leave. You certainly don't owe me anything."

"I'm here," Jack said.

She waited, looking up at him. "Are you?"

He put his hands on the curve of her shoulders and kissed her, her lips soft and slightly parted.

She said, "Are you here?"

She waited and he kissed her again because he wanted to, looking at her delicate face, the dark room behind her, and because he didn't know what to say.

She said, "What does it mean?"

"You analyze everything."

"Do you want to go to bed with me? Do you want to make love to me?"

He said, "Wait. Do you mean, have I been thinking about it? Or do you mean, let's go?"

Lucy smiled. "I always thought you had to be very serious about it. Swept away by desire."

"Yeah, you can do that. The whole idea . . . See, you have to like yourself first. If you do, then you're all set. You don't have to be serious, it can be a lot of fun."

"I've never made love to anyone."

He said, "Is that right?" And wanted to take it back; he shouldn't sound amazed. He said, "Well, no, I wouldn't think you would've. With your vow of chastity, of course not."

"I'd never really thought of it much."

"No, you were staying pure. . . ." He said, "But you've been thinking about it lately?"

"The first time," Lucy said, "do you know when it was?"

"Tell me."

"In the bedroom the other night, when I sat on the side of your bed. I thought about it after and wondered if that was why I came to you, because I wanted it to happen."

"I thought you just wanted to talk."

"I did. But while I was sitting there I was so aware that we were alone in a dark bedroom. I realized, this is what it's like to become intimate. This is the beginning of it and I loved the feeling. I wanted you to touch me, but I was scared to death."

"Well, listen . . . "

"I learned something about myself I never knew before."

"Boy, you come out of the nuns you come flying."

She was smiling at him again. She said, "I'll never forget you, Jack. You remind me so much of him . . . "

He knew who she meant. Not the other day when she said it, but he did now—just looking at her face, her smile, and feeling the goosebumps up the back of his neck.

She said, "Before he took all his clothes off and they called him *pazzo* and threw rocks at him. *That* Francis of Assisi. I'll bet he was just like you."

* * *

Roy called at five to ten. Lucy spoke to him for a minute and then handed the phone to Jack, her eyes wary as she said, "He's at the hotel," and continued to watch him as he took the receiver.

"Roy?"

"Listen, I'm almost directly across the courtyard from the guy's room. I sit in the dark with the door open a speck I'm looking at the elevator and can almost see 501. They put their new car in the garage across the street, carried five bank sacks into the room, and they been in there ever since. Little One's been going in and out—he says they've drunk three bottles of champagne and now they're working on cognac and talking about girls. If you could get what's her name, Helene, to bring 'em out for two minutes we could have this done."

"No, there's no way—"

"Knock on their door bare-ass and when they open it she runs over here and we take 'em."

"She's not in this."

He glanced at Lucy watching him as he heard Roy say, "Well, shit, everybody else is but her and she's done a lot more than most." They were in the sun parlor; Cullen across the room in his favorite chair, looking this way over the top of a magazine.

"Jack, is that Roy?"

Jack nodded and said into the phone, "What about the Indian?" As Cullen was saying, "I want to talk to him."

"He was downstairs a while," Roy said, "but he must've put the Chrysler away. Last time I checked, it was gone."

"He followed us to Gulfport."

"Yeah, what happened?"

"Nothing, I lost him."

"Well, what'd you find out?"

"Alvin Cromwell's got a banana boat lined up. He thinks he's going with 'em, tomorrow."

"Well, you did good, didn't you?"

"So they'll stay put tonight. . . . Roy, you drinking?"

"I had a couple. How'd you tell?"

"You aren't bitching about anything."

"Hey, well, listen. You don't like my first idea, I got another one. Little One goes in to bring 'em something or clear their mess, we go in with him. Shit, all four of us could hide behind Little One."

"Roy, I went into the presidential suite of a hotel one time—I'd been trailing this couple around for five nights and they were loaded, the woman with a different set of jewelry every time I saw her. She was advertising herself. Look at me, you all, how rich I am. I went in their suite and you know what I found?"

"You're making some point," Roy said, "but I don't see it yet."

"I found nothing. She kept her jewelry in a hotel safe deposit box. The guy even put his cash in there. The moral is, when you see one that's too good to be true, it ain't."

"Jack, you can't get five bank sacks in a deposit box or even the hotel safe."

"Did you look in the sacks, Roy?"

"All right, where would they hide it?"

"I don't know, but when they advertise it, come parading in with the sacks, you know it isn't in the room. We march in behind Little One and we don't find anything, then what? It's over with. We walk away, the cops pick up Little One, look at his printout, make him a deal, and we're back at the farm. Be there in time to plant soybeans."

Roy said, "I want to know where they could hide it."

"We wait till the morning," Jack said, "we'll find out. Don't use Little One for anything, okay? The man's clean and wants to stay that way."

Roy said, "You're no fun. Shit. Listen, send Cully to spell me and then you and Lucy come sometime after midnight, with both your cars. So we'll be ready at peep of day. Tell the guy at the desk we're having a party up here, 509. Shit, we may as well."

As soon as Jack hung up the phone Lucy said, "Who did you mean, 'She's not in this?' Me?"

"He was talking about Helene, using her again as bait."

"And you didn't like the idea?"

Cullen said, from across the room, "I wanted to talk to him."

Jack glanced over. "I'm gonna drive you down there, right now."

Lucy said, "If you've told her everything and you did use her, isn't she in it?"

"She did it as a favor, that's all. I'm gonna take Cully and then stop off at Mullen's and change my clothes. How 'bout I'll meet you at the hotel in a couple hours? Park in the underground garage, right across the street."

"Will she do anything you ask?"

He looked at her face raised to his, waiting, and said, "What do you want to know, Lucy? What she would do for me or what I might ask her to?"

The body Leo had prepared that morning occupied a moderately priced Batesville in one of the smaller visitation rooms. Jack studied the man's face in lamplight, surprised at his ruddy complexion and the way the man's sparse gray hair was combed down on his forehead like a Roman senator and fixed there. This was not Leo's work.

But Leo should be here. Or someone from the security service. Jack looked in the other visitation rooms. Rae-jeanne had said Leo must've received another body; otherwise why was he going to be late for dinner? It seemed, though, the man in the visitation room was the only customer. Unless the second arrival was up in the prep room and Leo was in his office. Jack had come in the side entrance. He could check, see if Leo's car was in back. Or he could run upstairs and look. He was going up anyway. Somebody was here. Jack knew that. There had to be. What he didn't understand was why, after having lived in this funeral home the past three years, he felt an urge to look over his shoulder. To turn around, quick.

The security man would be right here in the hall or in the small reception office, his thermos of coffee on the desk. But since he wasn't . . .

Jack went up the stairs, reached the dark hallway, and stopped when he heard the sound. Like a door closing quietly, with a faint *click.* The double doors to the prep room were closed. So were the doors to the casket selection room. He thought of the Beretta he'd lifted from Crispin Reyna, beneath the front seat of his car, and the colonel's Beretta, Jesus, that he'd had in his hand and put back in the drawer with the Indian in the bathroom, vowing never to go into somebody else's room again, ever. He was home now, but it was the same kind of feeling, that he shouldn't be here. Or *some*body shouldn't. He turned on the hall light. It didn't help much.

He'd check the prep room first because that casket selection room—shit, it was too easy to hide in there. He never liked that room. All those crepe-lined empty caskets waiting for people.

He opened the prep room door and jumped and made a sucking-in strangled kind of sound and then said, "Oh, shit," looking at Helene standing there with a put-on surprised expression on her face. Helene in jeans and a UNO sweatshirt, Helene's hair catching the fluorescent light as she stepped out of the dark.

She said, "Hi, Jack. What's wrong?"

"What're you doing here?"

"I'm on this weekend, till Monday."

"You're on *some*thing, I know that. Jesus."

"I don't do drugs anymore, Jack. My body is clean."

"Come on—what're you doing here?"

"What do you think I'm doing here, you jerk? I work here. Monday you'll have to have all your stuff out, 'cause I'm moving in."

"*Leo* hired you?"

"You know he's been looking, since you ran out on him. I did that man downstairs's makeup and he loved it. I mean Leo. He drove me home to get a few things, we came back, he asked me if I'd consider working here, and I said sure, I'll start right this minute."

"Last night you didn't even want to come in here."

"Yeah, well, I got over it. You know, maybe I just *thought* I was afraid. But once you get used to it . . . I saw you drive up, I thought, let's see if old Jack still has it together. You want a drink? Step down to my apartment. It isn't much, but I'm gonna fix it up. Do something with Leo's office, too. Upstairs, this place looks like it's been condemned. Leo said in a year maybe we could start on the downstairs, trade in that crappy furniture. He's nice, isn't he? Jovial."

"He's a peach of a guy. How much is he paying you?"

"I'm afraid that's none of your business. Actually he asked me how much I'd need."

"Leo?"

"I told him I'd let him know. I'll be doing the cosmetics and the hair, too, not just driving."

"Helene, this is no place for a girl like you."

"What kind of girl am I, Jack?"

"Wait'll a bad one comes in, person that was in a horrible wreck. Or you have to go to the morgue, pick up a floater they pulled out of the river, all bloated, eaten by fish . . ."

She said, "Jack, you're gonna make yourself sick. You want a drink or not?"

"I want to take a shower and change my clothes."

"I hope it helps your disposition. God."

Helene followed him to the apartment.

When she came into the bedroom she placed his drink on the dresser and leaned against it and watched him as he got out of his clothes.

"You have two and a half bottles of vodka on ice, but no beer."

"That can happen."

"You still have a nice body, Jack."

"What do you mean, still?"

"You aren't getting any younger, kid."

"I'm sure glad I came."

She said, "After you take your shower, you want to be friends?"

Asking him with a tone that was soft, familiar, the same mood in her eyes, watching him. He dropped his shirt on the bed and walked over to her.

"We're friends now."

"Are we good friends?"

"I think we're better than good friends."

"Do you know how long it's been since we made love?"

"A long time."

"Two thousand, two hundred, and fifteen days . . . give or take."

"No wonder I'm ready."

Close to him she said, "You sure are." She said, "I've missed you, Jack. Boy, have I missed you."

He shaved in a hot shower and washed his hair, turned the water off and came out to the sink, the steamy mirror. They'd have at least an hour. Taking the towel from the rack he opened the door half expecting to see Helene in bed or on it, waiting in some kind of put-on seductive pose, remembering her this morning—just this morning in her thin-strip panties doing her twist exercise, her breasts trying to keep up. . . . She wasn't in the room.

Rubbing his hair with the towel over his face he heard her voice and then heard it again. "Jack." He brought the towel down and was held by her expression, her eyes, with no trace of flirty funny business in them now.

"Someone's downstairs."

"You're sure?"

"I heard glass break."

TWENTY-THREE

Franklin had made up his mind on the way here: don't walk into something the way you walked into that bathroom. Don't announce yourself, either. Go in quick and point the gun at the guy before he knows what's happening.

But it didn't work the way he wanted. He had thought the door would be open because people came in here to see the dead; a woman missing her husband after she'd gone to bed, sure, and would want to be with him again. But the door was locked. So he had to break one of the small panes with the grip of his pistol and then had to hurry, it made so much noise, get to the guy before he knew what was happening and had his own gun in his hand.

Franklin was on the stairs now.

He came to the landing where it turned, looked up,

and there was the guy with his shirt hanging open at the top of the stairs, the light in the ceiling over him. The guy's hair looked wet. Franklin raised his pistol and aimed it at the guy because the guy was holding something in front of him, shining in the light, that looked like a short metal spear. The guy lowered it slowly, seeing he couldn't use it, and dropped it on the floor without being asked and stood with his hands at his side, not raising them.

Franklin said, "You suppose to put your fingers together behind your head."

But the guy didn't do it. The guy held his shirt open at the top of the stairs and said, "Look, I'm clean. I'm your prisoner, okay? But I'm not gonna put my hands behind my head or squat down or any of that shit. You want my shoes? I don't have any on, but if that's the custom I'll give you a pair. Come on." Now the guy was walking away and Franklin had to mount the stairs quick to catch up with him, the guy moving down the hall in front of him saying, "You still think you're in the fucking war? I'm gonna have to straighten you out, Franklin, if I can find out where you're coming from." They were going into the guy's room, where they first talked to each other five days ago. But now there was a woman here with red hair, her eyes open wide—the same woman who had been with the colonel last night at the hotel—and the guy was saying, "Helene, this's Franklin. I think you know each other. Franklin, sit down. We'll have a drink and get a few things straightened out here." The guy opening his refrigerator, but then turning to look at him saying, "Hey, Franklin? But first you have to put away the gun. Okay?"

"They called it the dinner for the freedom fighters, or something like that. It was in Miami, Florida, at a big hotel.

There was people at all the tables in the room and I was at the long table at the front," Franklin said. "First we have the dinner that cost five hundred dollars for each person. I think it was chicken. It was pretty good. Then we listen to speeches. One guy made a talk, he said my name to everybody that I was Miskito Indian fighting for the freedom of my people and everybody there clapped their hands. Then they presented statues of eagles to people who gave a lot of money. Then some of the people, different ones, came and talked to me. One of them, an Indian from the States, said to me don't believe it, is all a lot of shit what they tell you. Rich people came to shake my hand. You know what they said? '*At* a boy.' What does that mean, *at* a boy?"

"It means," Jack said, "what the Indian told you. They're giving you a bunch of shuck with the chicken à la king."

"One rich man said to me he gave twenty-five thousand dollars and wished he could join me in fighting for freedom, but his wife wouldn't let him go. I said to him to bring his woman. She can work with my woman in the camp."

"Atta boy," Jack said.

Helene said, "I don't believe this."

Franklin squinted in a frown, looking from Helene, sitting at the other end of the sofa, to Jack, standing by the refrigerator. "She means it's an amazing story," Jack said. "Go on."

"They had some people there a man said were refugees who escaped from Communist tyranny. He told them to raise their hands and everybody clapped."

"Yeah? Who were they?"

"They were some of the waiters working there."

"They give you a medal or anything?"

"They gave me a new fatigue uniform to wear at the dinner, the kind is different colors. They said it was okay to keep it. They gave me the chicken dinner, but I didn't have to pay five hundred dollars. They gave us ice cream, too."

"They brought you all the way from Nicaragua for a fund-raising dinner?"

"From Honduras. A man from the CIA brought me on the airline. I was suppose to go back, but I didn't. I stayed there." Franklin straightened. He pulled the Beretta out of the waist of his trousers saying, "It hurts, sticks in me when I sit down," and laid the pistol on the sofa between him and Helene.

Jack watched Helene staring at the bluesteel automatic, either fascinated or afraid to move; it was hard to tell. He liked it there, out in the open, the guy getting comfortable. "Take your coat off if you want."

"No, it's okay."

"Guy from the CIA brought you. You mean Wally Scales?"

"No, a different guy." Franklin's eyes open a little wider. "But you know Wally?"

Jack said, "I know him," giving Franklin a little shitty kind of grin, and left him wondering about it while he went into the bedroom. Jack came back with an aluminum-plastic deck chair he'd bought three years ago for $9.95, poured Franklin another vodka, gave Helene a look as he sat down, and felt her watching him. Helene knew him. He crossed his legs and wiggled his bare toes. He'd bet if he looked over at Helene again she'd roll her eyes.

"So you stayed and went to work for Crispin."

"He told me don't go back, he could use a freedom fighter because there was plenty Sandinistas in Miami."

"I heard one time you shot three guys. Or you were in on it."

"How do you know that?"

"Wally Scales knew it, didn't he?" He watched Franklin take a few moments, staring at him.

"Maybe he did. But I think you know more than Wally."

Jack sipped his vodka and let him think it.

"Crispin told me those guys were Sandinistas. He said we have to kill them or they would kill us. But the police told me, no, those guys were from Colombia and were doing drug business with Crispin a long time. They said he was a criminal."

"That's what I heard, too," Jack said. "But you were never in prison . . . "

"Never in my life."

"You shoot people—but that's what you do in war, huh, if you're a soldier?"

"Yes, of course. I told you that before. I come here, I want to know why you didn't kill me that time, but now I understand."

"I'm not in the war."

"Yes, like Wally. He can't shoot nobody either."

"No, they have you. They give you the shit detail and keep their hands clean. But why didn't you tell on me? When you caught me in the colonel's room?"

Franklin looked surprised. "Because you didn't kill me. See, then I know you're not Sandinista. If you aren't, then maybe it's not my business to think about it."

"You tell Wally?"

"If it is his business, he would already know it. If it isn't his business, why would I tell him? I see you more than I see him."

"And what does that tell you, Franklin?"

"I didn't know if you are a funeral guy or the police or what you are. But now, well, okay. You don't work at the same place as Wally but . . . Well, it's okay with me, I understand." He glanced at Helene. "I see her with Colonel Godoy at the hotel I thought she was his friend. But now I see she works for you. Okay, you don't have to tell me nothing." Franklin leaned over to push up from the sofa. "I wonder if I can use your toilet."

"It's in there."

Franklin stood up, walked into the bedroom.

Jack looked at the pistol lying on the sofa. Then at Helene as she said, "Jack? You're scary. You should've been an actor."

"I know it."

"He trusts you."

"I've got him confused, anyway, I know so much about him. He thinks I must be some kind of secret agent."

"He even likes you."

"You serious?"

"Jack, the way those guys treat him, those arrogant little assholes . . . You're probably the only person he knows who even talks to him."

"You think so?"

"They treat him awful."

"He's not a bad guy."

"He seems nice."

"Yeah, you get to know him."

"They're all short, aren't they?"

"He's tough though, you can tell."

"His suit's way too big for him."

"They screw up, he takes the fall."

"The poor guy."

"They use him and then they'll throw him away."

"But you're not, huh?"

"I'm trying to help him."

"Hey, Jack . . . "

"I am."

"He just flushed the john."

"Good, I'm glad he knows how to do that."

"Boy, if anybody should've been an actor."

"You really think so?"

"All the years you wasted, it's a shame."

"I'm doing all right."

When Franklin came back he stopped and looked at his gun lying on the sofa before he sat down. Then looked at Jack and seemed to smile. Jack got up and poured him another vodka.

"Are you a happy guy, Franklin?"

"I feel pretty good."

"Going home tomorrow, huh?"

The way Franklin grinned Jack knew the vodka was working. Sitting down again Jack said, "Let me ask you something, Franklin. Do you understand what the war's about, down in Nicaragua?"

"Sure, we fight Sandinistas."

"Yeah, but do you have a good reason?"

"They the worst kind of people," Franklin said. "They burn our homes, take our land, they kill some of us, and make us go live where we don't want to."

Jack said, "Oh."

There was a silence, Franklin watching him.

Jack said, "Let me ask you something else. You think

the colonel's gonna get on that banana boat tomorrow?
With those bank sacks full of money?"

It caught Franklin with his drink raised, about to take
a sip.

"And with his brand-new cream-colored Mercedes?
You think it's possible?"

Franklin kept watching him, but didn't answer.

"If he can't take it on the boat, you think he's gonna
drive it all the way to Nicaragua? That sixty-thousand-dol-
lar automobile. He isn't gonna leave it. Shit, he just bought
it yesterday."

Franklin said, "I thought it might be Crispin's."

"You did, huh? Then how come it's in the colonel's
name? He bought it, Franklin, that means he owns it.
. . . What'd Wally say about it?"

"Wally said only to call him if they leave me here."

Jack had to give that some thought. He said, "Go on,
take a drink and I'll tell you something else."

He watched Franklin swallow half the vodka in the
glass, make a face, squeeze his eyes closed and open them,
and wipe his hand across his mouth.

"Wally has your best interest at heart and I'm glad to
know that," Jack said. "You're a good guy, Franklin. We
don't want to see you get in trouble. But I think it's best if
you don't wait around."

Franklin cleared his throat. He said, "Leave here?"

Jack bit on his lower lip. "Damn, I wish I could tell you
exactly how I work. I 'magine it's confusing to you, all the
ins and outs of this kind of game. Hey, I even get a little
confused myself sometimes." He sneaked a glance at Helene, his audience, watching him with her mouth slightly
open, not moving a muscle. Jack bit on his lip again.
"Franklin, if I tell you something I shouldn't, will you

promise not to repeat it to anybody, not even to Wally?
. . . You'd have to promise me on your honor."

Franklin was nodding his head.

"Say it."

"Yes, I promise."

"On your honor."

"Yes, on my honor."

"Okay. First, do you know where the money is?"

"Maybe in that hotel room."

"You think so?"

"Maybe."

"Where else could it be? I was thinking maybe the car,
but that wouldn't be as safe as having it in the room, would
it?"

Franklin didn't answer. He seemed to shrug and Jack
wasn't sure if he liked the way the guy was staring at him.

"It doesn't matter. Here's the deal, Franklin. It looks
like the colonel and his buddy are gonna take off for Miami
with the cash. We think tomorrow." Jack gave him a sly
grin. "You kind of suspected that too, huh? Talked it over
with Wally? The possibility? But I'll bet he didn't tell you
what's gonna happen to those two assholes, did he? You
understand I can't give you the details, Franklin, they're
confidential. But I'll tell you this much. If you don't want
to spend the rest of your life in prison, convicted of a
serious crime, then you'll make me another promise, right
now. Will you do that, for your own good?"

Franklin seemed about to nod, ready to, but waited.

"I visited a state prison one time and I'll tell you, they
are no fun," Jack said. "All I'm asking is that you promise
me you'll get on that banana boat tomorrow morning and
go straight home to your family."

Now he was nodding.

"Doesn't that sound good? Get out of this mess and go back home? Man, it sure sounds good to me. I wish you a safe journey, Franklin. . . . "

He was still nodding.

"And God bless you."

Jack kept his reverent gaze squarely on the Miskito Indian. He didn't dare look at Helene.

TWENTY-FOUR

R oy opened the door bare to
the waist, showing Lucy the mat of black hair that covered
his chest. He moved his hand over it in a slow circle as he
said, "Well, I guess we're serious, huh?" He looked past
her toward the Nicaraguan's suite. "You hear anything
when you got off the elevator? Women screaming for
help?"

"Music," Lucy said, "that's all."

"They're still partying. Couple ladies of the evening
joined them a while ago."

Following Roy into 509 she said, "I thought you left
the door open so you could watch."

"What's there to see? They're not going anywhere.
Boy, it makes you wonder—couple of clowns like that sitting on two million bucks. But they're typical; you know it?

Guys that get into crime, most can barely write a note to hand the bank teller. Even the ones that appear fairly intelligent will turn stupid out of desperation. Like those two—I wouldn't be surprised they're telling the whores their business; showing off. That's the type they are. Even to letting 'em see the cash. I still think there's a good chance it's in the room. Hell, if I was the least bit sure, me and you could bust in right now and get it done." Roy walked into the bathroom.

Lucy looked at the double bed, still made but rumpled, the pillows pulled out, parts of a newspaper and a black knit shirt lying on the spread. She was aware of being alone with Roy; she could feel it and was self-conscious standing here in sandals, slacks, and her linen jacket, a straw bag hanging from her shoulder.

Roy faced the washbasin with a can of talcum powder, the bathroom door open. Lucy watched him rub his hands together, then raise them to caress his jaw and throat as he stared at himself in the mirror.

"I thought Cullen was here."

"He stepped out for the evening."

"Can I ask where he went?"

"You can," Roy said, "but you might not think it's nice, what he's doing, and I wouldn't want to tell on him. I hate snitches, even though they have their place."

"You fixed him up?"

"Hey, you don't miss much." Roy looked out from the bathroom. "Wasn't Jack coming with you?"

"He'll be here. He went home to change."

"Everybody getting ready for action," Roy said, rubbing talcum over his body, beneath his arms, as he came out of the bathroom. "Didn't forget your gun, did you?"

Lucy watched him, his chest gray with powder coming toward her. "It's in my bag."

"Lemme have a look at what you got."

She brought out the .38 encased in a tan leather holster, straps wrapped around it and tied. "Be careful, it's loaded."

"You mean," Roy said, "it isn't just for show?" Taking the holster from her, hefting it, he said, "Oh, my Lord, it's a shoulder rig. Just like the TV cops. Where'n the world'd you get this?"

"It's my dad's," Lucy said. "I have to carry the gun on me, don't I?" She felt awkward, again self-conscious, with Roy grinning, unwinding the straps.

"Yeah, this's what all the TV cops use, so you know they're cops and not insurance salesmen. Did you try it on? It's about the most uncomfortable thing you can wear, 'specially when it's hot out." Roy pulled the nickel-plated Smith & Wesson from the holster, released the cylinder, and snapped it back in place. "You ever fire it?"

"I know how it works."

"That's not what I asked you."

"My dad taught me how to shoot."

"When was this? It must've been before you went in the nuns."

"I was in high school."

Roy said, "When you were a little girl and not since, huh? Oh, man, this is some deal, I'm telling you. I'm anxious to see what Jack's gonna wear. You come in your new spring outfit and your shoulder holster, Jack, he's liable to show up in no telling what. Combat boots and bulletproof underwear, his face painted black. You all been watching TV? Meantime Cully's off getting his ashes hauled and doesn't care one way or the other we score or not." Roy dropped the gun and holster on the bed, picked up the black knit shirt, and pulled it over his head and down to his waist, tight, pushing his chest out, unbuttoning and unzipping his pants then as Lucy watched. He said, "Excuse me, but don't look and I won't show you nothing."

She said, "Roy, sometimes you overdo being yourself."

Roy said, "Two days, I can see you've enjoyed about all of me you can stand. Only I'm all you got, if you take a minute and look at it. How I ever got talked into this— I must've been in a weakened condition. Jack comes up to me, he goes, 'You never saw one like this before in your life,' and I'll give him that; nobody has. But you know in your heart you wouldn't stand to cop a dime off those guys if I was to drop out. Like you know you aren't gonna fire that gun in anger or to kill, 'cause aiming at a bull's-eye and a human being are two entirely different things. That's something else you're gonna have to leave to my judgment. I can't see Jack doing it, or Cullen. I doubt either one of them has the stomach. Jack's quick with his hands; oh, he'll pop you before you know it, but he's never used a gun, I'm sure, on another person."

"Have you?"

"Have I ever shot anybody? Twice I had to and they're both dead. But have you any idea what's gonna happen tomorrow?"

"No more than you," Lucy said. "All I know is we're going to do it."

"If you have to throw yourself in front of their car," Roy said. "All right, draw me a picture. They come out of their room tomorrow, go over to the garage, and get in the car, we assume, huh, and drive off. Then what?"

302

"They have two cars," Lucy said. "I think they'll just leave the Chrysler."

"Let's say they do."

"They get in the car and drive off and we follow."

"What about the cash—if it isn't in the room?"

"You said they went to five banks yesterday and came right back to the hotel. If they withdrew the money it's either in their room or still in the car."

Roy said, "*If* they withdrew it. You been thinking, haven't you? But I watched them. They came out of each bank with a full sack. You could tell."

"Or they came out with *some*thing in the sacks," Lucy said, "but not necessarily money. What if it was like a dry run today, to see if it's safe? Nothing happens, they withdraw the money tomorrow and they're on their way."

"That sounds pretty good. You haven't been just saying your beads, have you? All right, then what? Now we're coming to the good part. We follow them . . . "

"And wait for our chance."

"How do we know it when we see it?"

"They'll have to stop sometime."

"Okay, they pull into a rest area to go toy-toy. Or a filling station. We pull up alongside 'em. They see us. The next thing you know that nigger Indin's coming out of the car with his gun. We know he's their shooter, don't we? It's what he *does*. Now, are you gonna let the nigger Indin shoot you, or you gonna pop him first, or would you wait for me to do it, knowing if you wait too long you're dead? Or, you're in your typical shoot-don't-shoot situation requiring split-second judgment. Is that a gun in his hand? *Bam!* No, it was a flashlight, but a man is dead. These are some of the questions you have to ask yourself." Roy walked over to the dresser, scooped loose change into his hand and picked up his wallet. "Are we gonna drive all the way to Miami in pursuit of our dream? We are, then I have to get a bathing suit and some resort wear. How 'bout you?"

"You do like the idea," Lucy said.

Roy took a poplin jacket from the back of the desk chair. "What idea? That's the only thing keeps me in this deal—we don't have enough of a plan to know if it won't work or even to figure the odds. We're feeling our way along, is all. We're still playing—oh, man, isn't this exciting? This is serious stuff. We even got real guns, with real bullets in 'em." Roy slipped his jacket on. "I'm going around the corner and have a drink, pick up a few items we might need, check on Cullen. . . . Oh, and lemme have your car keys. I'll sit in it and watch theirs, just in case—since I'm doing everything anyway. Meantime you and Delaney decide if you can look right at a man and shoot him."

"I've already thought about it," Lucy said.

"Well, then think about him shooting *you.* If this deal's worth it. It isn't to me," Roy said. "I'll tell you right now, the time comes I see it's a no-win deal, I'm out. I am *sure* not gonna die for a bunch of lepers I don't even know."

They were in Darla's studio apartment over an antique shop on Conti. She said, "You know how much that'd cost you? All night and all *day?* I never had an all day."

Cullen said, "I don't care, you name it. You're the cutest thing I ever saw."

"Well, thank you. Usually during the day I relax. Do my hair and my nails . . . "

"You're a little lady of leisure."

"You kidding? I work my ass off in that place. I have to be there tomorrow at six."

"I'll stay till then. We can send out for Chinese, anything you want."

"Roy said—didn't he mention you just got out of prison or someplace?"

"Yeah, but I'd as soon not talk about it, ruin this beautiful evening."

"I meant, but how could you have any money?"

"I worked. I worked in the fields for a nickel an hour. I worked in the auto repair shop, got a raise to seven cents. I worked in the print shop for the same wage. I bought a few necessities, I bought home brew now and again and saved what I could. Twenty-seven years, you little honey, it can add up."

Darla said, "Well, you did pretty good, didn't you?"

"Put on the black stockings again."

"I thought you liked me nekked."

"Just the stockings and the garters, that's all."

"You think that'll do it?"

"I woke up with a hard-on this morning at six thirty-four. It's in there somewhere."

"I hope so, gosh."

"Yeah, it's gonna do it. Hey, anybody comes, don't answer the door."

"Nobody's gonna come."

"They might, you never can tell. Don't answer the phone, either."

"Well, I do get calls, you know. I'm not a hermit."

"You sure aren't. Oh, man, look at that. Come over here and tell me how you got so cute. Huh, how did you?"

"I just am, I guess."

The way Lucy had pictured it until this evening, she would see flashes of action taking place on a country road.

There are no houses within sight, only a scrub pasture, stands of pine, a ditch full of weeds where the two cars have come to a sudden stop, the blue Mercedes angled in front of the cream-colored Mercedes, dust still hanging in the air, in bright sunlight. She stands in the road, somewhat away from the others, and sees the Indian and the one from Miami brought out first, at gunpoint and with gestures, no words spoken. Now these two leave the scene. They're taken aside, disarmed, made to lie in the ditch—all that, whatever has to be done—because she sees herself alone with the colonel immediately after he comes out of the car. She waits as he makes his cautious appearance and looks about, bewildered—he can't believe this is happening— before he sees her standing in the road, alone, watching him. She's wearing her linen jacket over a prewashed denim shirt, slacks, sunglasses, her dad's revolver held at her side. Or with the gun in the holster. No, holding the gun, but not pointing it at him. Their eyes meet. The colonel stares, begins to frown. He doesn't recognize her, because he wouldn't imagine her being here. Only once have they met face to face, at Sagrado Familia when she was wearing khakis and a white scarf over her hair. He frowns harder as he looks at her and says, "Who are you?" Or, he frowns harder as he looks at her and says, "Tell me who you are . . . please." A silence comes over the scene, the dust settled now. She gazes at him without expression, removes her sunglasses, and on this day of retribution says quietly, "The sister of the lepers."

The shoulder holster was the first to go.

Then the conveniently desolate country road.

The holster went back in her straw bag and the road became an interstate highway with traffic in both directions, cars, motor homes, semitrailers. . . . And now the place where it would happen, at a rest area or a service station or the parking lot of a McDonald's, she saw in endless variations of several real places. The important part, facing the *contra* colonel alone, long enough for him to recognize her and realize *she* was doing this to him and why, could still happen. She would somehow have to make it happen; because the confrontation was more important than any other part of it.

But now, trying to see it happen closer to reality in time and place, picturing recognizable objects, signs, Exxon, McDonald's, the image in her mind began to expand, reach beyond the important part, the confrontation.

Sitting in the hotel room she saw the colonel standing by the car. She's delivered her line. She's with Jack and Roy and Cullen as they leave with the money. But now she looks back and sees the colonel still there, standing by his car as they drive off.

Jack watched Lucy walk past the bed to one of the matching armchairs by the window, the curtains pulled closed; watched her sit down and pick up her cigarettes from the low table between the chairs. A lamp on the table showed the room in soft light. Jack took a moment to look at the room. He liked the feel of it, the mood, faint sounds of music coming from outside. He wasn't sure about Lucy, though, changing again, silent at a time when he thought she'd be talkative. He wanted to tell her about Franklin, maybe one less to worry about. He was anxious to tell it, still feeling the vodka. Then wondered about Roy, Jesus, if he'd pulled out, and asked her. She drew on her cigarette, taking her time. She said no, he'll be back . . .

"But what if he did?"

307

"I'd have to give it serious thought," Jack said. "Is that what's bothering you?"

No, something else. She said, "We stop Bertie and take the money. But that isn't necessarily the end of it."

With the quiet delivery—she sounded fine.

Jack said, "You want to know what happens if he pulls a gun and one of us has to shoot him."

She was shaking her head before he finished.

"No. What happens if we *don't* shoot him? If we take the money and leave him standing there?"

"That's even better, isn't it? You don't want to kill the guy . . . do you?"

"But it wouldn't be the end of it."

Jack walked over to the other chair. He sat down and took one of her cigarettes.

"You haven't thought about that?"

"The way I've pictured it," Lucy said, "I skip through details, I see us bringing them out of the car, I see Bertie standing in the road. . . . He realizes what's happening to him. . . . I see it without a beginning or an end. It's the same way I remember photographs of people he tortured and killed and what I actually *saw* when he murdered the lepers. Do you understand what I mean? There's nothing that comes before or after. He kills people or commits acts of terror and leaves. That's the end of it. Nothing happens to him. All right, I see us stop him and take the money. . . . But that *isn't* the end of it. It continues on, and I don't know what he'll do."

Jack took his time. There were a few different ways to approach this.

He said, "Well, what's the first thing you think of? He calls the cops and tells them he's been robbed—if you don't mind my using that word, but that's the way they'd see it and write their report. An armed robbery was committed at such and such a time and place . . . "

"But it *isn't.*"

"If you don't get caught you can call it anything you want. But this game's like any other, you have to play by the rules. An honest criminal, if he's caught and convicted, will abide by the fact he's broken the law and is gonna do time. I've learned that's how you get through life without punching walls and hurting yourself; you abide by the facts of the situation, whatever it is. Didn't you know that? I thought you might've come across it in nun training. I knew a very successful burglar in the joint, a safecracker, he even paid his lawyer in advance, kept him on a retainer."

Lucy listened, but it seemed with some effort. She said right away, "I'm not going to argue with you about law. We're not criminals."

Jack said, "I don't like to think so either. In fact I'm convinced we're on the side of the angels, at least the avenging ones. But if we're ever brought up, don't be surprised if it's in criminal court. I suppose there could be a question of jurisdiction, depending on where it happens. We take these guys off in Mississippi and come back to New Orleans with the cash, that could make it federal, crossing a state line to commit a felony. I don't know, but what's the difference, we'd still say, 'What money? What're you talking about?' Whoever happens to ask. I accept the possibility of getting busted without giving it much thought, and not just 'cause it makes me break out in a cold sweat."

Lucy said, "Because you don't think it will happen."

"That's right, and you know why?"

"Because it's possible he won't call the police."

Jack smiled at her. "There you are. One reason being, he might be dead. The other, how does he explain what he's doing way out on the highway with the two million bucks? He's suppose to be leaving Gulfport on a banana boat. What does he tell his CIA pal, Wally Scales? Well, maybe he says he changed his mind, decided to ship out of Miami instead. Whether the CIA guy believes him or not is something else. But once you get into that area, another question comes up. If Bertie's gonna keep the money for himself, what does he say happened to it? Unless he plans to disappear."

Lucy was shaking her head. "He has an image of himself, he wears medals. The man likes to be seen."

"That's the impression I have. So he'd have to fake something and come up with a story, how he was ripped off. Sandinistas in New Orleans or some other guys, like Jerry Boylan. He stops somewhere this side of Gulfport, shoots a few holes in his new car, and calls Wally. . . . I don't know. I think he'd have to do something like that. Only now, if he actually does get ripped off and it's somewhere *past* Gulfport, he'd have to give it serious thought before he calls Wally. On the other hand, if for some reason he does recognize us, I think the only person he'd call would be you. Then we'd have a problem."

Lucy said, "Wait a minute. Why *wouldn't* he recognize us? He knows who we are."

"Yeah, but he won't really see us. You know that book you loaned me, *Nicaragua*, with the pictures of the young hotshot Sandinistas in their baseball caps and sport shirts? They're all wearing masks, bandanas, or scarves over their faces with eye holes. If you don't want to be identified, and we definitely do not, then that's what you have to do."

Lucy said, "But I *want* him to see me. That's part of it."

"Why would you?"

"He has to realize, he isn't simply being *robbed*, that it's an act of retribution."

"If we cover our faces," Jack said, "it's a stickup. If we don't, it's something else and we're the good guys."

She said, "Look, you can do whatever you want. But he has to know who I am. If he doesn't, I'll tell him."

"How come you never mentioned this before?"

"I thought it was understood."

"You tell Roy?"

"Did we talk about it? No."

"Roy was gonna look for Mardi Gras masks. He likes the idea of black faces, so the colonel'd think we're colored guys."

She said, "Jack, I'm very serious about this. It's important to me."

"Well, it's up to you. But if you tell Roy, I'm pretty sure he'll walk out."

"Why?"

"Come on—what've we been talking about? You *could* get picked up, the only one he identifies. The first question the cops ask is who was with you. Then they tell you what kind of a sentence you're looking at at some women's correctional. Then they lighten up, offer you a deal, and ask you again who was with you."

"You think I'd tell?"

"Roy wouldn't take the chance."

"I'm asking *you*," Lucy said. "Do you think I'd tell?"

"We had all week to talk about it. Now all of a sudden . . . it's a different kind of thing."

She said, "Jack? Do you think I'd tell?"

She stared at him, waiting, and he said, "I think they could pull your fingernails out, you wouldn't say a word. But you'd have to convince Roy."

311

"*If* it should happen," Lucy said. "But if you trust me, isn't that enough?"

Putting him on the spot—sitting here with a blue bandana in his coat pocket and a Beretta automatic shoved into his waist, ready to go. He said, "Maybe it is." They were this far. He said, "Do you know how you're gonna get the money down there?"

"Through the motherhouse," Lucy said. "Transfer it to the bank in León, where the sisters have an account."

"Are you going back?"

"To Nicaragua? I'm thinking about it."

"I didn't mean back in the order."

"I'm not sure what I am, but I'm no longer a Sister of Saint Francis . . . "

"Of the Stigmata," Jack said.

She seemed to smile, remembering. "When I was nineteen I'd say the word *stigmata,* whisper it, and get the chills and thrills." Looking at him, but within herself too.

She said she used to pray for a vision, an honest-to-God mystical experience, and believed, when she was nineteen, it would happen unexpectedly but soon. She said she had never told anyone before, that she used to concentrate, imagine herself weightless and then slowly raise her arms and go up on her toes trying to levitate like Saint Francis and be suspended by divine love. She said she would try to imagine what an ecstatic experience would be like and would think, if it isn't in the mind then it must be experienced through the senses, the body. Then she would wonder, if it's physical, would it be anything like physical love, making love to a man? The way she was looking at him now he knew what she was going to say. "But I don't know what that's like. It's something I have to find out."

Quietly telling him this in a room in the St. Louis Hotel at one-thirty in the morning, her eyes on him, waiting.

He said, "Lucy . . . "

He got up and stood looking down at her, it seemed like a long time before he offered his hands and brought her from the chair into his arms with a tender feeling, a good feeling. He said, "I'll hold you. Let me just hold you."

Close to him she said, "Can we lie down?"

TWENTY-FIVE

Roy was asleep in the back seat of Lucy's Mercedes, in the underground garage of the Royal Sonesta Hotel. He came wide awake and asked what time it was as Jack opened the door and slipped into the front seat.

"Quarter to eight. Where's their car?"

"Up past the second post and about six in. You can just see it. I moved this one," Roy said, "so we'll be pointing the right way. What're the banana pickers doing?"

"Nothing, yet."

"The broads stay all night?"

"No, they left. You could hear 'em."

"Jesus, quarter of eight already. Fucking stakeout, I never thought I'd be doing it again."

"You were sound asleep. It must not've been too bad."

"What would you know about it? Nothing."

"Where's Cullen?"

"Beats the shit out of me. I went up to Darla's hootch and banged on the door. No answer. He either had a heart attack in the saddle and she had to take him to Charity, or he pulled out."

"He doesn't have anyplace to go."

"He's a grown boy," Roy said. "He's dumb as a fucking stump, but he's still a grown boy. I took him to meet Darla, I said, 'Here you go, sweetie, see if you can fuck the old man's socks off.' She says, 'You don't have to use that kind of language.' I said, 'Yes, I do, 'cause you don't know shit.' How 'bout yourself? You and the sister have a nice time up there, Jesus Christ, while I'm down in the garage? Where is she?"

"Getting coffee."

"Well, I hope to Christ she brings me some."

"That's what she's doing, getting us coffee."

"You go over and listen at their door?"

"Since five this morning. They're sleeping in."

"I can believe it."

"The banana boat leaves sometime this morning," Jack said. "Even if they're not gonna be on it they have to make a move pretty soon, for show."

Roy was looking past Jack toward the Bienville Street exit, a square of sunlight against the ground floor of the St. Louis Hotel, across the street. A parking attendant sat on a high stool to one side of the garage opening. "I think they already have the cash," Roy said, "and I think we should do it here. Hitting 'em out on the highway somewhere is a bunch of shit and you know it."

"You get the masks."

"Fuck the masks."

"That means you forgot."

"I'm not gonna wear a fucking mask. If I don't do it for Carnival I'm not gonna get one for this. The guy doesn't know who I am. Tie a hanky around your face if you want and we'll keep Lucy in the car. She isn't gonna do us any good anyway. This's the place, shit, right here. I think they stashed it in their car. I had a tire iron we could find out in two minutes."

"Nobody'd be that dumb, leave it in the car."

"Nobody'd *think* they're that dumb. That's why it could be there."

"You look in the windows?"

"Yes, I did, Delaney. But I didn't look in the fucking trunk, 'cause the fucking trunk doesn't *have* a window."

"I'm glad you had a good night's sleep."

"They don't have it in there, fuck it. I'm going home and go to bed. Cullen might be smarter'n I thought. . . . Here she comes. I hope she brought us some brioche."

Jack said, "Look who's behind her."

Franklin de Dios was coming from sunlight into shade, down the ramp to the floor of the garage, as Lucy approached the car with two white take-out sacks, intent, hurrying. Reaching them, handing the sacks through the window, she said, "Franklin just came out of the hotel."

"He's right there," Jack said. "Now he's gone."

"He went down that first aisle. Watch," Roy said, hunched over close to Jack in the front seat. "He drives off, you better be with him. Where's your car?"

Jack had to think. "It's in that same aisle."

"You hear that?" Roy said, "He's starting a car." Now Lucy was getting in and Roy straightened, raising up. "Just wait, will you, for Christ sake? Jack . . . There it is, it's the

Chrysler. Isn't that the Chrysler? Jack, you gonna sit there or get on it?"

By the time he was out on Bienville, edging the Scirocco past trucks unloading and parked cars the black Chrysler was gone, somewhere up the one-way street, out of sight till Jack caught a glimpse of it turning left on Rampart and that surprised him. Where was Franklin going? Rampart turned into Tulane Avenue and Tulane became the Airline Highway and that would seem to answer the question. Franklin was going out to the airport, in Kenner. Yes, indeed, it looked as if Franklin was taking last night's advice and leaving town. If he'd rather fly than go by banana boat, that was okay. He probably had to stop off in Miami first, pick up his clothes and stuff.

Jack began to notice what a beautiful day it was: clear sky, not too humid. He pulled the Beretta out of his waist, digging into his groin, and slipped it under the seat. He might very well be driving this way again sometime in the afternoon, with a suitcase full of cash, following a week of activity that was certainly different. Man, each day something new and different. Having met some very unusual people. Having slept with two different young ladies, actually slept. . . . It was the tender feeling that messed him up with Lucy. He could see them taking their clothes off and still feel some tenderness. But when he tried to see himself lying between her legs he knew he couldn't do it, it would become something else and the tender feeling would be gone. He'd be performing and watching the performance, aware of her, yeah, seeing her, kissing her, but more aware of himself doing it, just doing it to her, and that wasn't what they were to each other. . . . He held her and listened to her breathing as she slept. The tender feeling was enough. She seemed strange because there was nothing put on about her; she was like a child in that way and knew more than he did; she knew how to walk into her dreams. He could talk to her but had to listen closely and think. Helene, when he talked to Helene things he said just came out. He could act foolish with her. He could act foolish making love to her. Or give her a certain look and she was with it. He had a feeling Lucy and Helene would like each other. Yes, indeed, and had a pretty good feeling in general, tailing the black Chrysler following signs to the airport and as far as the National car-return lot. Jack parked at the side of the road and watched Franklin come out of the Chrysler.

The guy had only a small flight bag.

Jack thought about getting out of the car, yell at him and wave good-bye. Do it quick, before the guy walked over to the shuttle bus. Or he could drive Franklin to the terminal, wish him a safe trip—even though he'd already done that. He thought, No, leave him alone.

And then thought, What's he doing?

Because Franklin was coming out of the car-return lot this way: Franklin in his black suit carrying his tan flight bag coming out to the road, up to the car, hunching over to look in the window with his pointy cheekbones and nappy hair, Jesus Christ, grinning.

"How you doing? You going back now?"

Jack had to nod.

"I wonder if you can give me a ride."

"I don't know if the boat goes to Honduras or to Costa Rica," Franklin said. "I didn't hear that from Wally Scales or from that other guy. What's his name? Lives there in the city where the boat is."

"Alvin Cromwell?"

"Yes, of course you know it. Yes, Alvin. It could go to

Costa Rica. Our leader is there, Brooklyn Rivera. I like to see him, but I rather go to Honduras right away."

"Why is that, Franklin?"

"So I can go back into Nicaragua with some friends of mine and visit people we know there."

"Go for a visit, huh?"

"They live in a concentration camp in the province of Jinotega, a place call Kusu de Bocay."

"Jinotega . . . "

"Maybe we can take them out of there. Help them have new homes and plenty rice and beans to eat."

They were on the Airline Highway heading back to New Orleans. Jack said, "You know the woman at Carville, who was in the coach with me? Her name's Lucy Nichols."

"Yes, I hear Colonel Godoy say that name."

"She worked in a hospital for lepers near Jinotega, the city."

"The city of Jinotega, I think it's far from Kusu de Bocay."

"The colonel came to the hospital and killed the lepers and burned it down."

"I believe it."

"Lucy wants to build the hospital again."

"Yes, that's good."

"She's a good woman."

Franklin didn't say anything and they drove in silence for a mile or so, Jack thinking.

"Yeah, I was pretty sure you were taking a flight. But you just went out to return the car, huh?"

"They call me, say to take it back. It's okay, I have time."

"But now you have to get to Gulfport."

Franklin didn't say anything and Jack thought of his

meeting with Wally Scales, keeping his mouth shut if the guy didn't ask a direct question.

"You know how you're gonna get there?"

"Yes, I know."

Man, it was work. "You gonna take a bus?"

"No, not take a bus."

"But you *are* gonna get on the boat."

"Yes, of course. Go home."

"But Colonel Godoy and Crispin, you're convinced now, they're not gonna get on the boat."

"Yes, I know that. What you told me and what Wally Scales told me."

Jack had to think. If he was supposed to know so much he had to be careful what he asked. They came to Tulane Avenue and followed it into Rampart.

"Well, I'm glad this's working out for you, Franklin."

"Yes, I think so."

"Yeah, I thought you'd be gone."

"Pretty soon."

"I followed you out to the airport."

"Yes, I know. It was kind of you."

"Yeah, I wanted to say good-bye. Maybe have a cup of coffee. Hey, after all that vodka we had last night, you feel okay?"

"Yes, fine."

Jack turned off Rampart onto Conti, one-way into the Quarter toward the river.

"We're almost back. Where can I drop you off?"

"Anyplace you want. I have to go back to that hotel."

Oh, shit. Jack took a moment. "I'm not sure that's a good idea, Franklin." Then began to think that it might, in fact, be a wonderful idea. "Why do you want to see them again?"

"I have to tell them I quit and say good-bye."

"You're not gonna say anything about your going on the boat. I wouldn't mention that."

"No, tell them I quit and say good-bye."

"They might be asleep."

"No, they call me. Crispin."

"He stayed there all night," Jack said. "They had some women stop in for a party."

"Oh, you know that?"

"Hey, Franklin, I even know what they haven't done yet, right?" Franklin was looking at him, grinning. He had a gold tooth. "I told you about it as a special favor, even though I shouldn't have. But that's okay, we're friends, right?"

"Yes, we friends."

"Listen, you go up to the room they're gonna be packing, I suppose. Or maybe throwing up in the bathroom after their big night, huh?" That got a grin. "Listen, while you're in there and they're not looking, you might have a chance to do me a favor, in return."

Lucy said, "He's back," and watched Jack's Scirocco, coming into the garage from the Conti Street entrance, roll past the row where Lucy's car was parked and come to a stop in the drive.

Close behind her, Roy said, "Who's that with him? Jesus Christ, he brought the guy back."

Lucy watched Franklin come out of the Scirocco and walk off toward the Bienville Street exit, carrying a flight bag. Now Jack was out, standing by the car with the door open.

"They had a long talk last night."

"Who did?"

"Jack and Franklin."

"About what?"

Jack was saying something to Franklin. Lucy watched Franklin look back and raise his hand to wave. Now he was going up the ramp to the street and Jack was looking this way, over the top of his car.

"They had a long talk about *what*?"

She watched Jack close his car door and walk around the back of it coming toward them, in no particular hurry but with an expression that was a good sign, alive, somewhat eager. While close behind her Roy was yelling out his window now, "Will you get over here, for Christ sake?"

Jack looked at Roy but wasn't going to be hurried. Lucy turned to face him as he hunched over and put his head in the window, close to her.

He said, "We might have it made," and then looked at Roy. "If you'll go over to the hotel, stand in the courtyard. After Franklin comes down, watch for the colonel. He comes flying out of the room, stop him. Give him some kind of official bullshit for about five minutes. *If* he comes out. He might not."

"Can I ask why I'm doing this, Jack?"

"Because you're our hero, Roy, and the colonel doesn't know that."

"And what're you gonna be doing, if anything?"

"Taking a peek in their car. Franklin's gonna see if he can get us the keys."

TWENTY-SIX

Franklin came off the elevator with his flight bag, stepped over to 501, right there to the left, and knocked on the door. He waited and knocked again and waited and knocked again. There were no sounds from inside. But they were here or downstairs in the dining room or somewhere, because that new car was still in the garage. He turned and saw a thin black woman in a maid's uniform that hung straight on her without shape, her hands resting on a cart loaded with towels and sheets, a plastic bucket and bottles of cleaning compounds. Franklin said to her, "Let me ask you, Mother, did you see them come out of here?"

The woman stood in profile watching him without appearing to watch him, her head only slightly turned.

"I work for them," Franklin said, "but I'm going to quit and I want to tell them."

The woman turned from the cart to look right at him now. She had something in her cheek he believed was snuff or tobacco.

"You gonna quit, uh?"

"I don't like working for them." He moved toward her a few steps, as far as the elevator.

"They don't treat you good?"

Franklin shook his head. "I don't like them. Do you think they in there?"

"I believe so. Where you from?"

"From Nicaragua."

"Yeah, I thought you from somewhere, the way you talk. You leaving, huh?" When Franklin nodded she said, "They leaving too?" When he nodded again she said, "Good. I never seen a mess like I have to clean up after that man. I see him, he don't give me the time a day."

"It's the way they are," Franklin said. "I wonder, Mother, if you can open the door for me."

"Sure, honey, I be happy to."

Franklin gave her a dollar.

Inside, he heard music and heard them talking in the bedroom as he looked around, saw the room-service table, the mess of dirty glasses and dishes, cushions from the sofa on the floor and smelled the odor of stale cigarette smoke. He crossed the sitting room to the desk in the corner. The colonel's briefcase was here, but not the car keys. The sacks from the banks, he noticed now, were on the floor beneath the desk. He placed his flight bag on the chair and stooped over to feel one of the round sacks and look at the metal clamp that held it closed. It would be nothing to open it. He straightened, looking at the desk again, wondering if he should open the colonel's briefcase that was made of alligator skin.

The colonel's voice said, in Spanish, "What are you doing there?"

Franklin turned. The colonel stood in his tight shiny red underwear, a few feet from the bedroom doorway.

"How did you get in?"

"I knocked on the door for an hour."

"How did you get *in*?" the colonel said in English this time.

"The maid, she used her key. I knocked on the door, but nobody heard me," Franklin said, looking at this man in his underwear sticking his chest out, scowling at him. Now Crispin appeared, coming out of the bedroom with a towel wrapped around his hips. Franklin wanted to ask them what they were doing in there with the radio music playing. Were they dancing? He almost smiled thinking of it.

"He says the maid let him in," the colonel said to Crispin. Crispin appeared sick, very thin; his bones showing. He crossed the room to the coffee table without saying anything and picked up a pack of cigarettes. Franklin looked at the colonel again, the man still watching him.

"Did you return the car?"

Franklin nodded.

"What? I didn't hear you."

"Yes, I return the car."

"Where is my receipt?"

"I don't have it. You didn't say."

"I told you get the receipt. Are you stupid?"

Crispin said in Spanish, "We don't need it."

"Whether we need it or not, I told him to get it."

"He doesn't know of receipts," Crispin said in Spanish. "He wouldn't know a fucking receipt if it bit him."

"I told him to get it—I wanted them to see who it was returned the car."

Crispin was smoking his cigarette now. "Yes, I forgot for a moment."

Franklin looked from one to the other.

At the colonel saying, "Because you drink too much and then you talk too much. You know nothing of self-discipline. You know how long you would last in the jungle?"

At Crispin saying, "Tell me about living in the camps, I didn't hear enough of it last night. Mother of God, telling those whores the history of your military life. You know what they cared about it? Nothing. You know where they want to go? Miami, that's where."

At the colonel saying, "Of course. You invited those whores to come with us. You don't remember that, do you? You were so drunk."

Franklin watched the colonel turn to him again and stare, as if thinking of something to say. But it seemed that all he could think of was, "Well, what do you want?"

"Should I carry something to the car?"

"I haven't packed my clothes yet."

Franklin, standing at the side of the desk, looked down and touched one of the bank sacks with his foot. "What about—should I take these?"

The colonel was watching him. He said, "Why? You think we have the money in those?"

"I don't know."

"He doesn't know anything," Crispin said, walking back across the room.

As he went into the bedroom, leaving them, Franklin

said, "But I don't think so. I think you keep it on your new car."

The colonel put his hands on his hips, above his tight shiny red underwear. "Oh, you do, uh? You're a pretty smart guy, Franklin. How did you become smart, from the missionaries, uh?" The colonel said over his shoulder into the bedroom, raising his voice, "Franklin says he thinks the money is in the car."

Franklin heard water running in the bathroom and Crispin's voice say, "Ask him how he knows that."

"How do you know that, Franklin?"

"I know you wouldn't keep it here."

"But we keep it in the car, with no one to watch it?"

"I think you have something watching it."

The colonel said over his shoulder, "He says he thinks we have something watching it."

Crispin's voice said, "What?" Franklin waited as the colonel repeated what he had said and then heard Crispin's voice say, "How does he know that?"

They're fools, Franklin thought. They don't know it or will ever know it.

The colonel, still with his hands on his hips in his foolish underwear, asked him, "How do you know that?"

"What difference does it make?" Franklin said. "I quit working for you."

Franklin saw the colonel's face change, become cold and made of stone, in the moment before he turned to his flight bag on the chair by the desk. Now he heard the colonel's voice, also cold, ask him, "What did you say? You what?"

Franklin brought his Beretta out of the flight bag and saw the colonel's expression change again, the eyes coming all the way open, as he aimed the 9-millimeter pistol at the center of the colonel's chest. "I said I quit," Franklin said, and shot him and watched him stumble back and throw out his arms as he fell to the floor. Franklin stood over the colonel, said, "Good-bye," and shot him again and saw his body jump. He heard Crispin before he saw him appear in the doorway with the towel around him, also with eyes open wide. Franklin said, "Crispin, I quit," and shot him in the chest and then had to step into the bedroom to say good-bye and shoot him again.

The car keys were on the dresser.

Roy had positioned himself where he could glance through the glass door into the lobby and see the elevator, turn his head only about 45 degrees and be looking up through the courtyard to the fifth-floor railing that was like a waist-high fence all the way around. He was looking up there now, ever since hearing that faint but distinct *pop* and then nothing and then *pop* and then two more, spaced, from off somewhere. They weren't loud ones, but he had heard those hard little sounds from off somewhere before and believed they had come from high up; though the sounds could have come from the street and down into the courtyard from above. None of the hotel guests having breakfast here had looked up or seemed to be wondering or talking about it.

There was a colored maid up on the fifth floor—he believed she was colored—standing by her cart and looking back toward the elevator. Roy watched her. If the gunshots came from up there she would have heard them. But now she seemed to have lost interest in whatever she was watching or waiting for, moving off with her cart, away from the elevator and that alcove where 501 was located. There wasn't another soul up there. No doors opening, people sticking their heads out to see what that was.

They might've caught the nigger Indin lifting the car keys, but they weren't going to shoot him for it.

The sounds could've come from outside the hotel. Roy accepted the possibility, but didn't believe it. Now some of the guests, he noticed, were looking up too, because he was. He needed a better place to watch from. He could go up to the room they'd taken, 509, stand in there with the door open. Shit, but he'd have to get a key.

Franklin saw the maid at the end of the hall as he waited for the elevator. He didn't go near the railing to look down, see if anybody was looking up; he didn't hear any noises or voices. The elevator arrived and he rode it down to the lobby and stepped off. He saw a man and woman standing by suitcases on the floor, talking to the doorman. Franklin walked over to the glass door to look into the courtyard. Everyone at the tables seemed busy having breakfast. He looked toward the registration desk, turned, and kept moving when he saw the guy waiting for the hotel clerk, the clerk talking on the telephone, the guy with his hands flat on the counter. It was the guy who had been with Jack Delaney. The tough guy with dark straight hair Franklin believed was police, sure of it from the way the guy spoke. Franklin hurried and didn't look back, hoping the guy didn't see him. He didn't want that guy to follow him over to the garage. He could have trouble with that one and he didn't want to shoot anybody else. Though he would if he had to.

They waited in the front seat of Lucy's car, both watching the square of daylight beyond the ramp. She said, "I might've mentioned it a few times before, but I don't see what this is going to get us."

"We're making Roy happy," Jack said. "He wakes up growling, but he has cop instincts. What seems to be, isn't always the case. Or the other way around."

"No one in his right mind is going to leave two million dollars in a car in a public garage. Even with the car locked."

"I told him that."

"Then we'll have to get the keys back to them."

"We won't worry about that—we can throw 'em in the lobby. I always thought I was patient, but I don't think I am."

"I thought you were, too."

"We'll just get started and I'll probably have to go to the bathroom. Once I was in a hotel room, guy and his wife lying there asleep, when all of a sudden I had to go. I hadn't even picked up anything yet. I went all the way downstairs. . . . But that was it, I was through for the night." He touched the front of his jacket. "You know what I did? Left the gun under the seat of my car. I better get it."

Lucy watched him open the door. "You won't need it for a while, will you?" Her gaze moved back to the garage opening, the square of daylight, and she said, "Jack, there he is."

Franklin came along the driveway past the first aisle of cars, past the second aisle of cars. . . . He saw Jack Delaney's old car, the door open, at the end of the next aisle and the woman's blue car in the aisle behind it. He saw Jack Delaney appear then, rising next to his car, looking this way, and raising his hand. Franklin didn't wave back to him. He turned into the aisle where the new cream-colored Mercedes was parked and walked toward it, not looking at Jack Delaney now, but knowing he wouldn't have time to get in the car and drive off. Jack Delaney would be in front of the car. He didn't want to hit him with the car, but he would do it rather than shoot him. He looked back again, quickly, and saw it would be difficult even if he tried. Jack Delaney was coming with a gun in his hand.

"Franklin—wait up!"

The guy had his flight bag in one hand and was unlocking the car door with the other. He had it open and was getting in by the time Jack reached him.

"Wait a minute, will you?"

Franklin hesitated and then came out, leaving the flight bag on the seat, raising his hands as high as his shoulders.

Jack pushed the door closed, out of the way. "Franklin, what're you doing?"

"I was going."

"With *them*? After what I told you?"

"No, not with them. I have to go be on the boat."

"You're stealing the guy's car? What're you gonna do with it?"

"Leave it there—I don't know."

"Wait a minute—what'd you tell those guys?"

"I told them I quit and said good-bye."

"Yeah? And what'd they say?"

"Nothing."

"Franklin, Jesus Christ . . . "

Lucy was coming. He could hear her leather sandals slapping on the cement, coming in a hurry. He glanced around. "Franklin's gonna swipe their car. You believe it?"

"We haven't met," Lucy said, looking at Franklin as

she came past Jack, between the Mercedes and the car parked next to it, offering Franklin her hand. He brought his hands down slowly and Lucy took one of them in both of hers. "I've heard a lot about you, Franklin. I had a friend who was Miskito we treated at Sagrado Familiar. You know the hospital for lepers? He stayed with us a long time. His name was Armstrong Diego. Did you happen to know him?"

Jack watched Franklin shake his head. The guy seemed a little awed or surprised.

"Colonel Dagoberto Godoy's men killed Diego," Lucy said, "and some of the other patients, with machetes."

"We're standing here talking," Jack said. "Franklin, what was the colonel doing?"

"Nothing."

"What do you mean, nothing?"

"They laying there, that's all."

"All right, Franklin, is the money in the car? . . . You're taking everything, aren't you?" Franklin seemed more resigned than cornered. Jack watched him nod his head, twice. Just like that. Ask him a question, you got an answer. Jack said, "You *are*?" And saw him nod again, twice. "I have to give you credit, Franklin, you're a pretty cool guy." Jack brought up the Beretta and held it level with the man's Creole Indian face. "Now you give us the keys. Hand 'em to Lucy."

Franklin's eyes didn't move from the gun barrel. He gave Lucy the keys without looking at her, letting her take them out of his hand. Jack didn't look at her either, paying close attention to the man's eyes, his solemn expression, until he saw Lucy beyond Franklin at the car's rear deck. Lucy was looking at the ring of keys, selecting one.

Franklin said to him, "If she opens it . . . "

"What?"

"She's going to be dead."

Jack said, "So will you if you move."

Lucy's voice said, "He has enough keys."

"She won't be dead from me," Franklin said, "but she'll be dead."

They stared eye to eye, Jack trying to hold the pistol steady. "I mean it. Don't move."

But Franklin was turning as Jack said it and now he yelled at him, "Franklin, goddamn it!" Aiming the automatic at the man's back and seeing Lucy, bent over, looking up, straightening as Franklin reached her, Franklin saying something to her and taking her by the arm. Jack saw her eyes, her startled look. He moved past the side of the car to the rear deck. Franklin was taking the keys from her. She was *giving* him the keys, glancing at Jack now as he reached the back end of the car and saw Franklin slipping a key into the lock.

She said, "Jack. Don't touch him."

Franklin, on his knees, placed the palm of his hand on the down-curve of the trunk lid, turned the key with the other hand, and let the trunk come open gradually, a few inches. He hunched in close to look in.

Lucy said, barely above a whisper. "It could be wired to explode."

"How does he know?"

"He thinks it is," Lucy said. "They've done it before. There was a priest in Jinotega, he opened his trunk and was blown to bits."

"He was gonna let you open it."

"But he didn't."

They watched Franklin raise the lid slowly, holding it, letting it come up a little more, feeling the tension of the mechanism. With the trunk open about eight inches he put his arm in to the shoulder, his face in profile against the cream-colored sheet metal, composed, feeling without seeing, his fingers working in there. He began to straighten then, getting his feet under him, raising the trunk lid with his shoulder as he stood up and turned to show them what he was holding, a hand-grenade, with one end of a straightened coat hanger hooked to its ring.

"MK-two," Franklin said, "they call a pineapple." He looked at Jack, offering him the grenade, and grinned. "You don't want it? Okay." He slipped it into his coat pocket.

Jack said, "You're a kidder, aren't you, Franklin?" He didn't know what else to say to him: the guy standing there with a grenade in his pocket; the guy could've let Lucy blow herself up. She was saying that to him now . . .

"Why did you stop me?"

Franklin, still grinning a little, a trace of it left, shook his head, Jack watching him. The guy didn't know what to say either, turning to the open trunk to raise the lid all the way up. Lucy looked in. She said, "Jack?" He moved closer and saw two full-size aluminum suitcases inside lying flat, side by side.

TWENTY-SEVEN

Roy got off the elevator and stood looking at 501 in the alcove. He stared hard, but the door wouldn't tell him a goddamn thing. So he followed the open hallway around to the other side of the courtyard, came to 509, and heard the phone ringing inside. Then he couldn't get the goddamn key to turn. The phone kept ringing in there. Roy hit the door with the heel of his hand, kicked it, yanked the knob toward him as he turned the key, and the door gave up and clicked open. He left it like that, got to the bedside table, and picked up the phone.

"Who's this?"

Cullen's voice said, "Roy? It's me. You all are still there, huh?"

"I think so," Roy said. "Lemme look. Yeah, we're still here." He brought the phone away from the table, as far as

337

the cord would let him—just enough—so he could look out the door toward the elevator.

"Nothing doing yet?"

"Naw, we're just sitting here fucking the dog, Cully. I expect same as you, huh? How's adorable Darla?"

"She's fine as can be."

"You wash yourself good after, you hear?"

"I was thinking," Cullen's voice said, "if I asked a doctor what he thought . . . "

Roy watched the maid appear with her cartload of towels and stuff, over there on the other side.

"You know, if I should take part in any kind of activity where I'm liable to become too excited or you get that ass-clutching feeling, man, you don't know what's gonna happen . . . "

The maid was creeping along toward the elevator, like she was sneaking up on it. Her head turned now, looking into the alcove at 501. The maid standing there, waiting.

"You know what I mean, Roy? I'm pretty sure he'd tell me I shouldn't ought to do it, with my history. Considering, you know, the old ticker isn't what it used to be. See, but I don't want to let you all down. . . . Roy?"

That maid wasn't moving from 501.

Roy said, "If you're gonna die, Cully, you may as well do it right there." He put the receiver on the phone, still watching the maid, laid it on the foot of the bed and left the room.

One of the aluminum cases lay flat on the bar in Lucy's mother's sun parlor. Jack touched the polished metal. He picked up his drink, his third vodka since arriving with Lucy, the first two finished off while she counted the money and they had the stand-up talk, argued, and finally reached an understanding. Now he was alone in the room. Very likely for the last time.

He'd left his car in the hotel garage for Roy. Later told himself it was the wrong time to be thoughtful; but now realized it didn't matter. Roy would be here soon, whether he drove or took the streetcar.

They had opened both aluminum cases still lying in the trunk of the colonel's new car. In each one a white T-shirt covered the stacks of currency: sleeveless T-shirts made of a thick, layered material Franklin believed was called soft body armor, bulletproof, that some of the *contra* officers wore. Jack remembered wanting to get out of there. The feeling, waiting for the colonel to appear. Wanting to know why they were standing there talking and then realizing, as Franklin pulled out one of the cases and handed it to Lucy, it was their deal. It was between the two of them and no one else; half to the Miskitos and half to the lepers. Jack wondering if it made sense. Still wondering, after all this, who were the good guys and who were the bad guys.

He heard Lucy's steps on the hardwood floor of the hall before she appeared in the doorway.

"Roy's here."

She turned and he heard her steps again, fading.

The house was quiet. He stood listening. She wasn't coming right back with him. As Roy walked in he probably asked what happened and she was telling him. Or as they came along the hall, Roy listening, stopping . . . Jack poured a scotch and moved toward the door with it. Hand it to Roy as soon as he came in. Take off his edge—if he had that dead look in his eyes. It was one of those situations, if Jack didn't know what was going to happen, he'd better locate something to use. His gun was lying on the bar. Roy would think it was funny if he tried to threaten him with it. There was a brass candlestick on the phone table that looked pretty good. . . . He heard them in the hall, their steps, and then heard Roy's voice. *"What?"* That one word. No doubt about it, Lucy was telling him . . . talking to him as they came in the room. Jack tried to hand him the scotch.

Roy pushed it away. "You let that nigger Indin have *half* the dough?" With the dead look in his eyes.

Jack placed the glass on the phone table, his hand and part of his sleeve wet. "It was the other way around, Roy. It was Franklin gave half to Lucy. He's the one had it."

Roy was heading for the aluminum case lying on the bar. "He *had* it? What does that mean? Those guys up in the room had it, too, and you know what the nigger did to 'em? He tell you? He popped 'em, man. Both guys, twice in the chest."

Jack said, "Franklin?"

"Your pal you had the long talk with's gonna do you a favor, go up and get the keys. He got the keys, all right, and shot 'em dead. And you let him drive off with a million *bucks*? Fucking Indin never even had on a pair of *shoes* before? Jesus Christ, Jack, what were you thinking?"

Lucy said, "He didn't tell us . . . "

Roy looked at her. "Had you known, would you given him *all* of it? I'd like to know how you people think. He's gone—that's it, huh? Jesus Christ, he even swipes the guy's car and you two watch him drive off." Turning to the aluminum case Roy said, "So what're we left with? I suppose you're gonna tell me she gets half. . . . " He opened the case, stared at the rows of currency. "How much's this, a million even?"

"A million one hundred thousand," Lucy said. She

went into her straw bag, lying on the sofa, and brought out a pack of cigarettes.

Roy looked past her at Jack. "You and I split half, or we cut this three ways? Fuck Cullen, he didn't help none."

"The way it turned out," Jack said, "you and I didn't help much either. I told you, Franklin gave the money to Lucy. I was there, I saw it. He didn't give me any or say, here, this's for Roy. Uh-unh, he gave it to Lucy. She thought we should have a piece of it, but I convinced her otherwise. Take it to Nicaragua, 'cause that's what this whole deal is all about anyway."

Roy said, "If bullshit was worth anything, Jack, you'd have the fertilizer market sewed up. What I see is, the schemers have been scheming again. Hell, I can hear you. Let's see if we can fuck old Roy. Tell him all the money's going to the poor lepers. . . . "

Lucy was shaking her head. "Roy, it *is*, it's for the hospital."

"He knows it," Jack said, "he's looking for an excuse, that's all."

Roy said, "Why even talk about it." He closed the case and lifted it from the bar. "If I can see it clear in my mind to take it off the Nicaraguans, I can surely take it off a you two, couple of lost causes." He started past Lucy. "You have any complaints, take it up with the police. Tell 'em what you been doing."

Jack put his hand around the brass candlestick, took it from the phone table to hold at his side.

Roy stopped a few feet away and opened his coat. "What're you gonna do, take a swing at me? Jack, I'd shoot my mother for a million bucks."

Behind him, Lucy said, "So would I."

She stood by the sofa holding her dad's nickel-plated .38 in both hands, arms extended.

Jack saw her as Roy, in front of him, half turned to look back.

Roy said, "Oh, shit, I forgot. You have your shoulder holster on? Show us. Jack, it's like TV cops wear."

Lucy said, "If you try to walk out with that I promise I'll shoot you."

Roy said, "Sister, if you had the nerve, you'd deserve the money." He turned, took two steps toward the door.

Lucy fired and Roy screamed.

TWENTY-EIGHT

Helene had the back end of the hearse open and the mortuary cot halfway out, trying to get the goddamn legs to fold down. Jack walked up to her and said, "Here," and released the catch. He said, "I'll get him." So calm about it. Helene watched him walk off, pushing the cot along the brick path through the garden. As he reached the shade trees a door on the patio opened and Lucy stood holding it for him. It didn't take long. Helene watched Jack bring the cot out with a man lying on it, then stop to say something to Lucy and kiss her on the cheek. He came through the garden to the driveway, to the back end of the hearse. It wasn't until Jack had the cot ready to load that Helene realized the man on it wasn't dead.

His eyes were open. There were towels wedged in between his right arm and his side. He was saying ugly things trying to look mean, calling Jack a name Helene didn't care for, usually said to women. It didn't seem to bother Jack. He slid the man into the hearse and slammed the door on him.

She said, "Jack, I can't pick up somebody who isn't dead, can I?"

He said for her to come on and waved to Lucy standing over on the patio. Lucy waved back.

They got in the hearse and left, Helene driving, Jack sitting back lighting a cigarette, not a care in the world. The first thing Helene wanted to know was why they didn't call an ambulance. Jack said because they'd ask how Roy got shot—reaching over and touching her just above the hip. Right there. Only on Roy it was a roll of fat. Jack said Roy would make up a story to tell at the hospital. Helene said, "Well, isn't he pissed?" Jack said, who cares? Roy couldn't tell on anyone without telling on himself. Jack asked her to save her questions till later. "Let's get old Roy to Charity."

At the emergency entrance they slid him out of the hearse and rolled him onto a gurney, Jack ducking questions from the orderly. He said to Roy, "You hurry up and get better, you hear?" The orderly was wheeling Roy off, so Helene missed what he said to Jack.

They drove off in the hearse. Jack said, "Go on up Canal. We'll stop by Mandina's and have one. How's that sound? Leo and I used to drop in there after a funeral, unwind."

Helene said, "If you think you're gonna get your job back, you're crazy."

"It's yours," Jack said, "if it makes you happy."

Helene gave him a look. He seemed so innocent sitting there, taking in the sights of Canal Street on a Saturday afternoon.